Sarah watched, breath suspended, while the mercenary tucked the doll under the sleeping child's arm, then melted back into the darkness.

Oh, God, she groaned to herself. Why did the man have to be so damned contradictory? Why couldn't he be totally evil, so she could hate him? Or totally good, so she could love him?

Her thought came zinging back to mock her. She wouldn't have loved him if he were a plaster saint, if he didn't possess the hard, biting edge that made him so different, so unlike any other man she'd ever known.

She loved him just the way he was.

Sarah flung up an arm to cover her eyes. She'd done some stupid, useless things in her life, and this ranked among the worst of them.

What in the world was she going to do about it?

What *could* she do about it?

Dear Reader,

We're back with another fabulous month's worth of books, starting with the second of our Intimate Moments Extra titles. *Night of the Jaguar* by Merline Lovelace is the first of a new miniseries, Code Name: Danger. It's also a fabulously sexy, romantic and suspenseful tale of two people who never should have met but are clearly made for each other. And keep your eyes on two of the secondary characters, Maggie and Adam, because you're going to be seeing a lot more of them as this series continues.

Award-winner Justine Davis presents one of her irresistible tormented-but-oh-so-sexy heroes in *Out of the Dark*, another of her page-turning titles. And two miniseries continue: Kathleen Creighton's Into the Heartland, with *One Good Man*, and Beverly Bird's Wounded Warriors, with *A Man Without a Haven*. Welcome bestseller Linda Randall Wisdom back to Silhouette with her Intimate Moments debut, *No More Secrets*. And try out new-to-contemporaries author Elane Osborn, who offers *Shelter in His Arms*.

As promised, it's a great month—don't miss a single book.

Enjoy!

Leslie Wainger
Senior Editor and Editorial Coordinator

Please address questions and book requests to:
Silhouette Reader Service
U.S.: 3010 Walden Ave., P.O. Box 1325, Buffalo, NY 14269
Canadian: P.O. Box 609, Fort Erie, Ont. L2A 5X3

MERLINE LOVELACE

NIGHT OF THE JAGUAR

Silhouette
INTIMATE™MOMENTS®

Published by Silhouette Books

America's Publisher of Contemporary Romance

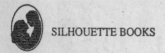 SILHOUETTE BOOKS

ISBN 0-373-07637-1

NIGHT OF THE JAGUAR

Copyright © 1995 by Merline Lovelace

Books by Merline Lovelace

Silhouette Intimate Moments

Somewhere in Time #593
*Night of the Jaguar #637

Silhouette Desire

Dreams and Schemes #872

* Code Name: Danger

MERLINE LOVELACE

As a career air force officer, Merline Lovelace served tours of duty in Vietnam, at the Pentagon and at bases all over the world. During her years in uniform she met and married the world's sexiest captain, who subsequently became the world's sexiest colonel, and stored up enough adventures to keep her fingers flying over the keyboard for years to come. When not glued to the word processor, Merline goes antiquing with her husband, Al, or chases little white balls around the fairways. Merline also writes historical romances for Harlequin Historicals.

To the man who has always been my dark, handsome hero—the one, the only, the wonderful, Al.

Special Acknowledgments

With special thanks to my super "technical advisers":

Dr. Larry Lovelace, whose medical expertise is exceeded only by his great sense of humor;

Colonel Bob Sander, U.S. Army (Ret.), who spent far more days in the jungle than he cares to remember,

and

Lt. Bill Price, Oklahoma City Police Dept. (Ret.), friend, security expert and a Jaguar at heart!

Prologue

Oh, God, please don't let them find us!

The terrified woman squeezed her eyes shut, as if that might block out the horror that had shattered the night.

A rattle of machine-gun fire assaulted her ears. Hoarse voices shouted. Someone screamed—a long, agonized cry for help. A pig squealed horribly.

The woman hunched lower behind the screen of spiky palmettos, her arms wrapped around the small, trembling bodies she was trying to shield, and prayed as she'd never prayed before.

The gunfire stuttered to a halt. Low, guttural voices called in the village. Then nothing. Heavy, dark, suffocating silence, unbroken except for a small whimper from one of the children cowering against her. A silence that lengthened, causing hope to claw at her chest. Maybe *they were gone! Maybe the attackers would melt back into the jungle they'd crept out of. She drew in a ragged breath and tried to shush the child pressed against her side.*

She flinched at the muted thud of footsteps nearby. A low voice. More footsteps, only a little way from their hiding place. Men trudged past. For a few moments, a few heart-stopping, desperate moments, she thought she and the children were safe. But then, a parrot screamed a protest at the passing men, startling a frightened cry out of little Teresa.

The footsteps slowed, then stopped. Stillness descended, heavy and waiting.

She pressed Teresa into her side, against the thick, sweltering folds of the robe she'd thrown on in the desperate hope it would give her and the children some protection. The little girl's terror infected the others. Ricci, only three, sobbed.

The palmetto fronds rattled, parted. Moonlight glinted on the evil-looking gun barrel that pointed right at her heart, and cast the lean face above it into sharp, shadowed angles.

They stared at each other, her eyes wide with terror, his narrowed and deadly.

Another face appeared at his shoulder. "What is it, gringo? Who's there? More of these peasants who resist our cause? Kill them!"

The man holding her in his line of fire drew in a deep breath. "It's a nun. For God's sake, it's a nun."

terrifying night clogged her throat.

Chapter 1

On a quiet side street just off Massachusetts Avenue, in the heart of Washington's embassy district, an elegant, Federal-style town house stood dark and silent in the pre-dawn April chill.

A discreet bronze plaque beside the front door caught the dim, fading glow of the streetlamps. Anyone brave enough or foolish enough to be wandering the capital's streets that early might have peered curiously at the plaque and learned that the structure housed the offices of the president's special envoy.

Those in the know—political correspondents, foreign diplomats, cabdrivers, and the bag people who slept on the subway grate on the corner—could have told the curious wanderer that the position of special envoy was another of those meaningless ones created several administrations ago to give some wealthy campaign contributor a fancy Washington office and an important-sounding title.

Only a handful of government officials with the highest compartmentalized security clearances knew that the offices of the president's special envoy occupied just the first two floors of the town house.

Still fewer were aware that the third floor served as headquarters for a covert agency. An agency whose initials comprised the last letter of the Greek alphabet— OMEGA. An agency that, as its name implied, was activated as a last resort when other, more established organizations, such as the CIA or the State Department or the military, couldn't respond for legal or practical reasons.

And only the president himself knew that the special envoy also acted as the director of OMEGA. The director alone had the authority to send its agents into the field.

One of those agents—code name Jaguar—was in the field now.

His controller paced OMEGA's high-tech communications center on the third floor of the town house. Her pale gray linen slacks showed the effects of a long day and an even longer night, as did her wrinkled red silk tunic, with its military-style tabs at the shoulders and pockets. Tension radiated from every inch of her tall, slender body as she took another turn, then stopped abruptly in front of the command console

Dammit, why didn't Jake report in?

Maggie Sinclair shoved a hand through her thick sweep of shoulder-length brown hair and glared at the unwavering amber light on the satellite receiver. "Are you sure there hasn't been any interference with our signals?"

The communications specialist seated at the side console sent her a pained look. "No, ma'am," he drawled in his soft Texas twang. "Not unless somebody's got something a whole lot more sophisticated than baby here."

He patted the steel gray console tenderly. "And no one does. If one of our agents in Saudi Arabia or Afghanistan or anywhere else on the planet so much as sneezes into his transmitter, I'll pull it down for you. No one, not even the *U*-nited States Air Force, can interfere with my signals."

Warming to his subject, Joe Samuels began to describe in loving, excruciating detail the power and frequency spectrums he could call up at will. Maggie listened with half an ear, having shared the small hours of the night with him and his baby many times before. She stared at the amber light, her thoughts on the man she was waiting to hear from.

Where was Jake? What was happening in Cartoza?

After more than two years as a special agent for OMEGA, Maggie had spent enough time in the field to develop keen instincts about an operation. Every one of her instincts was screaming that something had gone wrong with this one.

She should have heard from Jake hours ago. She was his control, his only contact at headquarters, and he hadn't missed a prearranged signal yet. The last transmission he'd sent had indicated that the big arms shipment would be tonight.

They were close, so close, to breaking up the international consortium that specialized in selling stolen U.S. military arms to unfriendly governments and revolutionary forces. Posing as an expatriate mercenary, Jake had infiltrated one of the rebel bands some weeks ago. The information he'd sent in so far had detailed how the weapons were being smuggled from various military arsenals across the U.S. He'd even pinpointed the isolated airstrips where the arms were being delivered.

But until tonight he hadn't been able to identify the middlemen, the Americans who arranged the shipments and took payment in drug dollars. Tonight, Jake had learned, the big money men were flying in with a special shipment. Tonight, he'd planned to be part of the group that met them. Tonight, OMEGA would take the middlemen down.

Maggie had placed surveillance aircraft on orbit and put a strike force on full alert, waiting for his signal. It hadn't come.

Resuming her seat in front of the command console, she reached for a foam cup with a neat pattern of teeth marks around its rim. She took a sip of cold coffee, then grimaced and set the cup aside. With a last, frowning glance at the amber light, she tugged a black three-ring notebook toward her. She flipped through the tabbed sections until she found the parameters for mission termination.

Maggie knew the criteria for ending an operation by heart. As the respective control and field agents for this mission, she and Jake had drafted them together weeks ago. But with his life on the line, she wasn't trusting anything to memory.

Ten minutes later, she pushed the notebook aside. She still had some latitude within the agreed-upon parameters. She'd sweat it out a few more hours yet, she decided. There was still a chance they could pull it off. The drop could have been delayed by weather, by mechanical problems with the plane, by any one of a hundred unexpected events.

Besides, Jake was good. Damn good. He had more field time than anyone in the agency, two years more than

Maggie herself. He'd been one of the first operatives re-cruited for OMEGA, a CIA transplant who'd helped train the dozen other transfers from various military and government agencies. He'd salvage the operation...if it was salvageable.

Still, the sixth sense Maggie had learned never to ig-nore in this business kept nagging at her. Her brows puckered in concentration, she stared at the console and willed herself inside Jake's head.

What was going on down there?

She was so intent on the unwavering yellow light that she didn't see Samuels acknowledge a positive palm-and-voice print. Nor did she hear the near-silent hum as the heavy oak door to the control center—protected by a bullet-proof titanium shield—slid open.

"Nothing yet?"

The deep, quiet voice, with its distinctive Boston ca-dences, made Maggie jump. She swiveled her chair around, thinking ruefully that she should be used to the way her boss moved by now.

And, she decided with a quick intake of breath, she certainly ought to be used to the sight of Adam Ridge-way in formal dress. She'd seen him in his special envoy persona often enough, looking incredibly distinguished and darkly handsome in white tie and tails tailored to fit his broad shoulders and lean, athletic body. Adam usu-ally stopped by the OMEGA control center after attend-ing one of his many diplomatic functions. Maggie had expected him tonight. Nevertheless, she had to force trapped air out of her lungs as she shook her head.

"No, nothing yet."

He flicked a glance at the row of clocks above the command console. "It's almost 4:00 a.m. down there."

"I know."

One of Adam's dark brows notched at her clipped response.

"I'm giving him another few hours," Maggie added, in a more measured tone.

He studied her face for a moment, then nodded. "All right."

The tight knot of tension at the base of Maggie's spine loosened an infinitesimal fraction at his quiet acceptance of her decision. She and Adam had had their disagreements in the past over her somewhat unorthodox methods in the field. But he'd never yet questioned her instincts about an operation. That he didn't do so now reinforced Maggie's confidence in her decision to delay terminating the mission.

Adam turned away, pulling at the ends of his white tie. "I'll be in my office downstairs. Call me if you hear anything."

The mischievous grin that was as much a part of Maggie's nature as her intense dedication to her job tugged at the corners of her generous mouth. She snapped a hand to her forehead. "Aye, aye, Skipper!"

Adam paused, his blue eyes gleaming at her atrocious approximation of a salute. "It's obvious we didn't recruit you from the military," he commented dryly.

Maggie grinned as she watched him stride across the room with the smooth, controlled grace of a man who had crewed for Harvard and still sculled on the Potomac every chance he got. She often teased him about his choice of a sailing craft, suggesting that someone with his wealthy background could afford a real boat—one with an engine, maybe, or at least an anchor.

When his black-clad frame disappeared into the darkness outside the control center, Maggie swung back to the console. Her lingering smile faded slowly.

The amber light emitted the same unblinking glow. Where the devil was Jake?

Two thousand miles away, Jake MacKenzie cursed viciously as he slashed at the strangler-fig root that had wrapped itself around his boot. His machete sliced through the thick elastic root with deadly efficiency, then slid back into the worn leather scabbard attached to his web belt. Jake reached up to adjust the night-vision goggles that photomultiplied light some forty thousand times, changing the inky darkness around him to an eerie luminous green. He plowed ahead, hard on the heels of the shadowy figure in front of him.

Christ! Everything that could've gone wrong tonight had! Not only had the plane they'd come to meet failed to show at the small airstrip hacked out of the jungle, but government troops had unexpectedly arrived in the area. Someone had better have a damn good explanation for that colossal screw up, Jake thought savagely.

As if that weren't bad enough, he and the band of revolutionaries he'd infiltrated had spent half the night detouring around the troops to get back to their camp, high in the mountains. Then, outside a sleeping village, one of the rebels had stumbled over some pigs. Startled, the stupid bastard had sprayed the squealing animals with his AK-47. Within moments, the night had erupted. Shouts from the nearby village, scattered small-arms fire and the answering stutter of the rebels' automatic rifles had split the darkness. Before Jake could stop them, the rebels had charged through the cluster of huts, firing on the peasants, who had so far stubbornly refused to support their cause.

They'd wanted to kill the terrified woman they'd found hiding in a stand of palmettos, too. Until they'd seen her black robe and veil and the kids clutched in her arms. Even these sleazers hesitated before pulling the trigger on a nun and three children. Still, Jake's acid observation, in quick, idiomatic Spanish, that a medical sister was the closest thing to a doctor in this remote part of the interior was probably what had saved her life.

So far.

Dragging the woman with them, the rebels had melted back into the jungle. The children, clinging to her like frightened monkeys, had stumbled along, as well. Within moments, an impenetrable wall of darkness had swallowed them. Not even the rugged all-terrain vehicles the *federales* used could navigate through the dense tropical rain forest.

And now he was stuck with them, Jake thought in disgust. Three orphans, according to the woman's frantic pleas to spare them. And a nun! An American nun, if her mangled, broken Spanish was any indication. As if he didn't have enough on his hands with this botched mission.

"Don't touch him!"

At the sharp, sudden cry, Jake dropped into an instinctive crouch and spun around. Through the thin lenses of the goggles—stolen from a U.S. military base, along with a shipment of high-tech arms—he saw the spectral shape of one of the rebels tugging at a child's arm.

"No! No, let her go!"

The man spit out a response, but obviously the sister didn't understand the guttural patois the rebels used. She snatched at his shirt, demanding that he release the child.

Jake straightened, his stomach clenching. The woman's black robe and medical expertise wouldn't protect her much longer if she riled these men. Or if they got to drinking. Or if—

A muted snarl from the man holding the child's arm told Jake things were fast getting out of hand. Cursing once more, he stalked back along the narrow, overgrown trail. He shoved up the goggles, which tended to blur items at close range, curled a hard hand around the woman's arm and jerked her away. The child, a girl of about five or six, cried out.

"Let me go!" The woman yanked against his tight hold, intent on the child.

Jake's grip tightened. "You may not realize how close you are to getting a knife in your ribs, Sister."

She swung toward him, her face a pale blur in the murky gloom. "You're an American?" she gasped in disbelief.

"More or less," he snapped.

"Wh-what are you doing with them?" She gestured to the group that now surrounded them, dim shadows against the darker blackness of the night, then repeated helplessly, "You're an American."

Jesus! Jake's fingers dug into her arm. "This is no time to be discussing nationalities. In case you aren't aware of it, my associates don't like *norteamericanos* much more than they do their own people who resist their cause. Come on."

She dug in her heels. "Tell that . . . that murderer . . . to get his hands off Teresa."

The wiry rebel understood English a whole lot better than the sister understood Spanish. He spit out a phrase Jake was glad the woman didn't grasp. The situation, he decided, was rapidly going from dangerous to nasty.

"The children are slowing us up. He's only going to put the girl on the packhorse, for God's sake."

She panted with a combination of fear and desperate determination. "For *his* sake, that's all he'd better do."

Jake released her arm, wondering what the hell she thought she could do if any of these men did try to harm the children. Bludgeon them with her rosary beads?

"Look, Sister," he warned, his voice low, "you'd better understand that you're in a pretty precarious situation here."

She drew in a ragged breath. "No kidding."

Jake sliced her a quick look, surprised at the terse response. Either convent life was an even tougher boot camp than he'd realized, or this was one gutsy lady. Unfortunately, he'd found over the years that gutsy tended to get people killed. If he was going to keep this woman alive long enough to figure out what to do with her, he'd better make damn sure she understood what was ahead.

"Don't think that veil you're wearing will protect you if you get their hackles up," he stated with brutal candor. "The only thing that saved you back there in the village is the fact that one of their pals died last week from a nasty case of gangrene. They've decided that it might be nice to have a *médica* around the camp to prevent such little unpleasantries in the future."

She gave a small gasp and put a shaking hand up to her throat. Even in the darkness, Jake could see the way her eyes went round with fear. Good, he thought savagely. She needed to be scared. He sure as hell was.

"I'd advise you not to push them too far," he added softly.

Muttering under his breath, the rebel beside them stooped and swung the girl onto the horse. Jake slung his weapon over his shoulder and lifted the littlest, a boy of about three or four, up behind her. The third child, a thin, wide-eyed boy of about eight, would have to hoof it.

The men drifted into the darkness to take up their positions in line. Jake tucked his weapon under his arm once more and waited for the signal to move on. The woman beside him glanced at the automatic rifle, and a look of revulsion crossed her white face, visible even in the darkness.

"How . . . how many of the villagers did you kill?"

Jake bit off an oath. He couldn't tell her that he'd tried to prevent the rampage. Hell, he didn't dare tell her anything. Talking to her at all was risky, given the group's simmering frustration over the missed drop. Although Jake had managed to convince these men that he'd sell his country or his soul or both for the right price, he was still a gringo, an outsider they didn't quite trust. With the least provocation, they'd turn on him like jackals after raw meat.

"How many?"

His hand tightened over the gun barrel. "As many as got in the way."

She put a hand over her mouth. "God will have to forgive you for what you've done," she whispered. "I can't. Those people were my friends."

Jake refused to allow any hint of sympathy or remorse to creep into his reply. "Yeah, well, I just might be the closest thing to a friend you've got left right now. And I'm telling you that if you want to survive the next twenty-four hours, you'd better keep moving and keep your mouth shut."

She swallowed and clutched the boy's hand.

"Stay in front of me from here on, where I can keep an eye on you," he ordered. "Don't step off the path, and keep a tight hold on the kid. There are a few surprises along the trail for anyone unwise enough to try to follow us. Now move it, lady... Sister.''

Gripping her skirt with one tight fist and the child with the other, she turned and fell into line.

As the small group traveled in heavy silence, the night sounds of the jungle they'd disturbed slowly resumed. Leaves rustled in the tall trees. Whistles and chirps seemed to come from every direction. Bats whirred through the branches high above, while whining mosquitoes circled Jake's ears. The crunching, tearing sounds of small animals and insects feeding drifted to him through the darkness. Once, far off in the distance, a jaguar screamed.

Jake managed a grim smile.

As the echo of the animal's cry died away, he mentally reviewed his options. There weren't many at this point.

He could abandon his mission right now and try to take out the dozen men with him on this botched operation. He calculated the risks to the woman and the children and abandoned the idea. It wasn't any more feasible now than it had been back in the village.

That left trying to brazen it out. When this little band got back to camp, Jake would have to convince the desiccated fanatic who led them that the aborted airdrop and the proximity of government troops were both just coincidence. That Jake himself had nothing to do with either—which he didn't.

At the same time, he'd have to find a way to protect this nun and her charges without blowing his cover. That might be a bit tricky, given the fact that he was supposed to be a conscienceless mercenary.

Still, he had no choice. There were already two other women in camp, one hard and pitiless and as dedicated to the revolution as the intense leader she slept with. The other was the vacant-eyed wife of one of the men, who didn't mind sharing her, for a price. Jake's gut wrenched at the thought of the games the men played with the un-comprehending, unresisting woman. His fingers clenched around the gun barrel at the thought of what they could do to the woman stumbling along ahead of him.

At that moment, he heard her call a strained reassurance to the little girl atop the plodding packhorse. Despite her own fears, and what she must know was a very uncertain future, she managed to soothe the whimpering child. A reluctant admiration for the woman's ragged courage tugged at him.

Maybe, just maybe, they could pull it off, Jake thought. More than just their lives was at stake here, he reminded himself. An entire country teetered on the brink of civil war, and all the horror that came with it. Cartoza was a small nation, but one of the United States' staunchest allies in Central America. Its government was dedicated to wiping out the drug traffickers whose insidious products were destroying the social fabric of all the Americas.

The U.S. President himself had activated an OMEGA response based on the information that the drug lords were financing shipments of stolen U.S. arms to the insurgents. The shipments had to be stopped before the friendly government toppled.

There was still a chance, a slim chance, of accomplishing that mission. If his controller at OMEGA didn't jump the gun and send in an extraction team, Jake might yet take down the middleman who was supplying the arms.

His lips twisted in a small, grim smile at the thought of his controller. By now, Maggie Sinclair would be pacing the floor, those long legs of hers eating up the cramped space in the communications center. Her brown eyes would be narrowed in intense concentration, her dark cloud of hair would be tangled from her unconscious habit of raking a hand through it whenever she was deep in thought. For all her worry, however, Jake knew, Maggie wouldn't panic.

The tight, coiled knot of tension between his shoulder blades loosened imperceptibly. Maggie wouldn't terminate the operation. Nor would she send in an extraction team. Not until she heard from him or figured out for herself what had happened. Jake had worked with most of the agents assigned to OMEGA, and Sinclair was one of the best.

Chapter 2

One more hour, Maggie thought. Two at the most. That was all she could allow herself. And Jake.

She took another sip of coffee, unmindful now of its cold, sludgelike consistency. Holding the cup at her lip, she began tracing a second ring of circular indentations around the rim. Suddenly a light flashed on the upper left portion of her console.

The front legs of Samuels's chair thwacked down on the tiles. "It's Big Bird!"

Maggie's heart pounded in sudden excitement. Big Bird! She should have known the surveillance craft orbiting high above the Caribbean would be the first to break the wall of silence surrounding Jake. The huge air force jet, with its Frisbee-like rotating radar dish, was officially termed the USAF Airborne Warning and Control System, but everyone had a different tag for it, some affectionate, some irreverent. No one, however, made fun of the vital information processed via its banks of on-board computers.

With the speed and skill of a magician performing sleight of hand, Samuels flipped a series of switches. The clear, calm voice of an air surveillance officer came over the speaker. Maggie hunched forward in her chair, listening intently.

An aircraft meeting the specifications Jaguar had called in earlier had taken off from a deserted airstrip in Alabama, Big Bird confirmed. Two F-15s had scrambled from a base in Florida to make a visual ID, then shadowed the slower-moving plane across the Gulf of Mexico. At the last minute, the aircraft under surveillance had aborted its landing in Cartoza, for reasons unknown at present. The report went on to provide a wealth of technical detail on the suspect's flight pattern, air characteristics and radar signature.

Maggie acknowledged receipt of the transmission and sat back, thinking furiously.

"So the drop didn't take place?" Samuels asked.

She met the communications specialist's steady gaze and shook her head. She wasn't surprised by his question. Everyone in the OMEGA control center during an operation was briefed on every detail. They worked as a team, together, twenty-four hours a day, throughout the duration of the mission. Everyone involved had a personal stake in the outcome.

"Get me a voice link to those F-15s," Maggie said. "I want to talk to the pilots and find out what—"

Another flashing light interrupted her.

Samuels verified the caller's credentials, then sent Maggie a wide grin. "It's the on-duty rep at the State Department crisis center. He has a report of some action in your sector of operations."

Maggie picked up the handset, adrenaline pumping through her veins. Although she far preferred fieldwork to acting as a control agent, she had to admit that being stuck at headquarters had its moments. Like now, when the reports started to flow in from a dozen different sources. From CIA, from Treasury, from any and all agencies whose intelligence networks OMEGA tapped into. She'd need a cool head, and the insight gained only through years in the field, to piece together the fragmentary and often conflicting bits of information that would soon pour in.

"State Department, this is Chameleon," she rapped out, identifying herself with the code-name she'd earned by her ability to melt into whatever locale she was sent to. "What do you have?"

Forehead furrowed in concentration, Maggie listened as the on-duty operations officer relayed information about a rebel raid on a small village in the interior of Cartoza.

"How many casualties?" she asked when he paused to consult his notes.

"Four. Three villagers and one suspected insurgent."

"Any positive ID on the insurgent?"

"No, the locals are still running their checks. I've got some vitals, though, if you want them."

Maggie gripped the handset. "Let me have them."

"Five feet seven. Black hair. Brown eyes. With an old, jagged scar on the left thigh, possibly from a knife. That's all I have right now."

Maggie slumped in relief. Jake certainly sported a shaggy head of black hair, and he'd acquired more than his share of scars over the years. But his eyes were a flinty shade of gray, not brown, and he stood a good five inches taller than the dead man.

"There's one more thing."

"What's that, State?"

"The villagers led the government forces to a newly dug, shallow grave containing the remains of a woman... an American woman, according to the garbled reports we got. With all the confusion of the raid, we haven't been able to confirm who it is. Was."

Maggie frowned at the console. "Who did you have down there?"

"We're not sure. The personnel folks are screening our data files now. Assuming she's not some tourist who took a wrong turn at Cancún and ended up in the middle of a revolution, we should know something within the next hour or so."

"Keep me posted, okay?"

"You got it."

Maggie replaced the handset, her eyes thoughtful. At this point there was no reason to assume a connection between the dead woman and Jake's operation. But she sensed instinctively that there was one, just as she knew that Jake wouldn't want her to terminate the mission until she was convinced it was necessary.

Twenty minutes later, she still wasn't convinced.

Although she hadn't yet heard from Jake, she'd sifted through enough fragmentary information to form a picture of what must have happened. The presence of the government forces in the area was a coincidence, an unscheduled military exercise. But their presence would have been enough to scare off the drop aircraft. Maggie guessed that the rebels had raided the village as a target of opportunity when the drop was aborted. There was a chance, a slim chance, that Jake's cover hadn't been compromised yet.

"Call me immediately if anything else comes in," she instructed Samuels. "I'm going to update the chief with this latest information."

She strode across the communications center and waited impatiently for the palm- and voice-print scanners to verify her identity. When the heavy door slid open, she took the stairs two at a time. She was in the the special envoy's reception area within seconds. Another synthesizer activated the door that led to his office. Maggie passed through a short corridor that contained every lethal protective device the enthusiastic security folks could devise.

The inner door stood open, but the sight of Adam on the special phone that recognized the distinctive voice patterns of only two men in the world stopped Maggie on the threshold. He waved her inside, listening intently, one hip hitched on the edge of the half acre of polished mahogany that served as his desk. Although he'd taken off his formal coat and white tie, he couldn't have shed his well-bred, aristocratic air even if he wanted to, Maggie thought. When she stepped inside his office, she caught the gleam of diamond studs winking amid the starched pleats of his shirt.

She also noted the slight narrowing of his vivid blue eyes. That was as close as Adam Ridgeway ever came to frowning. Not for the first time in the past two years, Maggie wondered just what it would take to shatter Adam's iron control. She herself had managed to strain it severely on more than one occasion, she acknowledged with an inner grin.

"The reports are just beginning to flow," he said calmly. "We still don't have a clear picture of what happened."

Maggie suppressed a smile at Adam's Kennedyesque pronunciation of *clear.* A gifted linguist, she delighted in the idiosyncrasies of American dialects as much as in the foreign languages that were her specialty.

The only child of an Oklahoma-bred "tool-pusher" whose job as superintendent of an oil-rig drilling crew took him all over the world, Maggie had spent her childhood in a series of exotic locales. By the time she won a scholarship to Stanford at seventeen, she'd been fluent in five languages and conversant in three more. Until two years ago, she'd chaired the foreign language department at a small Midwestern college. Then a broken engagement and the sense of adventure she'd inherited from her parents had left her restless and ready for change.

Three months after a call from her godfather—a strange little man her father had once helped smuggle out of a Middle Eastern sheikdom—she'd been recruited as an agent for OMEGA. Only later had Maggie learned that she was the first operative drawn from outside the ranks of the government. And that her godfather, now retired, was one of OMEGA's most intrepid agents.

Adam's conversation soon drew to a close. "I understand the urgency, Mr. President. I'll get back to you as soon as we know what happened in Cartoza."

Replacing the receiver, he folded his arms across a wide expanse of crisp white shirtfront. "All right, Sinclair, tell me what we have so far."

Briefly, succinctly, Maggie recapped the information she'd synthesized. When she mentioned the shallow grave and its occupant, Adam stiffened.

"We should know within an hour who she is," Maggie added. "State's running through their data base of all known citizens in the area. They've requested checks from Canada and the European nations, as well." She paused, chewing on her lower lip for a moment. "I don't know that there's any connection between the woman and our operation, but I have this..."

A small smile curved Adam's lips. "Tingling feeling in your bones?"

"More like a prickly sensation at the base of my spine," Maggie replied solemnly.

The smile disappeared. "Well, whatever it is, this is one time I hope your instincts are wrong."

"Oh-oh. Sounds like the call from the president added a new piece to the puzzle."

"Several pieces. Tell State to check the status of a medical sister who was working in Cartoza. From the Order of Our Lady of Sorrows."

"*Madre Dolorosa?* I read up on those sisters as part of my prebrief for this operation. It's a large order, headquartered in Mexico City, with branches throughout Latin America, the United States and Europe. Although the order is still very conservative in matters of dress and convent life, the sisters have been active in Central America. I'm not surprised one of their people was in Jake's area."

"Apparently the sister wasn't the only American woman in the area. Tell State to also check the status of a Peace Corps volunteer by the name of Sarah Chandler."

"Sarah Chandler?" Maggie wrinkled her brow. "Why do I know that name?"

"She's only been in the Peace Corps a short time. She arrived in Cartoza less than two weeks ago, in fact. Before that she was a rather prominent political hostess here in Washington."

"Oh, Lord! Not that Sarah Chandler!"

"Yes, that Sarah Chandler. The senator's daughter."

* * *

As she made her way back to the third-floor control center, Maggie's mind was racing. No wonder the president wanted to know what had happened in Cartoza. Senator Orwin Chandler of North Carolina was one of the most influential and powerful men on the Hill. According to Adam, the senator had already heard through his own intelligence sources about the rebel raid and had pieced together enough to know that the U.S. had some involvement or interest in the action. He didn't want any damn details, Chandler had informed the president. He only wanted assurances that his daughter was safe.

There wasn't any way the president could give Senator Chandler those assurances, Maggie thought grimly.

Not yet.

Tucking the sweep of her hair behind her left ear, she reclaimed her seat at the command console. "Okay, Joe, let's get back to work."

Despite his years in the jungle, Jake had never become accustomed to its lightninglike transitions from light to dark. In the evening, there was no dusk. Just a sudden graying of the air, then a blackness so swift and intense he couldn't see his hand in front of his face.

Dawn sliced through the canopy of fig and mahogany trees with the same startling speed. One minute he was stumbling along the narrow trail, straining to see the faint moving shadows of the men in front of him with the aid of the low-light goggles. The next minute those shadows had taken on context and contrast and the goggles instantly became superfluous.

Or at least that was the way it usually worked.

This morning, however, the figure directly in front of him refused to take shape. Jake shook his head, unable to appreciate the dedication that would lead someone to don a heavy, shapeless black robe in the oppressive heat of the jungle. His own khaki shirt already clung to him like a second skin, and the sun had only been up a few minutes. His jaw tight, he watched the woman lift her arm to wipe her face with a corner of a voluminous sleeve. She had small hands, he noted. Small and fine-boned, with short, blunt nails and work-roughened skin.

Frowning, he moved up alongside her. "That habit may have saved your life last night, but it's the worst possible getup for this climate. Your superiors ought to have more sense than to send you sisters into the interior wearing something like that."

She looked up at him then, and Jake saw her face for the first time in daylight. Framed by the limp white wimple and black veil, it was a composite of high cheekbones, an aristocratic little nose and a firm, pointed chin. Dirt streaked her forehead. Sweat and the pallor of exhaustion filmed her skin. But nothing could dull the impact of the most stunning eyes Jake had ever seen. Wide and luminous and a clear, translucent aquamarine in color, they shimmered like jewels in the morning light. They also, Jake noted, raked him with undisguised scorn.

"I wouldn't expect someone like you to understand matters of the cloth, Mr.... Mr...."

"You'd better just call me 'gringo,'" Jake replied, recovering slowly.

She turned away, declining to call him anything at all.

He fell back into line behind her. Jake swore under his breath, slowly, savagely. The beads of sweat clinging to his cheeks suddenly felt clammy. All hell was going to break loose when the men with him got a good look at the woman they'd taken.

It was too late now to even think about taking out the patrol strung out ahead of and behind them. They were within a mile of the camp. The intrusion-detection devices that ringed the hideaway had signaled their arrival for the past half hour. If gunfire broke out now, the rest of the rebels would be on the scene before he had the exhausted woman and her charges halfway back down the winding mountain trail they'd spent the past five hours trudging up.

His mouth grim, Jake reviewed his options.

He had only one, he decided as the narrow trail suddenly emerged from the tall, heavy forest into a debris-strewn clearing. He'd have to bluff it out.

The rebel camp sat high in the foothills of the Teleran Mountains, a line of jagged peaks extending from the Canadian Rockies all the way down through Central America. Dry and barren on the Pacific side, the mountains were greened by the trade winds on the Atlantic side. The moisture-laden winds dumped up to three hundred inches of rainfall a year on the steep slopes. The lush rain forest that resulted made for harsh living conditions and difficult travel, but, as Jake well knew, it provided excellent cover.

In classic guerrilla style, the band he'd infiltrated made maximum use of existing land features. They traveled under the screen of the thick forest canopy and carried with them only what they needed to fight with. For their base camp, they'd appropriated a cluster of tumbledown shacks that had once been an outpost of a vast coffee plantation. Abandoned by workers seeking more lucrative employment in cocaine-processing factories, the outpost had long since been reclaimed by the jungle. Only a few of the tin-roofed huts still stood, their wooden shutters gaping. The rebels used the most secure one to store their supplies. Their leader had claimed another for his personal use.

A narrow, sluggish stream cut across the far edge of the clearing, providing the only source of water for sanitation and drinking. Thin, barrel-ribbed packhorses, still the primary means of transportation this deep in the interior, cropped beside the stream. Overhead, camouflage netting stretched across the entire camp, shielding it from observation.

As the small group straggled into the clearing, Jake moved alongside the woman. "Keep quiet," he murmured. "And keep your head down."

She immediately flashed him a wide, startled look.

Christ! Those eyes were going to get them both killed. "Keep your head down," he all but snarled.

Stepping in front of her, Jake skimmed the gathering crowd for the thin, hawk-eyed leader who'd taken the name of the revolutionary hero he revered. He didn't have to search long. The only one in camp who adhered to any standards of discipline in his dress or personal hygiene, Che stood out among his scruffy band. The woman with him stood out even more. Her lush figure strained the fatigues she wore, but Jake knew better than to equate her rounded curves with stereotypical concepts of feminity. He'd seen her use the automatic rifle slung over her shoulder to deadly effect.

Stiff and unbending in his camouflage uniform, the leader stopped a few paces away and listened while the man nominally in charge of last night's fiasco stumbled through a muddled explanation in his thick mountain dialect. They'd already radioed in a brief report, but Jake could see that Che was tight-lipped with anger over the loss of the shipment of shoulder-launched heat-seeking missiles he'd been expecting.

When the man's muttered excuses ran out, Che turned cold eyes on Jake. "So, gringo, why do you think the government troops were near the drop zone last night?"

"Beats the crap out of me," Jake drawled, "but you'd sure better find out. I'm not risking my ass with these trigger-happy bastards of yours again unless you get some reliable intelligence that the area's clean."

Che's lip curled. "Or unless we up your fee, eh?"

"My fee doubled last night. I don't like working with amateurs."

A wash of color rose in the man's olive cheeks. "Watch yourself, gringo."

"You want me to show you how to arm these little toys you're collecting," Jake replied steadily, "you pay for it. The price goes up with every botched drop."

A muscle twitched on one side of Che's jaw. Jake held his look with a cold one of his own. After a long, tense moment, the rebel's gaze slid to the silent, black-clad figure. "Why did you bring her?"

Jake's voice deepened with disgust. "Because these fools you call soldiers of the revolution almost left her lying in the dirt in the village."

The leader sneered. "And that offended some long-lost religious sensibility of yours?"

"That offended my sense of self-preservation," Jake shot back. "The public outcry over a *religiosa*'s death would've caused a massive government manhunt for her killers. I didn't think you'd appreciate that, at least not until we get our hands on those missiles you want and even the odds a bit."

"You could've left her body in the jungle, where no one would find it."

"And the children's, too?" Jake shrugged. "You aren't paying me to murder nuns and children. If you don't want them here, you get rid of them."

Che's eyes went flat and black. For a heart-stopping moment, Jake feared he might have overplayed his hand.

"We might have need of a *médica*'s skills sometime in the near future," he offered casually.

Che made no effort to hide his suspicion as he glanced from Jake to the woman, then back again.

"You brought her, gringo," he said at last. "You're responsible for her. If she escapes or puts a knife through one of my men, you die."

Jake bared his teeth in a slow, twisting, menacing smile. "Then tell your men to keep away from her. Or they die."

Jake turned without another word and gripped the nun by the arm. The quick, questioning look she slanted him from beneath lowered lids told him she had understood little of the exchange. Just as well, he decided grimly.

The milling men parted as they walked to where the eldest boy stood protectively beside the packhorse. Jake reached up and lifted the little girl down first. She ran to the sister, burying her face in the black skirts. He scooped the toddler up, tucked him under one arm and jerked his chin toward the hut that served as a storage dump for the camp's supplies and the few personal belongings the men had with them. "Over there."

When he shoved open the door, trapped moist heat hit Jake in the face and sucked the air out of his lungs. He stepped inside and gestured to the others to follow. Setting the boy down, he nudged him toward the now-wilting sister, then tossed the bundles of gear belonging to the others out the door. That done, he knelt beside a military-style backpack propped against a crate stenciled with

U.S. markings. As he dug through the knapsack, Jake rapped out a series of low, hurried orders.

"Listen, and listen well. I'm going to go get some water and round up some food. Don't show your face outside this hut, and for God's sake don't try anything stupid, like slipping into the jungle while I'm gone. This camp is ringed with more booby traps and explosive devices than a nuclear storage site."

He straightened, canteens dangling from one fist, and eyed her for a moment. "I don't suppose you know how to use an AK-47—or, better yet, an APG?"

She ran her tongue over dry lips. "What's an APG?"

"Never mind."

A ripple of comprehension crossed her pale, strained face. She glanced at the crates, then back at Jake. "It's some kind of weapon, I gather. That's why you're here, isn't it? You sell guns to these men."

"No. I sell myself, or rather my expertise. These goons don't know how to operate half the weapons they're supplied by the drug lords who keep them in business. I show them."

A look of scorn settled in her eyes, deepening them to a shimmering blue-green that reminded Jake of a lake he'd once fished in upstate New York. It held cold, crystal-clear water, with a deceptive, unplumbed depth. The kind that invited a man to strip off and plunge in. The kind that invigorated and enticed and—

Jake pulled himself up short. Jaws tight, he whirled and slammed the door of the hut behind him. As he strode toward the sluggish stream, he couldn't decide what irritated him more. The fact that she hadn't made any effort to disguise her contempt, or the fact that such incredible, expressive and downright seductive eyes were wasted on a woman who'd taken a vow of celibacy.

Pushing the sister's image out of his head, Jake dropped to one knee beside the stream. He dragged the canteen in the slow, rippling water with one hand. The other he hooked in the web belt he wore low on his hips. His fingers drummed an impatient tatoo on the buckle.

Only Jake knew that the metal gusset next to the belt buckle doubled as an encrypting device, and that the pattern he tapped out formed a digitized code. The transmitter sewn into his belt was too small for anything other than a short emergency signal. But that signal would be picked up by the U.S. Navy ships cruising off-shore and relayed to the OMEGA control center within minutes.

Chapter 3

"**Y**es!"

Joe Samuels's shout brought Maggie running from the crew room, where she'd gone to splash cold water on her face.

"It's Jaguar," he told her, his eyes snapping with excitement.

Maggie expelled a whoosh of pent-up breath. Jake MacKenzie had survived the disaster of the night before. She headed for the command console. "Is he on the satellite receiver?"

"No. All I got was an emergency signal, relayed by the navy. Here it is."

Maggie's pulse leaped when she saw the three numbers Samuels had scrawled. Although she knew the emergency signals she and Jake had devised by heart, she went immediately to her black operations notebook and verified the individual digits.

Agent in place.

Stand by for further word.

"Way to go, Jaguar," Maggie murmured, grinning broadly. Her finger slid down to the clear-text explanation of the third digit.

Neutral on board.

Thoughtfully, Maggie tapped the notebook with her forefinger. Well, at least now she knew the location of the missing American woman. State had verified just moments ago the sketchy information the president had passed to Adam. There had been two American women in the village at the time of the raid—one a medical sister from the Order of Our Lady of Sorrows, the other a Peace Corps volunteer by the name of Sarah Chandler.

But which one had been buried in the shallow grave, and which one was now smack in the middle of Jake's operation? Until she gathered that rather vital bit of information, Maggie decided she'd better find out all she could about both of them.

Twenty minutes and as many contacts with various agencies later, she sat back in her chair and frowned at her two pages of scribbled notes. Scanning the profiles she'd pieced together, Maggie decided she didn't much like either one.

Sister Maria Augustine, age thirty-four. Formerly Helen Peters. Born in Pattersonville, Ohio. Joined the Order of Our Lady of Sorrows a year after graduation from nursing school. A highly skilled nurse practitioner who'd spent nearly half her life in Central America. As well known for her clashes with the bureaucratic government officials who regulated her medical station as for her outspoken criticism of the rebels who preyed on the people she served.

And Sarah Chandler, twenty-nine, daughter of Senator Orwin Chandler. Graduate of Sweet Briar College, with a degree in education she'd never put to use. A wealthy, pampered socialite whose affair with a married diplomat had caused a feeding frenzy among the Washington press corps when it was uncovered six months ago. And whose drunk-driving conviction a few weeks later had led to her disappearance from the Washington scene.

According to Maggie's sources, Senator Chandler had used his influence to convince the judge to give his daughter community service instead of a jail sentence. Again because of her father's influence, Sarah Chandler had been allowed to perform that service as a volunteer with the Peace Corps.

Maggie groaned and shoved a hand through her hair. Great, just great! Jake was stuck down there in the jungle with either a scandal-ridden socialite or a social activist of a nun on his hands. At this point, she wasn't sure which one she hoped it was.

Sarah Chandler sat on a fifty-pound sack of dried beans, an arm around Ricci's small body. Teresa clutched at her other sleeve with both hands, while Eduard, his face solemn in the sweltering haze of the hut, stared at her with wide black eyes.

Desperately Sarah tried to stifle the fear that had gripped her since the stutter of machine-gun fire had torn her from sleep so many hours ago and even now made her hair slick with sweat under the limp veil. Despite her best efforts, a series of tremors racked her.

Oh, God, what was she doing here? How had her life turned upside down like this in such a short time?

Humid, suffocating heat seared her lungs with each gulping breath. She glanced around the hut in mounting dismay. The panic she'd held at bay all through the long, terrifying night clogged her throat.

Her father was right! She could have worked out her shattering guilt over the consequences of her actions at home just as well as in the Peace Corps. She could've done community service in D.C., or in their home state of North Carolina, for that matter, anywhere other than some remote little village in the middle of the jungle. Sarah squeezed her eyes shut, seeing Orwin Chandler's big, hearty figure as he paced the paneled library of the Bethesda home they shared, puffing on the one cigar he allowed himself each day.

If she'd listened to her father, if she hadn't pitted herself against him for perhaps the first time in her life, she wouldn't be here in an airless shack, pretending a medical knowledge she didn't possess. She wouldn't be bound by horrible chance and circumstance to a steel-eyed mercenary who—

"Sarita?"

Ricci's wobbling voice pulled Sarah back from the brink of a hysteria engendered by delayed shock and total exhaustion.

"Sarita, tengo que ir al baño."

She stared at him, uncomprehending. Her formal Spanish, sketchy at best, seemed to have deserted her completely. Nor had she been in country long enough to gain any real understanding of the local dialect. The people she'd lived with these past weeks had hidden their smiles at her faltering attempts to communicate and replied politely in English. Even these children had a better command of her language than she did of theirs. Somehow, that made Sarah feel even worse.

"I'm sorry, Ricci," she said shakily. "Please, tell me again."

"I have to make the pee," he announced in English.

"Oh."

"Me also," Teresa chimed in.

Their simple needs steadied Sarah as perhaps nothing else could have. After a dark night of terror and a morning that had brought them to the grim reality of the rebel camp, they needed to make pee. Sarah reined in her incipient panic, reminding herself that she'd promised Maria she'd watch over these abandoned children until the church authorities came for them.

Maria! A stab of regret lanced through Sarah for the woman she'd grown so close to in such a short space of time. Strong, competent, no-nonsense Sister Maria, with her skilled hands and sympathetic brown eyes. Maria, who'd died so needlessly, so tragically, just two days ago after the Jeep she'd been hauling medical supplies in hit a tree root and overturned, crushing her underneath.

Ricci tugged impatiently on her sleeve. "Sarita!"

"Okay, honey, okay."

The ... the gringo had said not to go outside. Biting down on her lower lip, Sarah glanced around for a vessel the children could use. The hut was too small and too airless for them to just relieve themselves on the hard-packed dirt floor.

Aside from the stacked wooden crates she'd been warned away from, the only contents of the hut were sacks of coffee, rice, and the black beans that formed the main dietary staple in this region. Some dirty, ragged bedrolls had been tossed in one corner, along with a wadded pile of mosquito netting. Her gaze fell on the gringo's backpack, propped against the wall. Maybe there was something inside she could appropriate.

Tugging her arm free of Teresa's clutching hands, Sarah pushed herself off the cot and crossed to the bulging brown-and-green knapsack. Inside she found a cache of items necessary for survival in the tropics—quinine, a first aid kit, snakebite antidote, a plastic bottle of water-purifier capsules. There was also a shaving kit that held a few toiletries, as well as two small travel toothbrushes. Greedily grabbing one of the toothbrushes, Sarah set it and a squeezed-up tube of toothpaste aside, then dug deeper. She pulled out a poncho, vital in a country where torrential rains pounded out of the sky for at least an hour every day during rainy season, and a spare pair of the high, flexible rubber boots with thin soles necessary for walking any distance through the streams and soggy layers of vegetation in the rain forest.

Frustrated, Sarah turned to the side pockets. Her rummaging fingers extracted a clean, if wrinkled, khaki shirt from one pocket, a thick wad of socks from another, and from the last a couple of pairs of white cotton men's briefs.

Sarah fingered the soft cotton. To her consternation, a flush added to the heat bathing her cheeks as she stared at the Jockey shorts. Size 34, she read on the label. Unadorned, utilitarian, and utterly masculine.

For the first time, Sarah visualized the man she'd spent the past five desperate hours with as…as a man. A startling mental image of his lean, muscled body clothed only in these briefs gripped her. She remembered suddenly how his sweat-dampened shirt had clung to wide shoulders and delineated the taut muscles of his upper arms. How the web belt sporting a long, lethal-looking machete and a plain leather holster had hung low on his narrow hips. How…

"Saritaaaa!"

At the small, desperate wail, Sarah jumped. She crammed the briefs back into the side pocket and scrabbled in the dirt for the likeliest receptacle.

* * *

"They used my *boot?*"

The gringo's voice rose incredulously. He stood just inside the hut, canteens dangling from one arm, a mounded plate of beans and rice in either hand.

At the sound of his harsh exclamation, Teresa whimpered. Sarah wrapped an arm around the girl's thin shoulders and pulled her into her side.

"Well, they had to use something," she pointed out.

"They used my *boot?*"

"Oh, for—" Sarah bit off the impatient exclamation. What was the big deal? "You can rinse it out in the stream. After you provide something more suitable for the children to use."

He slammed the tin plate down on one of the crates. "There's a whole damn jungle right outside. They can use that!"

"You *said* not to leave the hut," she retorted, then belatedly remembered her role. "And I must ask you to refrain from taking the Lord's name in vain."

Under the dark stubble that shadowed his face, his jaw worked. Narrowed gray eyes glittered with an anger he made no effort to disguise. "Look, lady—Sister—we're going to lay a few ground rules here."

The unmistakable menace in his voice turned Teresa's whimpers to outright sobs. She burrowed into the smothering folds of the black robe and sent sharp little elbows poking in Sarah's side.

The scowl on the man's face deepened at the girl's sobs. He looked so fierce and threatening that Sarah's brief spurt of defiance evaporated. She gripped Teresa with a sudden feeling of panic.

His effect on the boys was no less dramatic. Little Ricci whimpered that they would die and buried his face in the thick black skirt. Eduard rose from his cross-legged position on the floor, sidled next to Sarah, and put a hand on her shoulder.

She wasn't sure whether the eight-year old meant to draw comfort from her or reassure her. Eduard rarely spoke. Even the skilled, patient Sister Maria hadn't been able to draw the boy from the silent shell he'd encased himself in since one of the villagers found him in the jungle several years ago, thin-ribbed, hollow-faced, and starving. His flat black eyes gave no hint of his thoughts or his emotions.

The touch of Eduard's small hand on her shoulder sent a wave of confused emotions through Sarah. She was ashamed of her sudden panic, yet too exhausted to summon the courage to combat it. And, worse, she was swamped by the enormity of the responsibility that had been thrust upon her.

She didn't know anything about children! She knew even less about jungle survival. How could she hope to escape and make it back to civilization dragging three kids? How could she defend herself, let alone them, from the furious man who confronted them? She wanted to burst into tears and bury her face in Teresa's tangled hair.

The gringo must have seen that he'd pushed her to the limit of her resources. The glittering anger in his eyes gave way to disgust. He rattled off something in Spanish that Sarah didn't catch and turned to dump the canteens beside the plate he'd slammed down a few moments ago. Reining in his temper with a visible effort, he shrugged off the weapon slung over his shoulder and propped it against the wall next to his backpack. He settled himself on the wooden box, his long legs sprawled out and his back against the stack behind him.

Whatever he'd said seemed to reassure the children. Or maybe it was his less threatening stance. In any case, Teresa's cries dwindled to gulping hiccups. Ricci's face appeared from the folds of Sarah's skirt. He glanced at the gringo, then at the food. After a moment, he pulled himself up and waddled over to the plates. Digging a grubby hand into the combination of rice and cold black beans, he proceeded to stuff the mixture into his mouth.

Wearily Sarah unwrapped her arm from the little girl's body. "Go on, Teresa. You must eat. You too, Eduard." She sent the older boy a glance she could only hope was calm and confident.

"You, also, Sarita," Teresa insisted, refusing to relinquish her tight grip on her sleeve. "You come, too."

Sarah nodded and started to push herself to her feet.

"Sarita?"

The deep voice rasped like rough sandpaper along Sarah's frayed nerves. She froze, wondering wildly if she should tell this man her real name. Did she dare trust him with the knowledge that she wasn't the medical sister he believed her to be? She straightened and brushed the straggling veil out of her face to look at him.

No. No way. Not this hard-eyed mercenary. If he bartered his despicable skills for the drug dollars these rebels paid him, she shuddered to think of the price he'd demand for the daughter of a United States senator.

"Sarita is what the children call me." Pulling the first name she could think of out of the air, she met his gaze. "I'm Sister Sarah Josepha. From the convent of Our Lady of Sorrows."

She managed to roll the convent name off confidently enough. In the few weeks they'd worked side by side in the small clinic Maria ran, Sarah had learned a great deal about her companion's religious background. Open, friendly, at times blunt and outspoken, Maria had held nothing back. Sarah had found herself envying the woman her dedication and sense of purpose.

"Our Lady of Sorrows," he murmured. "Appropriate."

Sarah stiffened. "What's that supposed to mean?"

He flicked a glance at the children, now crouched down in front of the food and busy filling their empty bellies. "Only that we're both going to experience a lot more sorrow than we can handle if we don't keep a real cool head for the next few days."

A sharp splinter of hope pierced Sarah's heart. "The next few days? Do you mean we'll only be here a few days? Then you'll let us go?"

"I don't know how long you'll be here," he replied flatly.

The hope in Sarah's chest exploded into tiny shards of a disappointment so painful she choked.

His brows drew into a dark slash. "Look, Sister Sarah, if it was up to me, I'd put you and the kids on a pack-horse right now and get you the hell out of Dodge. I'm not exactly thrilled to have the four of you on my hands while I'm trying to conduct a . . . business operation."

The hesitation was so slight that Sarah almost missed it. Bitterness and frustration curled her lip. "A business operation? Is that what you call it? There's a word for people like you, you know, and it's not *entrepreneur.*"

He rose to his feet and took a slow step toward her.

Sarah swallowed, but refused to back away.

"You've got a real mouth on you, for a nun," he commented softly.

He was so close Sarah could smell the tang of healthy male sweat emanating from his chest. She stared up at him, seeing the hard line of his jaw under the stubble that shadowed it. She realized suddenly that tall and lean translated into overpowering and rather dangerous at such close quarters. Rubbing damp palms down the sides of her skirts, Sarah took a deep breath and summoned up the last tattered remnants of her courage.

"Is that so? Just how many nuns do you know?"

Something glimmered in his eyes. Sarah couldn't tell whether it was surprise that she refused to let him intimidate her, or reluctant admiration at her stand, or amusement. The thought that her desperate struggle to contain her fear might amuse him sent her chin up another notch.

"Not many," he admitted. The ghost of a smile tugged at his lips. "In fact, I've only met one other. She caught me snitching fruit from the corner grocery store and whacked me over the head with her umbrella. When she marched me home, my staunch Methodist father agreed with the good sister that I needed a little more forceful guidance and took me out behind the garage. Since then I've tended to avoid your kind."

Waves of relief coursed through Sarah. She just might make it through this mess after all. Lifting her chin, she gave a disdainful sniff. "Obviously, both the whack over the head and your trip to the garage failed dismally to curb your ways."

"Obviously," he drawled, turning away. "Go eat. Then we'd better get what sleep we can before the heat gets too unbearable. I'll string some hammocks for the kids, and we can make do with the bedrolls."

"You're going to sleep here? With us?"

"Right the first time."

"I don't think that's either necessary or appropriate, Mr. . . . Gringo."

He didn't even bother to turn around. "What you think in this instance doesn't matter a whole lot, Sister Sarah. You see, that ferret-faced little runt out there who leads this band of so-called revolutionaries isn't exactly pleased that I dragged you back here. He's made me personally responsible for you, and I'm not a man who takes his responsibilities lightly."

Ignoring Sarah's inelegant little huff of derision, he looped the end of a hammock rope around an exposed wooden roof support. "Go eat," he ordered, in a voice that brooked no further argument.

While he moved about the small hut, Sarah joined the children. They scooted aside to make room for her around the impromptu table. Remembering his warning about things that went boom in the night, she lowered herself gingerly onto the edge of the crate, then glanced around for something to eat with. There wasn't anything except her fingers. Sarah wiped them on her robe and tried not to think of what might be clinging to either her skin or her skirts.

Her first scoop of cold beans and rice lodged in a throat still dry with the residue of fear and exhaustion. Sarah unscrewed the plastic top of one of the canteens and washed the lump down, grimacing at the taste of tepid water laced with chemical purifiers. She wiped the mouth of the canteen with her sleeve and passed it to little Teresa, then scooped up another few fingerfuls of food. Within moments, she was gobbling the hearty fare down as hungrily as the children.

After half a lifetime of dining at Washington's elegant restaurants and quaint eateries, Sarah had been surprised at how well she adapted to the steady diet of rice and black beans that formed the basis of every meal in this part of the world. In the evening the villagers augmented the dish with chicken or, occasionally, pork cooked in a spicy tomato sauce. When scooped up in still-warm corn tortillas and finished off with the plentiful fruits of the area, the food was nutritious and filling.

Or maybe Sarah's easy adjustment to it had stemmed from the fact that, for the first time in her life, she wasn't giving much thought to either her weight or her appearance. The humidity had wreaked such havoc on her once-shining cap of long platinum blond hair that she'd taken to simply dragging it back with an elastic band. Moreover, she'd found a degree of comfort and a strange sense of freedom in the baggy cotton trousers and shirts her Peace Corps sponsor had told her to bring. Sarah smothered a silent groan, wishing she could shuck the hot, sticky black habit and pull on one of those light-weight shirts right now.

Even Maria herself had rarely worn these suffocating robes, donning them only for infrequent visits to her chapter house in the capital city. In the interior she wore sensible lightweight cotton work clothes—and the bright red ball cap with the Washington Redskins logo embla-zoned on the front that Sarah had given her.

At the memory of the ball cap, Sarah's fingers stilled halfway to her mouth. She closed her eyes against the familiar wave of pain and guilt that washed through her. André had bought the ball cap for her on one of their delightful, illicit outings. Sarah had thought to use the anonymity of the huge crowd at a Skins game to teach the suave, sophisticated Frenchman a little about the Amer-ican national pastime. Instead, he'd shaken his head at her incomprehensible enthusiasm for what he consid-ered a slow, pedestrian sport and whisked her away

during the third quarter to a discreet little hotel to dem-
onstrate what he laughingly called the French national
sport.

She'd been so in love with him, Sarah thought in de-
spair. She hadn't stopped to think about the pain and
tragedy her selfish need for him could cause. She'd believed him when he caressed her and adored her with his
skilled hands and clever mouth. She'd—

"Don't forget to shake your bedroll out before you lie
down."

Sarah blinked and slewed around to see the gringo
stretched out, his long legs crossed at the ankle and a
floppy-brimmed camouflage hat covering his eyes.

"What?"

"Shake out the bedroll," he murmured, without re-
moving the hat. "It's a safe bet the last inhabitant was a
snake, either the slippery, slithery variety or one of his
two-legged cousins."

Sarah eyed the stained mat beside his in distaste.
"Maybe I'll share a hammock with Teresa."

"Suit yourself."

After the children finished their meal, Sarah wiped
ineffectually at the smallest ones' faces with the damp-
ened tail of her sleeve. Eduard disdained her ministra-
tions. He folded his thin body into the hammock, then
pulled Ricci in beside him. Sarah draped a tent of mosquito netting the gringo had rigged over both of them.

She approached the second hammock with the assurance of a woman who danced with a joyful, natural grace
and played a mean game of tennis. She soon found,
however, that negotiating her way into a swinging hammock with a child in one arm and heavy skirts draped
over the other took more than grace or coordination. It
took a skill she didn't seem to possess.

On her first attempt, the lightweight net swung out from under her, nearly dropping her on her bottom. On her second attempt, the knee she'd lifted to anchor the net swayed away, causing her to hop a few steps across the dirt floor on one foot to keep from losing her balance. Six year old Teresa clung to her neck, like one of those stuffed toys with the long, strangling arms, and giggled.

The sound tugged at Sarah's heart. She smiled down at the child. "Think that's funny, do you?"

Teresa put a dirty hand to her mouth to cover the gap from her lost front teeth. Her black eyes sparkled.

"Let's try this again. We'll do it scientifically this time. One step at a time."

Grasping the edge of the net in a firm hand, Sarah rose up on tiptoe and swung her hips into the net. She gave a startled squawk as the hammock rolled high up in the air and dumped her on the floor.

Teresa came down on top of her, giggling helplessly. Childish snickers from the other hammock told Sarah that Ricci was getting as much enjoyment out of this as Teresa. Even Eduard was smiling, she saw when she sat up and shoved back the once-starched white headband that held her veil out of her eyes.

So was the mercenary. He leaned on one elbow, the floppy hat pushed to the back of his head. Even through the draped mosquito net, Sarah could see the crooked slash of white teeth that cut the darkness of his unshaven cheeks.

Sarah had perfected a lot of skills during her years as a Washington political hostess. One of the most valuable was a ripple of musical laughter that went a long way toward minimizing any social disaster. André had often told her that her ability to smile and shrug off domestic crises that would mortify other hostesses was among her most charming traits.

So the answering smile she gave the gringo began as a well-learned, deliberate response to an embarrassing situation. But as her mouth curved, Sarah found relief from her fear and fatigue in the simple act. Her smile deepened.

For a moment, their eyes met, his gray and shadowed by black lashes, hers free of the fear that had haunted her for so many hours. They weren't mercenary and nun, but simply a man and woman enjoying a ridiculous moment. He broke it off first. Still grinning, he lay down again and tugged the hat over his eyes.

Sarah dragged herself to her feet and plunked Teresa into the hammock. "It's all yours, sweetheart."

The little girl grabbed at her hand. "Sarita!"

"Don't worry. I'll be right here beside you."

Gently disengaging her hand, Sarah pushed aside the mosquito netting draped over the stained, uninviting bedroll. She lifted the sleeping bag by one corner and shook it once, twice. Something fell out and scurried away between the stacked crates. Sarah gasped, then grabbed the other corner and shook the mat for all she was worth.

The man on the other bedroll grunted and rolled over on his side, his back to Sarah.

After a vigorous shaking, she laid the edges of the limp bedroll down and sat back on her heels, eyeing it distrustfully. When nothing moved under its surface and no hissing lump appeared, she smoothed it out with short, swift and very cautious pats.

"For Pete's sake, will you lie down?"

Sarah threw his broad back an indignant look. Slowly, gingerly, she stretched out, then reached up to tug the mosquito netting back down. It settled around them both like a white cloud, enclosing them in an airy, strangely intimate cocoon. After a few moments, the exhaustion seeping through her bones caused her rigid muscles to relax. She dragged her sleeve across her face to wipe away the moisture generated by her exertions and closed her eyes, sure she'd be asleep within moments.

She was wrong.

As tired as she was, her body wouldn't, couldn't, slip into blessed semiconsciousness. Instead, an insidious need crept through her, stiffening her limbs and keeping her eyes wide open in the hazy light.

The boys' breathing evened out. Little Teresa whistled once or twice through the gap in her front teeth, then snuggled down in the hammock and grew still.

Sarah stared up at the rusted tin roof. She listened to the scurry of forest mice scuttling up and down the walls in their never-ending search for insects. From a few feet away came the rumble of deep, sonorous breathing. Not a snore, exactly, but pretty darn close to it.

Desperately Sarah willed herself to ignore the sounds around her and go to sleep. She squeezed her eyes shut and began to count, as she'd done so often as a child, when her father had gone to some political fund-raiser or another and she'd lain awake in her big, flower-patterned bedroom, waiting for him to come home and read to her.

At two hundred and forty-seven, she gave up. Worrying her lower lip with her teeth, she rose up on her knees, then inched to her feet. She lifted her skirts and moved as quietly as possible across the hut.

She didn't even hear him move. She was just bending toward an object near the wall when a hard hand spun her around. The veil whipped at her face, causing the headdress to tilt haphazardly to one side of her head.

"What the hell are you doing?" Suspicion blazed in his eyes and singed his low, furious voice. "I thought you said you didn't know how to use a weapon."

"I don't!" Sarah gasped.

"Then why were you reaching for it?"

Sarah glanced down at the automatic rifle propped against the wall beside the backpack. "I wasn't reaching for your precious weapon!"

"So what were you after, lady?"

No *Sister Sarah* this time. No crooked grin that coaxed an answering response from her. At this moment, he radiated a hard, cold authority that made Sarah gulp.

"Tell me," he growled, giving her a shake.

The veil tilted farther over her ear, then fell off completely. He sucked in a quick breath, his narrowed eyes on her hair.

Sarah raised a hand defensively to the limp, sweat-slicked blond strands. "We...we don't cut it anymore. We haven't since Pope John's Vatican Council."

There'd been a Pope John. She was sure of it. And the Italian ambassador had talked at great length about a Vatican Council at one of the dinner parties Sarah had given for her father. She held her breath, waiting for the gringo's response.

His flinty gaze shifted to her face. "So you don't cut your hair anymore. That still doesn't explain what you're doing creeping around the hut."

She opened her mouth to reply, then shut it. She opened it again, but couldn't force out the words.

"I'm fast running out of patience," he warned softly, "and you don't want to be around when I do."

"I have to use the boot," Sarah muttered through clenched teeth.

Chapter 4

She needed to use the boot!

Drawing in a deep breath, Jake ran through his options.

He could risk taking her outside to go downstream, as the other inhabitants of the camp did. Or he could escort her into the jungle, no doubt with a trail of interested spectators tagging along behind.

No, options one and two weren't smart. He'd heard the murmurs among the men when Sister Sarah walked into camp. He'd caught the swift, slashing male assessment they'd given her when she glanced up at him, her eyes gemlike in a pale and dirty face.

Option three, he could let her use the damned boot.

What the hell? No doubt the acid from the kids' urine had already eaten through the special lining and destroyed the satellite voice communications device concealed there. One of the other OMEGA agents, a former air force jock, had told Jake about a C-130 transport plane that had gone down in Vietnam. Seemed the effluent of the farm animals being evacuated with desperate villagers fleeing the Vietcong had destroyed the cables under the aircraft's flooring. If urine could destroy the 130's metal-and-wire cables, Jake's transmitter-receiver was a goner by now. So was his boot, he decided wryly.

Releasing the sister's arm, he stepped back. "Be my guest."

Bright spots of color flaring in each cheek, she snatched up the rubber footwear. After a quick look around the hut, she marched behind a stack of crates.

Jake smiled grimly, wondering how he was going to explain this one to Maggie Sinclair—when, and if, he ever found a way to slip out of the camp and retrieve the backup transmitter he'd buried in a cranny of a towering strangler fig.

He settled back down on the bedroll and bent an arm under his head, thinking about the unexpected complication to his mission in the form of Sister Sarah Josepha. As he'd admitted earlier, he didn't know a whole lot of nuns, but the few he'd seen here in Central America were sure different from little Sister Sarah. Most of them wore sensible work clothes and no longer covered their hair with veils. They didn't drape themselves in old-fashioned, uncomfortable habits in an excess of zealous piety.

Although... Jake was forced to admit that none of the sisters he'd seen around these parts possessed quite the same combination of luminous eyes, tumbling white-gold hair and unconsciously seductive smile, either. At the memory of the way her smile had softened the angled planes of her face into a breathtaking beauty, he felt a slow, involuntary tightening low in his groin—followed immediately by a wave of self-disgust.

Maybe it wasn't overzealousness that kept her in those shapeless robes, he thought wryly. Maybe Sister Sarah exhibited a whole lot of common sense by covering up her undeniably attractive attributes so that they wouldn't distract her—or others—from the vocation she'd chosen.

Only the strategy wasn't working. Not right at this moment, anyway. Not for Jake.

He'd been in the jungle too damned long, he decided grimly. He'd forgotten the basic tenets of civilized behavior. He had no business thinking the thoughts he was about the woman who emerged at that moment from behind the crates and moved quietly toward the mat next to his. Jake heard her give the bedroll a few cautious pats before she settled in.

He came awake an hour later with the swift, instant alertness that had saved his life more than once. His senses collected immediate impressions for his brain to process. Heat, humid and oppressive against his skin. The scent of his own sweat. The sound of shallow, regular breathing. The feel of a hand on his arm.

Jake glanced down at the small white hand that rested palm up against his sun-browned skin. Sister Sarah was a restless sleeper, he noted with a tight smile. She lay sprawled on her back, her face turned away. As he watched, she twitched a little and twisted her head toward him. He sucked in a swift breath at the pallor of her face under its sheen of sweat.

Well, hell. So much for common sense. That heavy black habit had to go, before Sarita succumbed to heatstroke. Jake had better find something more suitable for her to wear in this stifling hut.

He rolled off the mat with the lithe, noiseless movement that had become second nature to him and reached

for the webbed belt that was always within reach. It settled around his hips with the familiarity of an old friend.
The leather holster slapped against one thigh, the machete against the other. Clamping the hat down on his
head, Jake left the shack.

Sarah awoke after a few hours' of restless sleep, groggy
and disoriented. She wasn't at her best in the morn-
ings—if it still *was* morning. Especially, she remembered
slowly, when she'd spent most of the night tramping
through the jungle.

She lay still, unwilling to move, unwilling to face what
came next. Maybe if she just kept her eyes closed, she
could convince herself she wasn't lying in an airless little
shack. If she didn't breathe in too deeply, maybe she
could keep the searing heat out of her lungs.

"Sarita."

Maybe if she just feigned sleep a little longer, Teresa
would stop tugging at her sleeve.

"Sarita, *el gringo* is gone. Is he coming back?"

Sarah opened one eye. The little girl's worried face
hovered against the filmy background of mosquito netting. Sarah turned her head to survey the empty bedroll
next to hers.

"Will he come back?"

The fear in Teresa's voice tore at Sarah's heart. According to Maria, the six year old had lost both parents
and two siblings in a devastating flash flood that all but
destroyed the village last year. Since then the child had
attached herself tenaciously to whoever offered security.

Maria had taken her into the clinic while church and
government officials worked through the lengthy, com-
plicated adoption process. In the interim, the little girl
had become the nun's second shadow, following her

everywhere. After Maria's death, Teresa had immediately transferred her attention to Sarah. For the past two days, Sarah hadn't been able to take a step without the dark-haired girl in the faded blue flowered dress beside her. When the rebels swept through the village—oh, God, was it only last night?—Teresa had clung to Sarah with terrified, instinctive trust. Frantic with fear herself, Sarah had thrown on Maria's robes in the hope they would protect her and the children. Running out of the clinic, she had sought safety for them all in the darkness of the jungle.

Only they hadn't found safety. And it appeared Teresa had already recognized the fact that her survival might depend on someone other than the woman whose sleeve she was tugging at.

"Will he, Sarita? Will he come back?"

"Yes, yes, I'm sure he will."

Sarah struggled into a sitting position. Only then did she see that Eduard was awake, as well. Unspeaking, he lay propped in the hammock, Ricci curled into a tight, sleeping ball beside him.

At the sight of his solemn face and unfathomable black eyes, Sarah felt again the enormity of the responsibility she'd so rashly assumed. Her dry throat closed as she fought the panic that threatened. How was she going to get them to safety?

She dragged in a deep breath. One step at a time.

"Why don't you go look in that backpack?" she suggested to Teresa. "Maybe there's a comb or a brush in it, and we can make you pretty."

While the girl fussed with the buckle on the knapsack, Sarah ruthlessly suppressed the memory of the mercenary's reaction the last time she'd appropriated one of his personal possessions.

The mercenary. *El gringo.*

Sarah made a moue of distaste as she washed her face with tepid water and a corner of her sleeve, then attacked her mouth with the toothbrush she'd appropriated earlier. If she was going to be stuck with the man until she got herself and the children out of this mess—and it looked like she was, she couldn't go on calling him "the mercenary." She searched for a name that would fit him, one she'd give him herself, since he wouldn't give her his. One that would suit a man too masculine and hard for handsomeness. Too lean and tough for politeness. Too lost to all concepts of right and wrong, she thought, for her to ever trust.

No, Sarah decided with an involuntary shiver. She didn't want to give him a name that reminded her of his disgusting profession. It would be better to come up with one that made him more human, more within her ability to manage. The image of her father's chief of staff flashed into her mind. Perfect.

With Teresa settled between her knees, Sarah went to work on her tangled hair with the black plastic comb the girl had found. She'd finished Teresa's and was attacking her own when the sound of the door swinging open caught her arm in midtug. She angled her head to see the gringo—Creighton, she reminded herself firmly—step inside.

A look of surprise crossed his face when he saw her sitting cross-legged on the folded-up mat, her long white-gold hair draped over one shoulder.

"Here," he said curtly. "Wear these when you're inside the hut."

Sarah arched a brow at his tone and caught the items he tossed at her. Obviously, the man didn't like her appropriating his comb any more than he did his boot. "I think it's better if I stay robed."

"I've got enough problems on my hands right now without you coming down with heatstroke. Put those on and keep them on. But only in this hut. When you go outside, cover yourself up. Especially that hair. Not that it'll help much," he muttered.

While Teresa scrambled to her feet, Sarah shook out the garments and held them up. Her eyes widened at the tattered skirt, in a bright pattern of pinks and greens, and the well-washed cotton blouse.

"Are there other women in camp?"

"Yes."

The terse reply irritated her. It was only a comb, for heaven's sake. "Wouldn't it be better if the children and I bedded down with these other women?" she asked stiffly. "Then we wouldn't have to...impose on you."

He flashed her a sardonic look and started to reply, but Teresa's timid voice interrupted her. "I want to stay with *el gringo*."

"Don't be silly, Teresa. We'll be more comfortable with the other women. Then *el*...then Creighton here wouldn't have to bother with us."

He frowned. "Creighton?"

"You remind me of someone by that name. Since you won't tell me yours—not that I really want to know it, you understand—I'll just call you Creighton."

His upper lip curled in distaste. "Creighton?"

Sarah struggled to her feet, yanking at the heavy skirts that threatened to trip her. "Really, I appreciate what you've done for us, but I think it would be better if you show me where the other women—" She broke off, gasping, as he moved to her side with the swift, silent grace of a jungle cat.

"You don't want to bed down with the other women, Sister Sarah. Trust me."

"I—"

"Trust me."

It took a moment, but Sarah finally got the message in his eyes. "Oh."

"Right. Oh."

After a moment, he tugged off his floppy-brimmed hat and raked a hand through his dark hair. "Look, I need you to just lay low until I figure out what the heck I'm going to do with you, okay? I don't trust any one of those scumbags out there."

"And you're suggesting that I should trust you?" Although she didn't say it, Sarah's tone indicated that she considered him just as much a scumbag as his so-called business associates.

He gave her a nasty smile. "I don't see that you've got a whole lot of choice, Sister Sarah."

Well, that much was true. She turned away, gripping the blouse and the gaudy skirt in both hands.

Jake stared at the fall of blond hair that formed such a startling contrast to the black of her robe. How in hell was he was going to keep the men's hands off her? he wondered with increasing desperation. How did he dare leave her alone in camp long enough to get to the backup radio transmitter that was hidden a couple of kilometers outside camp? He'd raised enough lewd remarks when he went to barter for some clothing with the husband of the vacant, glassy-eyed woman. The men's deep cultural inhibitions about abusing a *religiosa* were straining already.

"I'll be outside," he told her abruptly. "Send one of the children out if you need anything."

When he walked out the door, the tension knotting the muscles in Jake's neck kicked up another notch. Che was coming across the clearing toward the hut, his beefy, red-faced lieutenant at his side.

"So, gringo, you've rested from your night's adventure?"

"As much as I need to," Jake replied evenly. "Why?"

"I go to meet with our backer and arrange another drop." His dark eyes were carefully devoid of any expression. "Do you wish to accompany me?"

Jake felt a quick rush of adrenaline. His mission was to take down the American middleman who was scarfing up drug dollars in exchange for stolen arms smuggled out of the States. The narcs were supposed to take care of the elusive drug lords providing those dollars. But if Jake could get a bead on their location... Cold, sobering reality brought him up short. He couldn't leave the sister alone.

Jake gave a negligent shrug. "I'm not interested in where you get the dollars to pay me. Just that you get them."

He sensed at once that he'd given the right answer. Although Che's expression didn't alter by so much as a flicker of an eyelid, his hands shifted imperceptibly on his belt, to a less rigid grip.

Jake smiled grimly to himself. If he'd started out on the journey with the rebel leader, the chances were pretty good that he wouldn't have finished it.

"I will also discover why the government troops were in our area," Che continued. "Those who sent them will pay for it."

"Good."

If Che didn't find out through his sources, Jake intended to through his. There'd better not be another botched drop, or someone's ass was going to be in a sling, big-time. And it wouldn't be his. He hoped.

"Enrique is in charge in my absence. I'll send word of the new drop date and location as soon as I arrange it. You will go with the men, gringo, to inspect the merchandise before any money changes hands."

"Suspicious bastard, aren't you?" Jake offered with a half smile.

Che allowed a small answering twist of his lips. "Yes, my friend. I am."

As Jake joined the rest of the men squatting in the center of the clearing for the noon meal, a swift, heady feeling of relief coursed through his veins. With Che and half the camp gone, he ought to be able to manage the remaining dozen for a few days. Enrique, pig-eyed brute that he was, sported more brawn than brains.

Now, if Jake could just figure out how to keep the prickly nun and her charges safe without blowing his cover, he might just pull this damned thing off after all.

"I'm telling you, Adam, it's the only way."

Maggie paced the thick carpet in front of her boss's mahogany desk and sent him an impatient look.

Impeccably groomed and wearing a hand-tailored gray suit that had probably cost more than Maggie made in a month, Adam sat back in his black leather chair and listened while she stated her case.

"We haven't heard from Jaguar in almost twenty-four hours. Not since the emergency signal he sent yesterday saying he was in place and had a neutral on board."

"It also said to stand by."

Maggie swung to a halt in front of his desk. "That was before we got a positive ID on the remains. Now we know that Sarah Chandler is the neutral with Jake. What's more, we've had confirmation that three kids disappeared the night of the raid. Jake's got his hands full, if they're all with him."

"He's handled more difficult situations."

"True, but we've got a wild card in this situation that none of us anticipated—Senator Chandler. He's liable to mount his own rescue operation if we don't do something soon."

When Adam didn't respond, Maggie pressed her point.

"Remember how he chartered his own plane and flew into Somalia to negotiate the release of the downed chopper pilot last year? The one who just happened to be the son of one of his constituents?"

"I remember," Adam replied coolly. "Somalia wasn't our operation."

"No, but Cartoza is. Chandler could get Jake killed if he blunders in down there."

"So you want to go in instead and work the extraction, if possible?"

The fact that Adam didn't reject her plan out of hand told Maggie that he'd been considering alternative courses of action, too. Still, she'd have to talk fast to convince him to send her in instead of another agent. She knew he was reluctant to relieve her as Jake's control.

The relationship between field agent and controller was critical to any mission. The tie between them grew so intense, the ability to communicate instantly so vital, that the partnership transcended that of mere co-workers. It became a nexus, a bonding such as soldiers experienced in combat. But in this instance Maggie's instincts told her she could help Jake more on-scene than in the OMEGA control center.

"I won't break the communications loop. Samuels will relay Jake's transmissions to me real-time. And Cowboy can take over as controller for us both. He's recovered from his last mission, and knows almost as much about the area as any of us after his years as an attaché. Besides," she added, "he owes me one."

"I take it you're referring to the incident at Six-Shooters?"

Maggie glanced at Adam in mingled surprise and exasperation. "How did you know about that? That was personal, between Cowboy and me."

He merely quirked a brow.

"Okay, so you have your own sources."

She should've guessed Adam would hear how she'd rescued the handsome, easygoing Cowboy a few months back from the tough-as-nails EPA attorney who'd sunk her claws into him and refused to let go. Her disguise for that little private operation had been perfect. Not even Cowboy, as good as he was in the field, had recognized the streetwalker with the frizzy blond hair and thigh-high black plastic boots who'd sidled up to him in D.C.'s version of a country-western bar. Maggie's husky whisper that he didn't have to worry anymore, she'd been treated at the clinic for that little inconvenience, had made him sputter into his beer. It had made the attorney gasp, snatch up her purse and sail out.

The quick, irrepressible grin that was Maggie's alone flitted across her face. Among the dozen or so OMEGA agents, she was the acknowledged master when it came to impersonations. And the most outrageous. She'd perfected a chameleonlike ability to adopt the smallest nuances of any environment. That, combined with her ear for the rhythm and cadences of a local dialect, had gotten her in—and out!—of the most unlikely, impenetrable target areas. And she knew just the ticket to get her into Cartoza.

"If you agree that Cowboy can take over as controller, I have the perfect cover," she announced. "I'll go in as one of the sisters of Our Lady of Sorrows."

She caught the quick, involuntary glance Adam sent skimming down her figure. So her brilliant turquoise above-the-knee knit tunic with the picture of the latest addition to the Washington Zoo on the front wasn't exactly nunlike? So her tight black leggings hugged her calves? Adam knew that she could go from flashy to demure in the blink of an eye, or vice versa. She much preferred vice versa, Maggie acknowledged with an inner grin.

"I must admit, the idea of seeing you in a nun's habit is an intriguing prospect," Adam admitted, his blue eyes gleaming.

She leaned forward and placed both palms on his desk. "It's perfect, Adam. The sisters move freely in the country, and their chapter house in Cartoza's capital is less than twenty minutes by helicopter from Jake's last known location. Assuming he hasn't moved, and assuming the senator's daughter is still with him, I can get to the target area as soon as he calls for an extraction."

"And if he doesn't?"

"Then I'll do some intelligence gathering of my own among the locals, and at least be prepared if Senator Chandler decides to play his own hand."

"Jake hasn't called for backup," he reminded her, playing devil's advocate. "He might not appreciate you jumping into his operation."

She worried her lower lip a moment. "I know. But I just have this—"

"Prickling sensation at the base of your spine," Adam finished dryly. He rose and flicked down the cuffs of his icy blue silk shirt. "All right, Maggie. Go down to Cartoza. I think I can hold off Senator Chandler at this end for a while."

The cool assurance in Adam's voice convinced Maggie that he could hold off a half-dozen Senator Chandlers. For as long as he wished. Not for the first time, she wondered just where and how Adam Ridgeway had developed his air of authority.

In his public life, he was the son of a wealthy Boston philanthropist, had served a brief stint in the navy after college, and then settled down to the serious pleasures of an international jet-setter. His friendship with and *very* hefty campaign contribution to the dynamic young congressman who had become President had led to Adam's appointment as special envoy.

During his jet-setting years, however, Adam had also led a private, secret double life. The agents at OMEGA knew that over the years he'd provided the government with vital information that only someone who frequented the big-money world of casinos, Greek shipping magnates and international art auctions would have access to. But none of them knew exactly how he'd collected the bullet wound that scarred the flesh of his upper chest. Or how he'd gained his sharp, incisive knowledge of field operations, a knowledge that made them trust him implicitly with the lives they regularly put on the line.

Someday, Maggie thought, she just might find out.

Right now, however, she had a mission to prepare for. Flashing her boss a quick grin, Maggie whirled and left his office.

Adam's private secretary paused in the act of arranging a bouquet of daffodils in the crystal vase set on her delicate Louis XV desk. "Well, did you get the go-ahead?"

Maggie gave Elizabeth a thumbs-up. The gray-haired woman had worked for the special envoy since the position was created and was a favorite with the OMEGA agents. Multilingual, well-groomed and unfailingly polite, Elizabeth also qualified each year as an expert marksman with the 9 mm Sig Sauer Model P225 handgun she kept in a drawer at immediate hand level. Specially loaded with Glazer Teflon bullets, the weapon was devastatingly accurate at close quarters and would do serious damage to anyone unwise enough to try to force his way past the security screens on the first floor. Even the specialists who regularly tested OMEGA's state-of-the-art security systems joked that they wouldn't want to test Elizabeth.

She gave Maggie the motherly smile that so endeared her to the occasionally cynical and hard-bitten agents. "I'm glad to hear someone's going in, dear. I'll admit I've been worried about Jaguar. Although now I'll just worry about you, as well."

Maggie's eyes twinkled. "You always worry, no matter who goes in. You can rest easy this time, though. I'll be in and out of there before you know it. I'm guessing this little operation will be over within twenty-four hours—two or three days at the most."

Chapter 5

"Aaaarrrooo—ooo—gaaahhh!"

The distant, raucous roar brought Jake to instant awareness. He lay still in the predawn darkness as eerie, deep-throated answering calls echoed through the surrounding hills. A troop of howler monkeys were staking out their feeding area for the day, their deep bass wails warning other troops away from their territory.

Listening to the dominant male who lead the gravelly chorus, Jake felt a decided kinship with the shaggy-maned, bearded animal. He'd done everything but howl himself in the past twenty-four hours to keep the other men in camp away from his territory.

The big, pig-eyed lieutenant had wanted to put the blue-eyed *médica* to work on the fungal diseases and chafed skin common to men who traveled through the wet jungles. Jake had managed to convince him that the complaints could wait. She wouldn't be much use to anyone, as exhausted as she was. He'd won her a day, two at the most, he figured.

Not that Sister Sarah seemed to appreciate his efforts on her behalf.

After two days in this sweatbox, anyone else would've lost some of their starch. Not her. Although she'd exchanged her habit for the baggy cotton clothes he'd procured for her, she was as stiff-backed and prickly as ever. It still rankled when he remembered how she'd snatched the little three year old away last night. The boy had tugged on Jake's pant leg, asking if he really shooted people. Those damned beryl eyes of hers had flashed with scorn as she shushed the child and told him not to bother Señor Creighton.

Creighton, for crissakes.

Jake would have stalked out of the hut then, but a rumble of hoarse laughter outside had told him the men had decided to take advantage of Che's absence to hit the tequila. He wasn't particularly interested in watching the games they'd soon indulge in, nor did he dare leave the sister unprotected long enough to slip into the jungle and retrieve his backup transmitter. He'd have to try tonight. Tomorrow at the latest. Maggie wouldn't, couldn't, give him much longer than that.

Twenty-four more hours, Jake told himself. Forty-eight at the most. That was all he had. With luck, that was all he'd need. Che ought to have the new drop set up by then. As soon as Jake got word—and managed to retrieve his backup transmitter!—he'd tell Maggie to have an extraction team stand by. They'd swoop in and pick up the sister and the children the minute Jake led the patrol out of camp en route to the drop site. The extraction teams OMEGA used were good, a composite of elite special forces from the U.S. and the host country. The team would execute the entire rescue in radio silence, using silenced weapons and a swift, harmless gas that effectively precluded resistance. No one outside the immediate area would have any idea of what was going down. By the time Jake was a mile down the trail, the little nun beside him would be safely on her way back to her convent.

The thought made him frown in the darkness.

He lifted the net tent and rolled off the thin, lumpy mat. Dawn would come shortly, with its usual sudden swiftness. He might as well see about breakfast for his little extended family.

An hour later, Jake dropped a battered frying pan onto the crate that did double duty as a table.

"Here, I fried up some bananas."

An aroma of cinnamon and glazed sugar drifted across the already hot and humid air. The big cooking bananas, sliced lengthwise and fried to a crisp, would make a filling, nutritious breakfast.

Sister Sarah glanced up in surprise, and Jake struggled to contain his involuntary start. Even after a day and a night in the woman's company, he still wasn't used to the sight of her scrubbed, delicate face without the white wimple and black veil framing it. Or to the long blond hair she'd pulled back and tied with a narrow strip torn from the hem of her habit. Jake had never thought of himself as particularly conservative, but at this moment he wasn't sure he agreed with Pope Whoever's Vatican Council. Hair like that ought to be worn short, he decided irritably. Short and straight, in a style that didn't add several degrees of attraction to an already stunning face.

"I'll take the boys outside after they eat," he announced, in a tone that warned her not to object. He was in no mood for arguments after his long, hot, nearly sleepless night. And he sure as blazes wasn't about to offer up his boot again. The transmitter might be beyond repair, but rubber boots could save the life of someone tramping through the soggy, rotting vegetation that layered the rain-forest floor.

The primitive latrine Jake had rigged would suffice for her and the little girl, but the boys could darn well use the stream. Besides, they needed exercise. *He* needed exercise. He felt restless and edgy and caged. He wasn't used to sharing his quarters with a woman whose every move seemed to snag his gaze and whose breath fluttered softly in the darkness. Nor with three kids, two of whom, at least, appeared to be recovering from the terror of the raid. He turned away to dig out some water-purifier tablets for the canteens he'd just refilled.

Sarah bristled at the gringo's—at Creighton's—curt tone, but decided not to challenge his assumption of authority over the boys. Actually, it sent a spurt of secret relief rushing through her. After a day and a night with three small children, she was feeling an accumulation of stress that had nothing to do with their uncertain position in the rebel camp. Didn't kids *ever* run out of energy? Or questions?

Struggling to her feet in the overlarge, if blessedly cool, cotton skirt she'd donned yesterday, Sarah moved toward the makeshift table. The mercenary stepped back, but not quite far enough. Her bare arm brushed his. The feel of his warm, taut flesh, liberally sprinkled with wiry dark hair, made Sarah suck in a quick breath. She sent him a wide, startled look.

"Jesus!" he muttered, shifting his eyes back to the canteens.

"Please don't use the Lord's name in vain around the children," she admonished tartly.

His answer was a scowl.

Unsure what had put him in such a foul mood this morning, but sharing his sentiments, Sarah set out the battered tin plates and spoons their reluctant host had provided for them yesterday.

"Come on, children, you need to eat."

While the three youngsters gathered around the crate, Sarah scooped the bananas out of the frying pan. Her taste buds tingled at the delicious aroma. Breaking off an end of one banana, she popped it into her mouth. "Mmm . . . these are good."

Teresa's accusing black eyes stopped her in midswallow. Oh, hell. She'd forgotten again. Sarah gulped down the sweet, glutinous mass.

"I was just testing them, Teresa. In case they were too hot for you to eat. But they're okay. You can say grace now."

The little traitor shook her head, then smiled shyly up at the tall man standing beside her. "*You* say it, Señor Creighton."

Sarah wasn't sure which she enjoyed more—the pained expression that crossed his lean, unshaven face whenever one of them referred to him by that name, or his startled look at the thought of leading a prayer. Good, she thought with malicious satisfaction. Let him struggle with the words for a change. She'd stretched her own skimpy knowledge of Catholic prayers, gleaned from Maria in the past two weeks, about as far as they would go.

He cleared his throat, then said gruffly, "Thanks Lord. Let's eat."

His fervent efficiency won grins of approval from the smaller children. Even Eduard managed a smile.

Raising a brow, Sarah passed him a plate. "Is that the best you can do?"

"I'm a little out of practice," he admitted, showing a flash of strong white teeth against his dark stubble.

"It's time you got back into practice," she pontificated, throwing herself into her role. "You have a lot to ask forgiveness for."

The sardonic look that made his eyes shade from misty gray to dark flint passed over his face. "More than you know, Sister Sarah."

They didn't speak during the short meal, except to answer Teresa and Ricci's seemingly endless stream of questions.

Yes, Sarah was aware that Teresa's back tooth was loose.

Yes, the sun streaming in through the broken shutters made a pattern just like a big striped iguana on the dirt floor.

No, Ricci shouldn't add the insect he'd crunched between his fingers with such delight to his mashed bananas.

"C'mon, big guy." The mercenary scooped Ricci up under one arm. "Let's go outside and see if we can find you bigger game. You too, Eduard."

Sarah breathed a sigh of relief as the door shut behind two of her charges. And to think she had laughingly suggested to André one rainy, love-filled afternoon that they make lots of children. Lots of little miniature Frenchmen, with their father's heart-stopping smile and gallant Maurice Chevalier charm.

At the memory, the pain that lingered just below the surface of her consciousness seeped into her heart. Why hadn't she guessed from the way André kissed aside her attempt to picture their future, that he didn't want children? Not with Sarah, anyway. Why hadn't she realized he had no intention of leaving the four he already had, or their mother? How could she have been so stupid? So incredibly gauche? How could she ever forgive herself for making another man's wife try to take her own life?

"Sarita, will you comb my hair?"

Sarah nodded, swallowing to relieve her tight throat. She sat on the now-cleared crate and tucked Teresa between her knees. She'd managed to put a measure of her pain behind her when a soft knock sounded on the door.

Sarah snatched Teresa to her chest. She stared at the door, her heart pounding in painful thumps.

The gringo—Creighton—wouldn't knock. Nor would the boys.

Another soft thump of knuckles sounded against the wood.

Moistening her lips, Sarah called out, "Yes? Who is it? *Quién es?*"

The wooden door slowly inched open. A heavyset woman with thick black braids and a dull expression in her brown eyes stood on the stoop.

"What do you want? *Qué quiere?*"

Her eyes on the little girl, the woman held out a small bundle. *"Para la niña,"* she mumbled.

"For Teresa?"

Sarah scrambled to her feet, trying not to trip over her overlarge pink-and-green skirt. Now she knew who it belonged to. Her unexpected visitor wore a similar one, although its purple-and-blue hues were considerably more faded. Moreover, her stained blouse showed ragged, poorly stitched rips. With a flash of insight, Sarah realized the gringo must have bought or bartered for this woman's best outfit. Maybe her only other outfit.

And now she was offering something for Teresa. Perhaps a clean shift to replace the sweat-stained one the child wore. Or, better yet, some underpants. Sarah had washed the youngsters' underwear last night. The items refused to dry in the humid, muggy heat. Even chubby, smiling little Ricci had protested at putting the damp things on again.

Sarah gave the little girl a gentle push. "Go ahead, honey. Take it."

Teresa hesitated, then stepped forward. She lifted the bundle out of the woman's hand and scuttled back to Sarah's side. Her nimble fingers made short work of the string wrapped around it.

"Oooh! Look, Sarita! Look!"

Eyes shining in delight, Teresa shook out a dress in bright red cotton. Ruffles embroidered with colorful flowers and birds decorated the neckline and the full skirt. A sash of sunshine yellow looped around the waist, its long, dangling ends also embroidered in gay colors.

Teresa took a few dancing steps around the hut, the dress held up against her thin body. Excitement and the unguarded joy of a little girl shone in her face.

Sarah smiled and turned to thank the silent woman. For a moment she thought she saw a flicker of... of something in the woman's eyes as they rested on Teresa, but as soon as Sarah spoke they immediately became flat and dull.

"It's beautiful. Thank you. *Muchas gracias, señora.*"

The woman stood silent.

Teresa overcame her shyness and went forward, chattering in rapid-fire Spanish. She put out a small and rather grubby hand and laid it on the woman's arm.

Sarah's keen eye caught the convulsive way the woman's fingers folded over Teresa's, as if she wanted to impress the feel of the girl's small hand in her flesh. Then she whirled and was gone.

Teresa shrugged off her sudden departure with the cheerful unconcern of youth. "I will wear this dress now," she announced, prancing around the hut. "To show Señor Creighton how pretty I am."

Señor Creighton again!

"You'll be a lot prettier if you let me wash you first."

Teresa's wide smile faltered at the bite in Sarah's voice. Ashamed of herself, Sarah gathered the girl into her arms.

"I'm sorry, *niña*. It's . . . it's the heat."

The little girl sniffed.

"Come," Sarah coaxed, "slip out of that old dress, while I get the canteen and a cloth of some sort. I'll wash you, then we'll see if we can find something pretty to tie in your hair, okay?"

Showing her gap-toothed smile once more, the little girl complied. Sarah dug through the backpack she now had no compunctions about raiding and pulled out a pair of the white cotton briefs. With a small smile, she reached for a canteen.

She soon had the girl as clean as possible under the circumstances. The red dress was a little loose on Teresa's small body, so Sarah wrapped the sash twice around her waist and tied it with a big bow. The girl played with the flounces on the full skirt while Sarah worked the comb through her thick black hair, then parted one section of the crown and tied it with a strip torn from the mosquito netting to form a jaunty ponytail.

"Okay, sweetie," Sarah told her, patting her fanny. "You're done. You look very pretty."

Her hands holding out the sides of her skirt, Teresa twirled around once or twice.

"Okay, Sarita," she said after a moment, unconsciously imitating Sarah's slang. "Now you. Your hair needs the comb, also."

It needed a whole lot more than a comb, Sarah thought ruefully. Her lips twisted in a wry smile as she imagined her hairdresser's reaction if he were to see her now. Jonathan would no doubt take it as a personal affront that she'd let the shining mane he labored over with such devotion get into this condition.

She reached up and untied the strip of cloth binding her hair. Wincing, she began to work the comb through the sweat-tangled mess. At last the pointed plastic teeth glided smoothly. Sarah reached up and slid both hands behind her neck, then lifted the heavy weight high up on her head. She arched her back in a slow, luxurious stretch.

The door to the hut crashed open, freezing Sarah in midstretch. Shirtless, his broad chest streaked with blood, the mercenary strode in. He held Eduard's thin body high in his arms. Ricci stumbled in behind them, his lips puckered and trembling.

Openmouthed, Sarah stared at them. Creighton's eyes narrowed as he took in her uplifted arms and less-than-nunlike pose, but he didn't slow his stride.

"Shut the damn door," he growled. "Then come over here. Eduard sliced open his arm."

"What?" Sarah let her hair fall and jumped up. Slapping her palm against the door, she rushed to the man's side. "How? How did he cut himself?"

He laid the boy gently in the hammock. "The machete slipped."

"You allowed a child to play with a machete! A *machete?*" Sarah's voice rose incredulously as she shoved him aside.

"He wasn't playing. He was clearing some overgrowth from the stream behind the hut. The damned vines tripped him up."

Sarah gasped at the bright red that stained the khaki shirt wrapped around Eduard's forearm.

"I don't think he sliced through any muscle. The cut's deep, though. You'll have to suture it."

He turned away, missing Sarah's sudden stricken expression. The hand she'd reached out toward the bloodstained khaki shirt trembled violently.

"I have some disinfectant powder in my backpack," he called over his shoulder. "But no sewing kit. I'll have to see if I can round up a needle and some thick thread for you to stitch it with."

Sarah gulped down the lump lodged in her throat. She'd probably only threaded a needle once or twice in her entire life. She'd certainly never sutured anything or anyone. Nor had Sister Maria in the two short weeks Sarah assisted her in the clinic. Sarah had watched her set a broken leg, administer a good number of inoculations and sit up two days and nights tending a new mother stricken with postpartum fever. But the nursing sister hadn't stitched anything.

Sarah met Eduard's wide, unblinking stare and bit down on her lower lip, hard. There was no way she was going to fumble around and inflict unnecessary pain on this child. A man like the gringo, whose life depended on his resourcefulness, would have far more skill at stitching wounds than she did. Regardless of the consequences, she had to tell him that she wasn't a medical sister.

Sarah turned around, only to blink as he shoved a plastic bottle into her hands.

"Here, dust him down while I go find a needle." He spun on his heel and was gone before she could force out the admission trembling on her lips.

Unwrapping the bloody shirt with shaky fingers, Sarah gasped at the sight of the long slash running almost the entire the length of Eduard's forearm. Another inch or two more, and he would've sliced through the veins at his wrist. Bright red blood welled up from the laceration and trickled down his arm to splash against his chest.

"Madre de Dios," Teresa whispered, standing on tiptoe beside Sarah to peer at the wound.

"Does Eduardo die, Sarita?" Ricci's wobbling, childish treble galvanized Sarah into action.

"No. No, of course he won't die. Teresa, get me that wash rag we just used. Be sure to wring it out in clean water first."

She wrestled with the top to the plastic bottle of disinfectant powder. The blasted thing was childproof, of course. She finally got it open, then set the cap back on loosely while she dabbed at the seeping blood with the damp briefs. To her untutored eyes, the edges of the wound gaped hideously, exposing a layer of glistening muscle underneath. She pressed the edges together with trembling fingers, holding them with one hand while she dusted the whole area with the other.

Blood welled sluggishly through her spread fingers, smearing the power. Jaws tight, Sarah wiped it away, clamped the wound together again, then sprinkled more dust. Sweat beaded on her brow and trickled down her cheek. Sarah leaned back, afraid it might drip into the wound, yet kept her tight hold on Eduard's arm. The awkward position made her back strain.

It seemed like hours before the gringo returned.

"Where have you been?" Sarah snapped.

"The only needle in the entire camp is so rusty I wouldn't use it on my boot." He flashed her a sardonic look. "Of course, you have different standards when it comes to the care and maintenance of boots."

Sarah started to tell him indignantly that this was no time to start with his selfish possessiveness again, but he forestalled her.

"You'll have to do it the native way."

"What native way?"

He lifted his hand, and for the first time Sarah noticed the short length of bamboolike stalk he held. Both ends were stuffed tight with leaves.

"You'll have to use ants."

"Ants? Are you crazy?"

His eyes narrowed. "How long have you been down here, anyway?"

"Not . . . not long."

"Not long enough, obviously. When you've spent as much time in the jungle as I have, you'll learn not to dismiss native customs with such contempt."

"But . . . ants?"

"The Maya used soldier ants more than two thousand years ago to close wounds. Lots of folks around here still follow their example. A buddy of mine says African tribes do the same with driver ants. Now, do you think you can set aside your modern medical prejudices long enough to hold the edges of the skin together while I work?"

Sarah shot him a venomous look, forgetting her decision of a few moments before to confess all and throw herself on this man's mercy. It appeared that her lack of medical knowledge was totally irrelevant, anyway.

"There's no need for sarcasm." She bit the words out, her hands still clamped around the boy's arm. "My concern is for Eduard. I *have* been down here long enough to know that those ants you're talking about sting. Badly. They can kill small animals, and even the occasional human."

His gray eyes slanted toward the silent boy. "Eduard's man enough to handle the sting. Aren't you?"

The boy met his steady look and nodded slowly.

What was this? Sarah wondered, astounded. Some kind of macho male bonding? Since she didn't have any better option to offer, however, she kept her mouth shut and watched the tall, sweaty, shirtless man next to her.

He pulled the leafy plug out of one end of the tube and tapped it on his palm. Sarah's eyes widened at the sight of the huge ant that fell out. It was as big as one of her native North Carolina's crickets. And far more fearsome.

"Here, plug this back up." He shoved the tube into Teresa's hands and turned to Eduard. "Ready?"

The boy nodded once more.

Grasping the ant between his thumb and forefinger, the gringo held its head against Eduard's flesh, on either side of the cut. The big, sickle-shaped mandibles bit into the skin. When the jaws clamped shut, they drew the flesh together. Eduard jerked, but made no sound.

Leaving the head in place, the mercenary pinched off the ant's body and tossed it aside. He reached for the tube once more and swiftly, competently, repeated the procedure. Sarah moved her hands up Eduard's arm as he worked, clamping the skin together while man and insect closed it. Within moments, a neat track of black "sutures" traced up Eduard's wound.

Sarah straightened her aching back. She stared down at the wan, sweating boy, her heart aching for him. She'd been bitten by a soldier ant only once since her arrival in Cartoza, but she remembered how long and how fiercely it had stung.

"When the bleeding stops completely, we'll pat mud around the bites to draw out some of the sting."

Sarah looked up at the man beside her. "More ancient Mayan remedies?"

His cheeks creased. "No, this one's from Field Manual 90-5. The army's handy-dandy guide to jungle operations."

Sarah glanced over at the crates stenciled with U.S. markings. "How convenient. The weapons you and your friends steal come complete with a set of manuals."

She regretted the tart words almost as soon as they were out. They sounded petty after what he'd just done for Eduard. Then she reminded herself that Eduard wouldn't be here in the first place if it wasn't for this steel-eyed mercenary. She had to remember that the man frowning down at her sold his technical knowledge for cold cash to murdering rebels. Lifting her chin, she returned his scowl.

Jake fought the urge to tell her that he wouldn't need to steal the manual. He knew it by heart. Every word. Hell, he'd written most of it. He used to teach it, along with his hard-earned survival skills, at the army's special forces school. A lifetime ago. Before he'd lost his wife to his career, then his career to his own impatience with the inflexibility of a peacetime army. Before OMEGA had lured him into the dark, dangerous, lonely world of clandestine operations.

Did he dare trust her? Should he tell her now that he wasn't the man she thought he was? Jake opened his mouth, then clamped it shut. No, it was safer for her, for the children, for all of them, if he didn't. Not yet.

Jake knew he couldn't keep her confined in this little hut much longer. She needed out—for her own health, if not that of the men who grumbled about their various aches and pains. He'd have enough on his hands trying to minimize Sister Sarah's impact on the gorillas out there without worrying whether she might inadvertently let slip that Jake wasn't the man they thought he was.

When he'd confirmed the date of the drop and set up the extraction, Jake would tell her what to expect. Until then, he'd just have to put up with her scorn, even if it did sting every bit as bad as any ant bite he'd ever experienced. The sister needed to go back to the convent and get a few more lessons in forgiveness for her fellow man, he thought.

And she damn well needed to get back in that black habit.

Jake's jaw tightened as his gaze dropped to the swell of creamy flesh showing above the loosened neckline of her blouse. The image that had greeted him when he carried Eduard into the hut flashed into his mind.

Sister Sarah, with her arms raised to hold the fall of blond hair off her neck.

Her neck arched, as if in invitation.

Her blouse molded around high, firm breasts that Jake had no business noticing.

Sweat popped out on his brow. He edged past her, grabbed one of the tin plates and stalked toward the door.

"I'll go get the mud."

Chapter 6

By midmorning, the primitive sutures and soothing mud had done their job. The swelling from the ant stings had disappeared, the cut remained closed, and Sarah felt competent enough to wrap Eduard's arm in a strip of light gauze bandage she'd found in the bountiful knapsack.

When the boy fell into a light doze, the gringo tugged on his wrinkled spare shirt and left the little hut—to check on the status of his so-called business activities, Sarah supposed.

By noon, Eduard showed little effect from his injury, other than his bandaged arm. The younger children, who'd remained quiet and subdued until now, began to get restive. Sarah tried her best to divide her attention between the three of them, but found herself running out of stories and energy and patience. When the gringo returned some time later to check on them, she greeted him with something very close to relief.

One dark brow arched, but he refrained from commenting on her change of attitude. "How's your patient?" he asked, ducking his head to step closer to the hammock.

"Your patient, you mean," she said with a small, frazzled smile. "He's doing fine."

"Good enough for me to take him outside?"

"*Sí.*"

They both swung around at the soft affirmative, startled to hear Eduard speak.

He didn't say anything more. He just swung his thin legs over the edge of the hammock and sat up, his injured arm cradled in the makeshift sling Sarah had fashioned from a strip torn from the mosquito netting. Sarah started to protest, but Eduard looked at her with a silent plea.

"He has to make the pee-pee," Ricci informed them, with a three-year-old's utter lack of reticence.

The gringo laughed and strode over to help the boy out of the hammock. "Then maybe we'd better take a trip before lunch. Come on, Squirt. You too."

Sarah bit her lip, marveling at the careful yet assured way he handled Eduard. Ricci trailed happily out the door after them.

"Me, also," Teresa chirped. Red skirts swirling, she jumped up and ran out before Sarah could stop her.

Oh, well, let him handle her for a while. He certainly seemed capable of it, Sarah thought wearily. Sinking down on the handy crate, she stared at her grubby hands. Although she'd washed as best she could, mud rimmed her nails. She flipped her hands over once or twice, examining them. The long, polished tips she used to spend so much time and money on were gone, as was the smooth, tanned skin. A spasm of regret for her former life shot through her. Sarah clenched her hands into fists.

She leaned her head back against the wall of the hut and closed her eyes, wishing herself away from this place, away from the children who were more responsibility than she'd ever dreamed they could be. Away from the man who overnight seemed to have become the center of her universe.

He was unlike any of the men she'd ever known, Sarah thought resentfully. So different from the suave, urbane men she'd charmed and flirted with. And he was a universe away from the laughing Frenchman she'd fallen in love with.

Eyes closed, Sarah waited for the familiar pain that came with any memory of André. A ripple of hurt eddied through her, but it lacked the intensity of the waves that had swamped her in past weeks. And André's image seemed less sharp, less vivid, than before.

Instead, a different image imprinted itself in precise detail on the inside of Sarah's lids. Hard-eyed. Lean-hipped. Broad chest bare under the unbuttoned edges of the wrinkled khaki shirt. In her mind's eye, Sarah noted the swirls of black hair scattered lightly across the gringo's pectorals. The soft black pelt narrowed to a thin line as it angled down his chest and traced its way over a flat stomach, then disappeared into his waistband. A sudden, insidious desire to run her fingertip along that line of dark hair snaked through Sarah.

When she realized where her thoughts and her mental image had taken her, Sarah's eyes flew open. Startled, she sat bolt upright on the crate. Good Lord! She had to be more stressed than she realized. She couldn't feel anything remotely resembling physical attraction for a man like him. This liquid heat curling low in her stomach had nothing to do with him. Nothing! She was just tired. Just stressed by all she'd been through. Or maybe she was feeling something like the hostage dependency syndrome that formed a frequent topic of conversation at the dinner parties she'd hosted or attended. Among the Washington elite, international terrorism and diplomatic kidnappings were a very real concern. The State Department even offered courses on dealing with captors to senior officials traveling abroad.

That was all that was between her and this mercenary, she reasoned, a sort of sick dependency relationship. Circumstance had thrown her into his company. Some lingering shreds of conscience had led him to offer what protection he could to a fellow countryman. But Sarah couldn't let herself forget why he was here. She couldn't let herself become emotionally dependent on him. She couldn't, *wouldn't,* allow herself to feel any attraction for him.

She didn't even like him! He was scruffy, and unshaven, and as dangerous as any of the men he associated with, and...and she had no idea what his life was like outside this jungle. For all she knew, he had a wife and a houseful of kids tucked away in New Jersey. Which might explain why he was so good with Teresa and Ricci and Eduard.

The thought sent a rush of mingled pain and determination through Sarah. She'd made a fool of herself once, and hurt a lot of people in the process, herself included. She wouldn't do it again.

Nor, she decided with a rush of determination as she glanced around the hut, would she sit here any longer like some weak, gutless wimp, totally dependent on a man she couldn't allow herself to trust. She was Sarah Chandler, she reminded herself. Daughter of one of the most powerful men in Washington. A personality of some force in her own right for many years. Her reputation might be a bit tarnished these days, and her self-esteem a little dented, but, dammit, she wasn't stupid, and she wasn't going to wallow in her misery any longer. She'd done that once, with disastrous results. Once she'd tried to find an antidote to her shame and hurt in alcohol. Once she'd lost control of herself to the point that she'd plowed her Mercedes into the side of a D.C. metro transit bus. Not again. Never again.

Surging to her feet, Sarah marched over to the stack of clothing, hers and Teresa's, folded neatly atop one of the crates. Within moments, she'd shed her borrowed clothes and the suffocating black robe enfolded her from head to toe. She tied the limp strings of the wimple at the base of her neck, making sure no tendrils of hair escaped it or the black veil. Drawing in a deep breath, she headed for the door.

The reminder that the men outside would expect her to exercise her supposed medical skills made her pause with one hand on the warped wooden door. After her near panic with Eduard, however, Sarah had had time to reflect. She realized that there couldn't be any serious injuries or maladies awaiting her treatment in the camp. If there were, she would have been forced to attend to them before now. Two weeks with Maria had taught her how to administer penicillin, if necessary, and treat minor jungle ills. Assuming that they even had any medical supplies in camp. After the fiasco with the needle, Sarah wondered.

As soon as she stepped outside, she felt an immediate sense of relief. Air marginally cooler than that inside the hut swirled through the clearing. The camouflage net strung across the camp like some huge, rippling parachute provided a measure of shade. She waited while her vision adjusted after the dimness of the shack, then peered around the littered clearing. Debris from the abandoned, tumbledown huts lay interspersed with empty tins and crates the rebels had discarded. The packhorses cropped desultorily beside the stream. Sarah caught a flash of red in the bright, dappled sunlight and lifted her skirts to head for Teresa.

The black-robed figure was halfway across the clearing before Jake saw her. Surprised and furious that she would disobey his order to stay inside, he jumped up and strode to meet her. Before she could get a word out of her mouth, he grasped her arm and spun her around.

"What do you think you're doing? Get back in the hut."

She pulled her arm free. "No."

"No?" He stared at her, clearly taken aback. "What do you mean, no?"

"No."

"Look here, Sister Sarah—"

"No, you look. I'm tired of not being able to breathe in that stifling shack. I'm tired of being afraid to face these men. And I'm particularly tired of the way you say that."

Jake reared back, astounded at the sudden attack. "The way I say what?"

"The way you say 'Sister Sarah.' In that half-mocking, half-patronizing tone."

He glanced from Sarah to the hut and back to Sarah again, trying to figure out just what the hell had happened in the fifteen minutes or so since he'd left her alone.

"I can't stay inside any longer," she told him, her eyes luminous in their intensity. "I have to get out. I have to move around. I won't allow myself to be more of a prisoner than I am."

"Let's just review our options here," Jake growled. "I could damn well drag you back to the hut." In fact, he thought, it would give him a good deal of satisfaction at this moment to pick little *Sister Sarah* up, carry her back inside, and dump her on her keister.

"You could," she acknowledged, her gaze locked with his.

He jerked his chin toward the children squatting by the stream. "Or I suppose you think I could just stand guard over you and the kids, like some medieval knight protecting his lady."

One delicately arched brow told him just how little she considered him a knight in shining armor.

"Or I could let you live with the consequences of your sudden spurt of independence, which is..." Out of the corner of one eye, Jake caught sight of the beefy, pig-faced lieutenant strolling across the clearing toward them. "Which is what I'll have to do. We just ran out of options, lady."

Jake slanted her a quick look, relieved to see that she at least had the sense to wipe the determined expression from her face and dull the impact of her vivid eyes.

The man called Enrique stopped beside them. Hooking his hands in his belt, he rocked back on his heels and gave the sister a narrow, appraising glance. "So, gringo, your little *religiosa* has decided to make an appearance?"

"The heat in the shack grew too much for her," Jake replied with a shrug. "She needs air."

"Or perhaps occupation for her hands, eh?"

Jake saw her swallow quickly, then firm her lips. "Perhaps," he agreed, accepting the inevitable.

The lieutenant lifted a hand to scratch his chest. "When the men get back from patrol, I will tell them to bring their complaints to her. Myself, I'm healthy as a horse. Although..." His big paw stilled its absent movement. "Maybe I'll find a pain somewhere that needs attention, eh?"

"I'd suggest you stay healthy until Che gets back," Jake drawled. "He left you in charge of the camp, remember? And me in charge of the woman."

Enrique didn't miss the unsubtle reminder. He eyed the man opposite him lazily, as if debating whether or not to challenge him. Jake didn't alter his own easy stance, but the hairs on the back of his neck prickled. His .45 was nestled in the holster attached to his web belt. He'd left his automatic rifle propped against the wall inside the hut, however. He wouldn't make that mistake again.

"Have you heard from him?" Jake asked casually. "Che said he'd radio in as soon as he arranged a new drop."

"No, but we should hear from him soon. Unless the *patrón* was not there when he arrived. Then Che must wait until he returned."

Jake's mouth twisted. For too many years, the great landowners had oppressed the people of this region, paying them slave wages for backbreaking labor on their coffee and banana plantations. Now a new generation of powerful barons had gained financial dominance—the drug lords who operated the processing plants hidden in Cartoza's deep, protected valleys. They were slowly gaining a stranglehold over the economic fabric of the country that was more pervasive, more devastating, than that of the old landowners. Even Che, a man dedicated to overthrowing the current government in favor of a people's democracy, depended on a *"patrón"* for funding. So much for the revolutionary's political purity, Jake thought cynically.

"Let me know when you hear from him. I'll be around."

"So will I, gringo," the man replied, his eyes on the nun.

Pig-face would take some watching. Close watching.

Jake shepherded the sister back toward the children. "I think we need to review a few of the ground rules here, Sister Sar—" He stopped himself, remembering her objection to the way he said her name.

She waved an impatient hand. "Oh, just call me Sarah. It's . . . it's permitted in most orders now, you know."

"No, I didn't know."

Jake frowned, not at all sure he wanted to drop her title. He hadn't realized that he'd been so patronizing when he used it, but at least it had kept a nice, neat barrier between them. Sarah sounded far too . . . human.

"Why don't you just join the kids by the stream?" he suggested curtly, uncomfortable with this business of names. "I'll go see if I can find something other than beans for lunch."

He recrossed the clearing some time later, juggling two cans of tuna fish that had cost him an infrared starlight rifle scope. The scope's loss wasn't critical, since Jake had another that slid onto the special grooves in the barrel of his .45. With a little modification to the mounting, it could be fitted to the automatic rifle, as well. Still, he was running through his equipment at almost as fast a clip as Sis—as Sarah was running through his personal possessions.

He tossed a can in the air, then almost missed catching it as he halted in midstride. Eyes narrowed, Jake searched the shadowed spot beside the stream where he'd left his charges. They weren't there.

Spinning on his heel, he strode to the hut and yanked open the door. Even before his eyes adjusted to the gloom of the interior, Jake knew they weren't inside. No little girl's giggles echoed in the silence. No little boy demanded that Sarita take him in her lap. Tossing the cans aside, Jake grabbed his automatic rifle. In a movement so swift and instinctive it took less than three seconds, he pressed the magazine release, checked that the clip carried a full compliment, then snapped it back in place. Jaw clenched, he headed back out the door.

He hadn't heard any screams. There hadn't been shouts. Any muted laughter or disturbance among the men. A swift, gut-wrenching fear rose in him that Sarah had decided to carry her unexpected streak of independence to the extreme. Despite his warnings, she might have taken the children and tried to slip out of camp. It would be easy enough. The rebels didn't mount much of a guard. They didn't need to. One of the skills Jake had "sold" them was how to arm the ultrasensitive intrusion detection devices that now ringed the camp's perimeter. The motion sensors concealed tiny built-in computers that differentiated between sizes and shapes and body heat. Small animals wouldn't set the sensors off, but humans would. Even humans as slender and slight as Sarah....

A cold sweat chilled Jake's body. If detonated, those devices wouldn't leave a whole lot of Sarah and the children for the jungle scavengers to feast on. He cursed silently, savagely. He shouldn't have left them alone. Even for a second. He shouldn't have—

"Señor Creighton! Señor Creighton!"

At the sound of Teresa's high-pitched shriek, Jake dropped into a crouch and whirled. The scampering girl stumbled to a halt a few paces away, her mouth dropping at the sight of the gun leveled at her. A short distance behind her, three other faces registered varying degrees of surprise and shock.

Jake's breath hissed out. He raised the barrel skyward and straightened slowly. His eyes blazed at Sarah, searing her small, delicate face, her incredible eyes, her high cheeks and full, pink lips, into his mind, to replace the image that had knotted his stomach just moments before.

"Where the—?" He bit off the blistering words he would've used with any other person in similar circumstances and tried again, spacing each furious syllable for maximum emphasis. "Where...in...the ...*hell*...have... you...been?"

She blinked, clearly taken aback at his vehemence. "We've been with Eleanora. At her lean-to."

"With Eleanora. At her lean-to. Who in the *hell* is Eleanora?"

"Oh, for Pete's sake. What's gotten into you?"

Jake rubbed his hand down his mouth and chin, feeling the rasp of bristles against his palm. He couldn't tell her what had gotten into him. Not yet. The stomach-twisting, heart-pounding fear he felt for her had been too raw, too intense. Too far outside the range of emotions he'd allowed himself to experience for too many years. Jake wasn't quite sure how his emotions, not to mention his life and his mission, had seemed to spin out of control from the moment he parted those damned palmetto bushes and found her crouched behind them.

"I take it Eleanora is the woman who gave Teresa her red dress?" he managed, in a more moderate tone. "The one whose husband sold me those clothes for you?"

It was a pretty safe guess. The only other female in camp was Che's comrade cum mistress, who was with him on his little trek to the *patrón*'s hacienda right now. So much, he thought, for keeping Sarah and the kids away from the camp's other female residents.

Sarah nodded. "She offered to share her lunch with us. It was delicious. Some kind of fresh meat I didn't recognize, with nuts and rice, all mixed together."

Jake had a pretty good idea what the meat was. Except for wild pigs and small, bear-like kinkajous, few mammals inhabited the wet floor of the rain forest. Eleanora had probably cooked up a nice lizard or snake casserole. Before he could tell Sarah so, however, Teresa stepped forward to tug on Jake's pant leg.

"Look, Señor Creighton." Her face regained the excitement it had held before the momentary fright the gun had given her. "Eleanora gave me a dress for the doll you made for me. Look. Look!"

Jake hunkered down and looked. The mango root he'd found beside the stream earlier this morning and carved into a somewhat squash-faced baby now sported a frilly little skirt and kerchief. After duly admiring the root's new wardrobe, Jake straightened. Teresa and Ricci scampered off. Eduard followed more slowly.

Sarah tilted her head, eyeing him thoughtfully. "It was kind of you to make Teresa that doll."

"Yeah, well, it's just a root."

"You're very good with the children." She hesitated. "Do you have a family waiting for you at home? A daughter Teresa's age, perhaps?"

Jake thought of the series of empty, echoing apartments, sparsely filled with rented furniture, that he'd called home since his divorce so many years ago. He hadn't needed or wanted anything more, hadn't had time for anything more.

"No, there's no one waiting," he answered with a shrug. "And it's easy to be good with these kids. They expect so little of life that they're grateful for whatever crumbs fall their way."

She nibbled on her lower lip for a minute, processing the bits of information he'd given her. "You're a man of many talents, Señor Creighton."

"Look," he said with a tight smile, "if I'm going to call you Sarah, you have to stop laying that Señor Creighton bit on me."

"Then what shall I call you... other than gringo?"

"Try Jack."

"Jack." She rolled it around on her tongue experimentally. "Jack. It suits you. Is that your real name?"

His smile eased into a grin. "No, but it's close enough."

"Someday I'm going to find out just who you are."

She'd said it lightly, in jest, but the words seemed to hang between them. A troubled expression crossed her expressive face, as though she'd belatedly realized that knowing too much about him might not be too wise. A man on the wrong side of the law in at least two countries wouldn't want many people walking around who knew his identity.

"Why don't you show me what medical supplies the camp has on hand?" she said quietly, turning away. "And tell me what I can expect to encounter when the patrol returns."

* * *

All in all, Sarah thought later that night, she'd handled her first face-to-face encounter with the scruffy band of guerrillas pretty well. She'd kept her head down, her eyes on her work, and her conversation to a minimum. Jack had augmented her sketchy Spanish, translating for her when she couldn't fully grasp the explanation of the symptoms. Luckily, she hadn't been presented with any scabrous sores or debilitating injuries. She didn't have anything more serious than a severe case of warm-water foot immersion to deal with.

Despite its innocuous name, warm-water foot immersion was a potentially dangerous disease. It occurred frequently in areas with a lot of streams or creeks to cross. Sarah had been briefed on it during the first aid course she took as part of her Peace Corps training. Since so much of Cartoza was covered by soggy rain forest, Sister Maria had been particularly knowledgeable about the condition. If left untreated, it was painful and could eventually lead to permanent crippling. But if the sufferer's white, wrinkled, bleeding feet were kept dry and dusted with powder regularly, the condition would soon clear up. Sarah passed her instructions through Jack to her patient, a thin, stoop-shouldered rebel named Xavier, who seemed more interested in her blue eyes than her medical skills.

Now, after sharing another meal with Eleanora, Sarah had cleansed Eduard's cut, rebandaged it, and settled her charges for the night. Shielded by the stack of crates, she'd changed out of the sweaty habit and once more wore the loose cotton blouse and skirt. She sat on her bedroll, knees drawn up, and plucked at the bright pink-and-green material of her skirt.

"Did you see the bruises on Eleanora's arms?" she asked quietly.

Jack's hand stilled momentarily on the shiny nickel-plated revolver he was cleaning. His eyes were shadowed as he sent her a glance across the dim hut, which was lit only by the tiny flame dancing over the Sterno can beside him.

"I saw them," he said.

Sarah crossed her arms on her knees and rested her chin on them. "I don't think that evil little man she's with is really her husband. She doesn't speak much, except to Teresa, but from something she let slip, I think her father sold her, *sold her,* to him when she was just thirteen or fourteen."

"From your work with the church, you must know that it happens a lot down here, especially in the interior. Crops fail, a family has too many children to feed—"

"Knowing about it doesn't make it any more acceptable!"

He refused to be drawn into that argument.

"Eleanora seems so desperate to touch Teresa." Sarah nibbled on her lower lip for a moment. "I think she must have lost a child of her own."

Setting the pistol aside, Jack leaned forward and regarded her intently. "Listen to me, lady. You've got enough problems of your own right now without taking on Eleanora's. We both do."

Sarah lifted her chin from her knees. "Maybe it's time we talked about those problems. I know mine, but I'm not sure I understand yours, or where you're coming from. Why are you protecting me and the children? What's in it for you, Jack?"

She hadn't meant to sound accusing or disdainful, but the contempt she couldn't suppress crept into her voice.

He stared at her for a moment, then shrugged and retreated behind the shuttered screen of his eyes.

"Maybe you didn't understand the little discussion Che and I had when we hauled you into camp. The government forces are putting enough pressure on his little band of cutthroats as it is. If I'd allowed the trigger-happy bastards to kill you the night of the raid, the public outcry over a nun's murder would have tripled the intensity of the air patrols. I wasn't eager to have the *federales* descend on this camp, guns blazing, until I'd hightailed it out of here."

Sarah's heart turned over in her chest. "Just when do you plan to do that—hightail it out of here?"

"When my business is done."

"What happens to me and the children when you leave?"

Across the dim, shadowed interior their eyes locked. Silence dragged out between them until Sarah felt it in every pore, every nerve.

"I don't know yet," he finally replied. "You'll just have to trust me."

"Trust you..." She stared at him, unspeaking, for moments longer. Then she turned away and reached for the rolled-up mosquito net. It fell between them, a filmy curtain that shut out his face and shut Sarah in with her doubts and fears.

Jake slid the .45 back into its holster, his throat tight. He wanted to tell her. Christ, his gut ached with the need to tell her. But he didn't dare. Not yet. As he doused the Sterno "candle" and slid into the bedroll beside hers, however, Jake swore that he'd erase that faint, lingering contempt in her eyes if it was the last thing he ever did.

He lay awake in the darkness, one arm crooked under his head, wondering just why it was so important to him.

The children's steady breathing joined the chorus of night songs from the jungle outside. Sarah shifted on her pallet, her hips twisting this way and that as she sought a comfortable position. After a while, her soft, breathy sighs told Jake she'd slipped into slumber.

She was some restless sleeper.

He smiled in the darkness as she mumbled incoherently into the bedroll and twitched her hips once more. But the smile froze on his face when Sarah flopped over on her back. She flung out an arm, touching him as she had the first night in the hut. Only this time her hand didn't just rest on his arm. This time she clutched at him in an unconscious, reflexive reaction to the contact, then followed the touch of her hand with a snuggle. There was no other word for it. She twisted across the space between their bedrolls and snuggled up against his side. Her breast pressed against the wall of his chest. Her cheek rubbed against his shoulder, seeking a comfortable position.

Common sense told Jake to slide his shoulder out from under her head and turn his back to her. Or at least nudge Sarah back over onto her own thin mattress. He didn't do either, however. Instead, he lay still, feeling the wash of her breath against his neck. Hearing the little smacking noise she made as she settled once more into sleep. Reminding himself that she was off-limits. The scent of her surrounded him, all sun-warmed, musky female.

Despite every reminder, despite every stern warning to control himself, Jake felt his senses flicker, then ignite. His groin tightened, slowly, painfully. It took every ounce of discipline he possessed, but Jake resisted the fierce need to curl his arm about her shoulder and press her even more firmly against him. He lay still and unmoving, cursing the tattered remnants of a conscience that wouldn't allow him to roll over and cover her soft body with his own.

He was still wide awake when a booted foot slammed against the door to the hut.

"Hey, gringo!"

Jake had rolled out from under the net and was on his feet before the second kick banged against the wood.

"Che wants to speak with you!" Enrique shouted unsteadily through the door. "Hey, *americano!*"

A third kick sent the door crashing back on its hinges. Enrique stumbled inside, his flashlight waving wildly. Its sharp, powerful beam caught the startled, frightened faces of the children clutching at their hammock edges. It swept over the bedrolls, then jerked back to pin Sarah in its piercing glare. Her silvery blond hair tumbled over her shoulders as she sat up and raised a hand to shield her eyes. Jake stifled a groan at the sight of her high, firm breasts clearly silhouetted against the thin cotton blouse.

Enrique didn't make any attempt to stifle his reaction. He gaped, openmouthed, for several seconds. Then a slow, hoarse chuckle sounded deep in his throat. "So this is why you've not joined us to drink tequila and exchange war stories these past nights, gringo. Your *médica* has been tending to your aches privately, eh?"

His thick, slurred phrasing told Jake there wasn't a hope in hell of them talking their way out of this.

"I, too, have such an ache, gringo." Enrique held the flashlight on Sarah with one hand while he fumbled at his belt buckle with the other. "You go talk to Che, and I will see that my pain is treated, eh?"

Jake had only one option.

He took Enrique down.

Chapter 7

A single, swift chop to the neck, and Enrique's knees buckled. Before he hit the dirt, Jake bent and caught the big man's weight across his shoulders. It happened so fast, so quietly, that the only evidence of any struggle was the flashlight bouncing on the dirt floor.

"Get that," Jake grunted, staggering back a step under the weight of the unconscious man.

Sarah scrambled to the end of the bedroll and caught the spinning metal cylinder. Her hands shaking wildly, she directed the beam at Jake. He winced and turned his head away from the blinding light.

"Point it at the ground, for God's sake, then hand it to me."

When she'd complied, he tried to give her and the children assurances he was far from feeling himself. "Don't worry, we're going to bluff our way through this."

"Bluff?" The word came out in a strangled squeak. "How?"

"I'm guessing Che wants to talk to me because this dumb son of a b—because Pig-face here is too drunk to understand the specifics on the drop. Che's probably furious with him and wouldn't object too strenuously if I put him out of action for a while." Jake smiled grimly. "You may get the chance to practice a few of your medical skills on this goon when he wakes up. *If* he wakes up."

Sarah's blunt-tipped fingers dug into his arm as he swung away. "Be . . . be careful."

"I always am. But it probably wouldn't hurt if you say a couple of prayers in the next few minutes."

In fact, Jake thought, it wouldn't hurt if she said a whole basketful of them. Using the flashlight to guide him, he made his way across the clearing to the shack Che had designated as his headquarters, kicked open the door and strode inside. Half a dozen startled faces turned at his entrance. With a twist of his shoulders, Jake dumped Enrique's inert bulk on the floor. His compatriots gaped at the sprawled body. Ignoring them, Jake crossed to a rack of portable communications equipment arrayed on a rickety table.

"Get Che for me," Jake rapped out to the man seated on a stool before the radio. "Now."

"He's . . . he's standing by."

With a jerk of his head, Jake motioned for the man to vacate his seat. Picking up the hand-held mike, he pressed the transmit button. "This is the gringo. What have you got?"

"Arrangements have been made for another shipment. Our supplier will deliver it personally. He was most unhappy that the last shipment was diverted. There will be no mistakes with this one.''

Che's voice bore the sharp edge of anger and frustration. Poor bastard, Jake thought cynically. He had to choose between a lieutenant he couldn't rely on and an *americano* he despised.

''It will arrive at approximately 1100 hours on the twenty-seventh,'' the rebel announced.

The twenty-seventh! Jake swore viciously under his breath. That was three days from today. He had to make it through three more days in this camp. Three more days of keeping Sarah and the kids safe. Two more nights of lying beside her.

''Give me the coordinates.''

''Enrique has them,'' Che said coldly.

''Enrique may not survive the night,'' Jake drawled. ''He's starting to annoy me, big-time.''

Che drew in a swift, sharp breath, audible even over the radio. ''Enrique will survive long enough to lead you to the drop site. After you show us how to operate the missiles, I don't care which one of you puts a bullet in the other's head.''

''That's what I like about you, pal. You're such a warm, caring son of a bitch. So tell me, what did you find out about the *federale* presence in our sector?''

Jake smiled to himself at the frustration that almost sizzled through the receiver. ''It appears it was an unannounced exercise. A stupid scheduling mistake by some staff officer at the headquarters. The *patrón* is most displeased.''

''Just tell him to make sure it doesn't happen on the twenty-seventh. One more screwup and even your *patrón* won't be able to afford my fees.''

The radio went dead. Jake tossed the mike onto the tabletop and swung around on the stool to survey the occupants of the room. They stared back at him with varying degrees of anger, wariness and interest on their faces. Pig-face lay sprawled in the dirt before them, like one of the huge, hoglike tapirs he resembled.

"Is that tequila?" Jake asked, nodding to the cloudy bottle standing on the table amid a litter of grease-stained cards and half-full glasses.

"*Sí,*" one of the men answered cautiously.

Jake rose and stepped over Enrique's bulk. "Pour me a drink. It may be a while before your friend here wakes up and we settle matters between us."

A thin, slumping man who'd been one of Sarah's patients picked up the bottle. He sloshed tequila into a dirty glass, shoved it toward Jake, then jerked his chin toward Enrique. "Why do you fight with that one?"

"His ugliness annoys me."

A ripple of laughter greeted the sardonic response. By the time Enrique began grunting and twitching, the men at the table didn't make any effort to hide their amusement at his graceless return to consciousness. Jake concealed his satisfaction behind an impassive face. He'd spent half his life leading men. He knew that few soldiers would respect or follow someone who'd been made to look ridiculous in their eyes. And the picture Enrique presented when he finally sat up, slack-faced and drooling spittle, inspired very little respect.

"So, Enrique," Xavier called out, "the gringo says your face offends him. I can see why."

The bellows of laughter that accompanied this sally sent a wave of mottled red across the face under discussion. "Perhaps you won't laugh so much when I tell you that I saw the little *religiosa* in his bed," Enrique snarled.

"While we make do with Pablo's slut of a wife, this one has been plowing between those tender white thighs."

The sideways glances the men sent Jake contained surprise, suspicion and a faint hint of disapproval, followed swiftly by hot, avid interest.

Jake didn't entertain much hope of convincing the big, red-faced man that he'd been hallucinating, but he figured it was worth the try. "You're a pig, Enrique. And you're drunk. You let your filthy mind run away with you. You frightened the woman and disgusted me."

Enrique lumbered to his feet. "I know what I saw. You thought to keep her to yourself, eh, gringo? No more. After tonight, we all share her. Except you, of course. Tonight you die."

He fumbled for the pistol in his holster.

Jake didn't alter his loose-limbed sprawl. One hand toyed with the tequila glass, the other rested negligently in his pants pocket.

"You cannot kill him, Enrique," a short, frowning rebel protested. "Che has said he must be at the drop site in three days."

In a few succinct words, Enrique dismissed his leader. He pulled out a big-framed .45 with a silver replica of the Mayan sun calendar on its decorated grip. Chairs tumbled over backward as the men scrambled out of the line of fire.

"And do you also expect your *patrón* to perform that particular unnatural act?" Jake inquired lazily. "He will be no more pleased than Che if you make him waste the money he's laying out for the shipment."

The casual observation brought even the drunken lieutenant up short. Enrique knew as well as Jake that the drug lords would be far more relentless and exacting in their retribution toward one who crossed them than Che would ever be. The guerrilla leader wouldn't hesitate to put a bullet through an enemy's forehead. The drug lords' henchmen would make him beg for it.

Enrique hesitated, the .45 wavering in his big paw. After a long, tense moment, he jammed it back in its tooled leather holster. "Maybe I won't shoot you, after all. Maybe I will just cut off your *cojones.*"

"You can try, my snout-nosed friend. You can try."

Jake loosened his grip on the weapon in his pocket. The palm-size .22 carried five hollow-point rounds, any one of which would've put Enrique down. Jake wouldn't need them now. Tossing down a last swallow of tequila, he rose.

A feral light sprang into the lieutenant's eyes at the sight of the easy target. His hand moved toward the belt hooked over the back of a nearby chair.

Jake's razor-sharp machete sliced through the air. Its lethal, specially balanced blade pinned the leather belt to the chairback and toppled the chair over with the force of the throw.

"No knives," Jake told the startled lieutenant. "No guns. Let's settle this in a way that will give satisfaction to us both."

A slow grin spread across Enrique's red face. "You're right, gringo. I will much enjoy feeling my fists smash into your face. Almost as much as I will enjoy your woman squirming and thrashing beneath me."

Jake could have ended the farce that followed at any time, but he took a savage pleasure in reducing Enrique to a staggering, gurgling, bloody hulk. His rational mind argued that he needed to destroy the last shreds of confidence the other men placed in the lieutenant's authority. A primitive, wholly male instinct, however, wanted to make sure Enrique understood what the consequences would be if he touched Sarah.

Jake didn't escape totally unscathed himself. For all Enrique's bulk and drunken state, he packed the power of a bull behind his hammerlike fists. When the big man lay sprawled on the dirt floor once again, Jake hooked a foot around a chair leg and dragged it to the table.

"Now, my friends," he panted, dragging the back of his hand across his bleeding lip, "let's finish that tequila."

Jake closed his eyes as clear liquid fire slid down his throat and curled in his belly. He sagged back against his chair, enjoying the heat, the feeling of satisfaction, even the pain that throbbed in his chin.

He should go back to the hut. Sarah would be wide-eyed and trembling with anxiety, he knew. He also knew that there was no way he could soothe her fears and stretch out beside her right now. Not with his blood pounding in his veins and the remembered feel of her body next to his battling with the last remnants of his conscience.

Sarah sat in rigid, unmoving silence. The flickering light of the Sterno lamp surrounded her and the children in a small circle of gloom. They huddled against her, clinging to the black robe she'd hastily pulled on. It had saved them once before. With a sick, wrenching fear, Sarah hoped it wouldn't have to save them again.

When no shots or screams sounded for what seemed like hours, the children's fear slowly eased. Sarah's, however, mounted with each passing moment. Where was he? she wondered with increasing desperation. What would she do if he didn't return? Oh, God, he had to return. She squeezed her eyes shut and repeated for the hundredth time the prayers he'd suggested.

Only gradually did Sarah realize that more than just self-preservation motivated her fervent prayers. It wasn't the lean, unshaven mercenary she wanted to see step through that door. She wanted to see Jack. Or, better yet, the Señor Creighton Teresa idolized. The man who'd carved a doll out of a mango root and tucked a delighted, squealing three year old under his arm. The man who coaxed even the still, silent Eduard to speak. The man who made Sarah's breath catch when he creased his cheeks in that damned crooked smile of his.

The man who finally returned, however, wasn't any of the ones Sarah had prayed for. She gave a glad cry of welcome when she saw his shadowy but unmistakable form silhouetted in the door, then gasped when he stepped into the little circle of light. Brownish dried blood covered most of his face and spattered his bare chest. Even in the dim sputter of the tiny flame she could see the dark bruise that covered one side of his jaw.

At her startled gasp, he attempted what must have been meant as a reassuring smile but ended up as a grimace of pain. He staggered a bit as he put a hand up to his jaw.

"Oh, my God!" She pushed herself out of the children's grasp and flew across the hut to take his arm. "Move, children. Let him sit down on the crate. Teresa, get me the cloth we use to wash with. Eduard, you find the disinfectant. The little bottle of liquid antiseptic, not the dry powder we used on you."

"It looks worse than it is," Jack muttered as she helped him ease down. "Most of the blood belongs, uh, belonged to Pig-face."

"Did he die?" Ricci asked, wide-eyed and tremulous.

Sarah bit her lip as she took the canteen and the white cotton briefs from Teresa. That a three year old should have such a fixation with death tore at her heart.

The gringo tried again. This time he managed more grin than grimace. "No, Squirt, he didn't die. But he'll probably wish he had when he wakes up."

"Good!" Eduard's low response made up in ferocity what it lacked in volume.

Jack's head swung toward the boy. "You didn't like old Pig-face, either, huh?"

"For pity's sake," Sarah said, turning his chin back to examine it. "Hold still."

With a rush of relief, she saw that he'd been right when he said most of the blood wasn't his. Aside from several swelling bruises, she discovered only one laceration, along his jawline.

"Tilt your head back so I can clean this," Sarah ordered, hoping against hope that she wouldn't have to perform an ant-optomy.

He propped his head back against the wall. Eyes closed, he allowed her to tend him. She wiped the last of the dried blood from the underside of his chin, then took the bottle of antiseptic Eduard handed her.

"Ouch!"

Sarah blinked. Somehow she hadn't thought this tough-as-unchewed-leather mercenary would be so sensitive to pain. Gentling her touch, she dabbed at his chin once more.

"That stings."

The plaintive complaint sounded so much like that of a little boy that Sarah couldn't help smiling. She moved closer to his side and slipped one arm around his neck. Cradling his head against her shoulder as she would Eduard's or Ricci's, she swabbed his cuts.

But the body pressed against hers wasn't Eduard's or Ricci's. It was long and sleekly muscled and musky with the scent of a man. Sarah felt a stir of awareness at the feel of him leaning into her. Her swift, instinctive reaction quickly gave way to another emotion, however. An unexpected tenderness welled up in her heart. For so many days now, she'd drawn from this man's strength. For so many nights, she'd fallen asleep knowing he was beside her. That he would now wrap an arm around her hips and lean into her for support filled her with soft, sweet warmth.

She was so bemused by the feeling that it was some moments before she realized his head had turned a few degrees, until his cheek rested on the slope of her breast. And that his arm had slowly tightened, drawing her even closer into the heat of his body. It took a moment more before she registered the fact that the hand on her hip no longer just rested there. Through the heavy fabric of her robe, his fingers kneaded the swell of rounded flesh.

"What are you doing?" Sarah gasped, pushing herself out of his hold.

"I..." A wave of confusion crossed his face for a moment, to be replaced almost immediately by a scowl. His arm dropped. "Damn, it was the tequila."

Sarah was so disturbed by the sensations his touch had aroused that she didn't even chastise him for his inappropriate language.

"Tequila? Have you been drinking?"

"A little." He met her incredulous stare, then shrugged. "Hell, a lot."

Sarah's mouth sagged open, then closed to a thin, ominous line. "You mean we've been sitting here in the dark, frantic with worry, and you've...you've been swilling tequila with that rabble out there?"

At her accusing tone, a tinge of red rose in his cheeks. "Look, I was just cementing my relationship with the boys. So they wouldn't come looking for Sister Sarah to tend their 'aches,' as well."

Sarah stood rigid while a slow, fiery fury flowed through her veins. He'd been drinking, while she sat here terrified, praying her heart out for him! He'd been schmoozing with his cretinous pals while she blocked out every despicable aspect of his character and painted him as a cross between Santa Claus and an unshaven Pierce Brosnan! He'd stumbled in, covered with blood, and made Sarah's heart leap in fear. She'd cradled him to her breast like some hurt child. Now he had the nerve to sit there, his head tilted up at her belligerently, and scowl at her as though the whole thing had been her fault.

Acting on pure impulse, Sarah tipped her hand and poured the entire bottle of disinfectant over his cut.

"Jesus H. Christ!"

This time Sarah would have chastised him, if she hadn't been so startled by his reaction. His drinking hadn't dulled his reflexes, she discovered. With the deadly speed of a bushmaster, he uncoiled his long body and sprang up. A hard hand grabbed her outstretched wrist and twisted it up behind her.

Off balance, Sarah stumbled against his bare chest. The soft, springy pelt she'd fantasized about brushed her cheek. She tried to push herself away with the flat of her palm. He held her easily with one hand, which only added to Sarah's pounding, white hot anger.

"You want to explain that little bit of medical malpractice, *Sister Sarah?*"

"Figure it out for yourself, gringo."

She realized her mistake as soon as the words were out. There wasn't anything even remotely nunlike in the way she challenged him, eyes flashing, fury radiating from every inch of the body he held pressed against his own.

His eyes narrowed. In the dim light, Sarah couldn't see their expression, but she felt his body stiffen against hers. The hand holding her wrist behind her back tightened, and her breasts were crushed against a solid, unyielding wall of hard, male flesh.

They stared at each other, unspeaking, until a small whimper shattered the tension arcing between them.

"Please, Señor Creighton, you and Sarita, you must not fight."

Teresa's tearful voice brought them back to the reality of a small, airless hut and three frightened children. The hold on Sarah's wrist loosened, then fell away. She stepped back and drew in a long, shuddering breath.

"I'm . . . I'm sorry," she stuttered.

His eyes were guarded, curiously so after his blazing anger of moments before.

"I was petrified, sitting here in the dark, not knowing what was happening. I . . . I said every prayer I knew for you." She stumbled through the apology, not really sorry, but shaken enough by what had just occurred that she felt the need to reestablish their previous relationship.

His jaw worked for a moment. "Well, I suppose I have to thank you for your spiritual intervention, but I'll damn sure let you know when I want any more of your medical attention. Now let's see if we can get some sleep for what's left of the night."

The children managed to drift back into quiet slumber, but they were the only ones. Jake lay still and tense in the darkness, waiting for dawn to slice through the cracks in the tin roof with its characteristic suddenness. He could tell from Sarah's lack of movement that she wasn't sleep. She lay with her back turned stubbornly to him, too far away to touch, too close for him to ignore the prickling sensation her mere presence caused within him.

He knew the knife-edged tension that kept him awake was the culmination of the night's events. The brawl with Enrique. The knowledge that the drop was set and Jake could finally contact OMEGA. The fiery tequila. The feel of Sarah's hips cradled in his arm.

The desire that had been curling in Jake's belly since the moment she'd snuggled up to him all those hours ago suddenly jackknifed. He gritted his teeth, straining to keep a leash on his rampaging libido. Drawing up one knee to ease the coiled ache, he cursed himself and her in the darkness.

Didn't she know better than to hold his head against her breast like that while she swabbed his cuts? Didn't she know that every time she even brushed his arm, fire streaked all along his nerves? Couldn't she sense how it twisted his gut every time she feathered her fingers through her hair?

For all that she wore a nun's habit, wasn't she still woman enough to recognize the effect she had on a man when she flashed those magnificent, fury-filled eyes up at him? At that moment, Jake had come so close to forgetting who she was and where they were that it scared the hell out of him.

His jaw clenching, Jake played and replayed that strange confrontation in his mind.

He'd dealt with enough people in his time to know that no human being ever really fit a stereotype. The toughest first sergeant he'd ever worked with had had an almost pathological fear of heights. The sweet, honey-haired second-grade teacher he'd dated for a while after his divorce had kept a library of porno flicks just the other side of kinky. Maggie Sinclair, with her long legs, sparkling brown eyes and infectious grin, could put a bullet through the center of a target forty-four out of forty-five times.

So it didn't bother Jake that Sarah wasn't exactly a younger version of Mother Teresa. He could accept that she sported a fall of silvery-blond hair under the black veil. He understood that she was only human, like when she alternated between quiet competence and frazzled weariness with the children. He knew that the fear and strain of waiting for him tonight had toppled many of the barriers between them, causing her to blaze up at him like any outraged female confronting an errant male.

Still, that confrontation bothered him. And he didn't know why.

Jake's mouth settled into a tight line. Maybe it was his own internal alert mechanism that had activated this indefinable tension that shimmered right below his skin's surface. Maybe his body was signaling that he'd gotten too close to this operation, too emotionally involved with Sarah. He needed to back off, to avoid any repetition of the fierce, primal protectiveness he'd felt when Enrique threatened her. He sure as hell needed to avoid any more physical contact with her. From here on, he had to concentrate more on his mission and less on this woman who intrigued, irritated and aroused him in equal measures.

That was it, Jake decided. He had to get this operation moving forward again. As soon as he could slip out of camp, later today, he'd reclaim his backup transmitter and reestablish contact with his OMEGA control. Now that he knew the approximate time of the drop, he could work out the details of the extraction and strike with Maggie Sinclair.

Some of Jake's tension eased at the thought of Maggie. Once again he thanked his lucky stars she was the controller for this operation. Not that the others weren't good—damn good. But Maggie and that sixth sense of hers were in a separate category altogether. Of course, her uncanny instincts were probably going bananas right now. No doubt she'd worn a track in the tile floor of the control center with her pacing over the lack of contact with Jaguar.

Jake wiped away the trickle of sweat that signaled the imminent arrival of another hot, humid dawn, then grinned wryly in the dark. At least Maggie was doing her worrying and pacing in air-conditioned comfort.

Chapter 8

Maggie couldn't remember the last time she'd been so hot!

It was still early morning, just an hour past dawn, and yet her heavy black robes were already sticking to her back. She sat on the sticky vinyl seat of the bus taking her into Cartoza's capital and fanned the air with one hand. The sleeve of her habit flapped energetically but stirred up a lot more dust than breeze. Despite the heat and the crowd packed belly to belly in the wheezing, huffing bus, however, Maggie felt a familiar drum of excitement beating in her veins.

She was back in the field!

After an intense session with Cowboy to get him up to speed and a hurried outfitting by the OMEGA uniform specialists, she'd left Washington just after midnight. An air force jet had flown her to her insertion point at a base in neighboring Costa Rica. From there she'd boarded a commercial flight into Cartoza's only airport, thus establishing her cover as a newly arrived medical sister.

And now she was back in the field!

So what if sweat rolled down her ribs? So what if her stiff black habit scratched and the white wimple got in her way every time she unthinkingly tried to rake a hand through her hair? Maggie would've endured far worse— and had in the past—to feel the intensity and awareness of everything around her that came only with being in the middle of an operation.

Settling her small brown suitcase more comfortably across her knees, she made sure the blue steel Smith & Wesson .22 automatic pistol tucked in her sleeve didn't show, and sat back to enjoy the ride into the capital. She'd stay at the sisters' chapter house today, until she heard from Jake. Or until outside pressure or circumstance made her decide to go in for Sarah Chandler.

As the bus bounced over the rutted road that led out of the airport, chickens squawked, babies cried, and deafening music blared from a loudspeaker. The old woman next to Maggie smiled at the din, then held up a gnarled, arthritic hand to display the rosary beads she clutched. It didn't take Maggie long to realize that the old woman wasn't saying her rosary just to pass the time. She was probably praying fervently that she survived the trip. Maggie herself muttered a few prayers as the bus careered along the narrow, twisting road that led from the airport into the capital. On one side, lush vegetation in more shades of green than Maggie had ever seen climbed up the steep hillsides. On the other was a sheer two-hundred-foot vertical drop to the sparkling blue-green Atlantic. Sure that the bus would sail off the road at every turn, Maggie tried to focus on the bright flashes of brilliantly colored flowers on the right and ignore the empty stretch of air on the left.

When the bus turned inland and approached the tumble of shacks that formed the city's suburbs, she breathed a sigh of relief. Almost immediately, Maggie realized that she'd relaxed too soon. Cartoza's capital clung to the steep slopes of the Teleran foothills like barnacles on a ship's keel. Huffing and groaning, the bus crept up one almost perpendicular street, then plunged down the next, in wild defiance of any and all traffic laws. Pedestrians shouted curses and jumped out of the way, horns blared, and thick exhaust fumes from poorly refined fuel added to the collection of odors trapped in the bus.

When she wasn't bracing herself against the seat in front of her, arms stiff and eyes squeezed shut in anticipation of her imminent demise, Maggie caught glimpses of adobe-covered buildings plastered with posters advertising everything from Diet Pepsi to the topless dancers at Café La Boom Boom. After countless stops to let off and take on passengers, the bus finally puffed to a halt before a pair of tall wooden doors set in a pink adobe wall.

"El convento!" the driver bellowed back over his shoulder.

"Thank the Lord," Maggie muttered, easing her way past the old woman.

A firm tug on the bell rope soon gained her access to a shaded, flowering courtyard. After paying her respects to the senior sister, she was shown to a small, sparsely furnished room kept in readiness for transients. As soon as the door shut behind her escort, Maggie sank down on the bed, tugged off her veil and raked a hand through her thick mane.

Seconds later, she pulled up the antenna on her hand-held secure-transmission satellite communications device. The transmitter-receiver, called a transceiver for short, was small and thin, not much bigger than a lady's compact. It switched from transmit to receive mode at the slightest touch of a finger.

"Nothing from Jaguar yet," Cowboy relayed, his voice as clear as if he were calling from across town instead of bouncing a signal off a low-orbiting satellite.

Maggie knew that she would've been contacted instantly if Jake had called in, but she still couldn't help feeling a stab of disappointment. That, combined with fatigue and the accumulated tension of the operation, made her sag for a moment. It was probably just as well she wasn't jumping right into action, she reflected. She wouldn't be much good to Jake if she let her instincts become dulled.

"Roger," Maggie replied, acknowledging Cowboy's transmission. "I'm going to grab a few hours' sleep, then reconnoiter."

"I'll hold the fort," he replied.

Slipping out of the black robe, Maggie placed her gun on the handy night table and stretched out on the cot in her underwear. True to her cover, she wore plain, unadorned white cotton panties and bra, which the uniform specialists had assured her were *not* easy to find in D.C. on such short notice. The thick adobe walls gave the small room a cool, dim cast. Within moments, she was asleep.

Half an hour later, a raucous, booming bellow sent her leaping from the bed, .22 in hand. She dropped into a crouch, weapon held straight out, then swung it in an arc across the width of the room. A second bellow thundered through the walls.

The sound of scurrying feet outside drew Maggie toward the door. Opening it a cautious crack, she saw several sisters hurrying down the hall. A young, olive-skinned novice in a gray dress stopped at her signal.

"Excuse me. Is that a fire alarm?"

"It's the bell for midmorning prayers," the young woman explained. She glanced pointedly at Maggie's underwear and uncovered hair. "You have only five minutes before you must be in place."

"Mmm..." Maggie thought she just might skip midmorning prayers in favor of her first few hours' sleep in almost two days.

"Of course," the novice said earnestly, "if you miss these prayers, just listen for the bell after next. It calls one to a special half hour of contemplation and prayer before lunch."

Maggie stared at her in gathering consternation. "You mean the bell rings like that all morning long?"

"Oh, yes, Sister," the young woman assured her. "All day long. Every thirty minutes, from five-o'clock wake-up to ten o'clock last prayers. It is, perhaps, a trifle loud, but one gets used to it."

Not in this lifetime, Maggie thought. She closed the door and leaned against it. Jake had better call in, and soon!

"Xavier and I are going into the jungle to check the intrusion-detection devices."

Sarah's hands stilled as she stared up at Jack's shadowed face. The black plastic comb hovered over her dull, limp hair.

"Xavier?"

"The man whose feet you treated." His mouth twisted in a mocking smile. "He's supposed to be my assistant."

"How long will you be gone?"

"Not long. Here, take this."

She glanced at the small, toy-size gun he held out to her and repressed a shudder. She hated guns, and the violence they caused. Her mother had been killed in a hunting accident when Sarah was just a baby. The senator hadn't allowed a gun anywhere in the house since. Sarah had never touched one in her life. Lowering her hands, she clasped them tight in her lap. The sharp teeth of the comb bit into her palm.

"I...I don't..."

His mouth tightened at her reluctance to take the weapon. "Look, Sister, I'm not asking you to violate some deep-seated religious principles here. You don't have to shoot to kill. If anyone comes into the shack, just aim the thing straight up in the air and pull the trigger. I'll be back before the echo dies away."

"Couldn't we just go with you?"

"I can't take you out of here just yet," he said sharply. "I told you, I've got some business to conduct in a few days."

"I wouldn't dream of asking you to put our welfare ahead of your *business*," Sarah retorted, acid dripping from her voice. "I just want you to take me and the children a little way upstream."

"And leave you alone? To try and make it out on your own? Don't be stupid. One misstep and you'd all be monkey bait."

Sarah glared up at him. "I wasn't thinking of escape. I wouldn't risk the children's lives by trying to find my own way through your booby traps. I just thought that I could bathe them while you did your...your business."

The undisguised scorn in her voice tightened the skin across his cheeks. He closed his fingers around the gun.

"They need a bath," Sarah insisted. *She* needed a bath, too. Badly. But she'd settle for dangling her feet in some cool water and splashing what she could over her face and arms.

Sarah set her jaw as she waited for his response. His shuttered gray eyes gave no clue to what he thought. He'd been so withdrawn this morning, so reserved. Ever since they'd rolled back the mosquito netting and gone about the business of seeing to the children's needs, Sarah had sensed a change in him. She wasn't sure exactly when she'd become so attuned to this man's moods, but she knew that something had changed between them last night. Irrevocably.

Maybe he was still suffering from all that tequila he'd downed, Sarah thought irritably. Or maybe he was still angry about the way she'd poured that disinfectant on him. Or maybe he was finding the prospect of protecting her and the children more of a strain on his patience and his admittedly tattered conscience than he'd bargained for.

Too bad.

Sarah wasn't any happier about being stuck in this camp than he apparently was, but until she figured out a way to get herself and the children back to civilization, she wasn't letting Mr. Mercenary off the hook. He was stuck with them. And they were stuck with him.

"All right," he answered finally. "There's a pool about a kilometer from here. Far enough away to give you some privacy, but still well within the perimeter defenses."

Sarah scrambled to her feet before he could change his mind. "Good! I'll gather a few things while you go get the children. They're with Eleanora."

One dark brow rose cynically as she headed for the backpack she now considered her own. He didn't comment, however, and stepped out the door.

The prospect of being out of the hut and the oppressive camp for even an hour lifted Sarah's spirits. Her unease over Jack's strange quietness vanished as she dug through the pockets of the backpack for the few remaining toiletry items.

She felt like a child being given a special treat, like an adventurer setting off on an exciting journey instead of just trudging a half or so mile upstream. Sarah smiled, remembering the vacations she'd taken with her father at five-star resorts. The junkets provided by lobbyists who were currying his favor. The yearly trips to Europe to buy clothes and enjoy the hospitality of the ambassadors and diplomats she'd entertained in D.C. None of those jaunts had thrilled her as much as the prospect of this little excursion.

She threw on the black robe and rolled her few supplies up in the cotton blouse. The blouse was so big and baggy on her, she could wear it while she was bathing the children and still be covered from neck to knees.

Hearing Teresa's childish giggles, Sarah pulled open the door and watched the little procession cross the clearing. Ricci was perched on Jack's shoulders, his black hair covered by the floppy-brimmed camouflage hat. Silent, unsmiling Eduard walked beside them. Teresa danced along in her bright red dress, holding on to her precious doll with one hand and Eleanora with the other. Bringing up the rear was the thin, stoop-shouldered guerrilla whose bleeding feet Sarah had treated yesterday. He grinned and pointed to his boots with the tip of his rifle.

The cavalcade came to a halt. Jack nodded toward the heavyset, expressionless woman beside him. "She says she can help you with the children."

Sarah flashed Eleanora a wide, grateful smile. As much as the children tugged at her heartstrings, they still overwhelmed her at times. She'd gained a whole new appreciation of motherhood in the past few days. The younger children's constant demands for her attention, their swift mood swings from happy to tearful, the utter lack of privacy, even to go to the bathroom, had added to the stress of her ever-present uncertainty and fear.

"I managed to round up some soap," Jack added, handing her a much-used bar.

Sarah grabbed it with an involuntary cry of delight. She didn't want to know what he'd had to barter or promise for it. It was one thing for him to sell his knowledge of stolen weapons for cash, she admitted to herself with rueful honesty. It was another thing altogether when he sold it to benefit her or the children.

From the way his lips twisted cynically, Sarah guessed that he'd noticed this apparent inconsistency in her rigid contempt for his business dealings. Shrugging, she tucked the soap inside her bundle.

"Okay, troops," he said dryly, "fall in. Stay behind me on the path once we leave the clearing, understand?"

"*Sí, Señor Creighton,*" Teresa trilled.

Jack rolled his eyes, then led the way out of camp.

When Sarah saw the small pool, she gasped in surprised delight. Until this moment, she'd never realized that the jungle could be so incredibly beautiful and seductive.

A ribbon of water tumbled down one of the steep hills that surrounded the camp and collected at the bottom to form a silvery, glistening basin. Feathery ferns the height of small trees formed a lush green backdrop for the pool. A single beam of sunshine sliced through the dense canopy overhead, illuminating the brilliant scarlet and yellow trumpet flowers that basked in its light.

"The pool's shallow enough for the kids to wade in," Jack said, drawing her wide-eyed gaze away from the delightful scene.

"What about snakes and such? Is it safe?"

"A safe as anything is in the jungle," he replied with a shrug, "but I'll check it out for you."

He slid his machete from the leather scabbard and spoke a few words to the rebel, who nodded and moved toward the far side of the pool.

"While Xavier and I are gone," Jake said in a quick undertone, "Eduard will stand guard. Just to make sure no one else has decided to follow along and drop in on your little party uninvited."

Sarah bit her lip and glanced down at the eight-year-old. Eduard needed to bathe, as well, but she knew he would resist if she tried to coax him in. He was such a quiet, contained little boy. He didn't seem to want cuddling or attention, as the younger ones did, and he shied away from allowing Sarah to help him with any personal needs.

"We men will take a turn later, when you're done," Jack said deliberately.

Eduard sent him a grateful man-to-man look.

"But..."

"Don't worry, I won't let his arm get wet. I've spent enough time in the jungle to know as much about blood flukes as you do."

He knew a whole lot more than she did, Sarah thought ruefully as she watched him walk toward the pool. About blood flukes—whatever those were—and about the jungle and young boys. In his own quiet way, Eduard seemed to have developed a severe case of hero worship. More of that male bonding, Sarah supposed.

She shook her head, wondering at the contradictions in the man. Over the past few days, she had found herself by turns disgusted by him and grateful to him. She'd laid awake at night, aware of his uncompromising masculinity but unwilling to acknowledge its effect on her. He cold-bloodedly dealt in death, and yet ...

And yet he'd provided her what safety he could in this precarious situation. Moreover, he was so kind to the children, in his brusque way. Teresa preened like a little banty rooster in her bright dress whenever she caught his eyes. She refused to go to sleep unless the root he'd carved for her was tucked into the hammock with her. Little Ricci followed him about with the eagerness of a happy puppy.

Sarah frowned as she watched the object of her thoughts hunker down on a flat rock and slap the water gently with a stick to see what creatures, if any, he disturbed. Why should it surprise her that she couldn't reconcile the complexities in his nature? For all her much-touted charm and skill at playing the Washington social game, she'd failed miserably to understand what drove the one other man who'd swept into her life with such devastating impact.

Now there was a contrast, Sarah thought dryly. André, with his impeccable manners and skilled lovemaking. And this...this soldier of fortune, with his hard gray eyes and his soiled khaki shirt stretched across his broad back. The rolled-up sleeves displayed the tanned, muscled arms that had wrapped around her with such lack of gentleness last night. Sarah shivered, remembering the feel of his body pressed against hers.

"Sarita! Can we go in now?"

"Can I make the pee-pee in the water, Sarita?"

Sarah glanced down at the two children dancing around her, one thin and wiry, the other stubby and plump. "Why don't you make the pee-pee before you get in the pool?" she suggested with a smile.

"Can we go in now? It is safe," Teresa insisted, tugging on her sleeve.

The mercenary rose, confirming Teresa's opinion. "The water's clean. Just don't leave the clearing. Xavier and I will be close enough to hear you if you scream, but far enough to give you privacy. Thirty minutes long enough?"

"Thirty minutes is fine."

He tipped two fingers to the floppy brim of his hat, then started back around the pool to join Xavier.

"Now, Sarita? Now?" Both children tugged on her sleeves now as they hopped from one foot to the other in their eagerness.

Smiling at their antics, Sarah glanced up and caught Eleanora's eye. For a brief, unguarded moment, the other woman shared her enjoyment of the youngsters' unrestrained eagerness. Almost as quickly as it had appeared, however, the flash of awareness in Eleanora's eyes faded and her features took on their habitual vacant flatness.

"Okay, okay," Sarah said, laughing. "Let me get changed, then Eleanora and I will take you in."

She edged behind a screen of ferns to shed her black robe and the panties she intended to wash. As she pulled on the baggy blouse, she pondered what she now guessed was a deliberate shield erected by Eleanora. Sarah bit her

lip, ·imagining what it was that the older woman retreated from behind that dull passivity. Jack's warning
that she had enough problems of her own without add-
ing Eleanora's to them sounded in Sarah's mind. She
wanted to heed his warning. She *needed* to heed it. But
when she knelt beside the older woman to undress the
wiggling, squirming children, Sarah knew the warning
had come too late. Just what she could do about Eleanora's plight eluded her at this precise moment. But she
would have to think of something.

The children waded into the pool, shrieking at the cold
and jumping up and down. Their small hands beat the
water and sent silvery spray flying everywhere. Laughing, Sarah sat down on the flat rock beside Eleanora. She
rucked the hem of the long blouse up over her knees,
dangled her feet in the water and let the children splash
and play. Within seconds, the two women were almost as
soaked as the youngsters.

The cool water felt wonderful. Sarah longed to slip off
the rock and join the kids. Her fingers clenched around
the soap. Maybe after they'd cleansed the children, she'd
slip into the pool, blouse and all, and wash her hair.

Out of the corner of her eye, Sarah caught a blur of
khaki. She looked up to see Jack emerge from the jungle
on the far side of the pool. He stopped abruptly, his body
slowly tensing as he stared at her. Even from this distance, Sarah could see how his skin stretched tight across
his cheekbones and his eyes devoured her.

Her heart slamming up against her ribs, she glanced
down and saw how the wet blouse clung to her breasts
and thighs. The soaked cotton molded her, shaped her,
revealed her.

Sarah's first instinct was as old as time. A feminine
response to the danger she sensed in the man stripping her

with his eyes. She lifted her arms, intending to shield herself. Then a second urge—as old as, and even more powerful than, the first—gripped her. The woman in her responded to his hunger, and an answering need shivered down her spine.

She'd been ashamed for so long. Of her complicity in another woman's tragic attempt to end her life. Of her inability to deal with the relentless media in Washington, who'd hounded her every move. Of her own ineptness during these weeks in Cartoza. Jack's hot male look stripped away her shame and doubt and fear. What was left was basic. Elemental. Cleansing in its raw power. Whatever else she might or might not be, whatever strengths or inadequacies she possessed, Sarah Chandler was a woman.

Her arms dropped to her sides. Slowly she straightened her shoulders.

Jake held himself rigidly still. A bead of sweat rolled down his cheek. Hard and aching, he fought the urge to stalk around the pool, haul her up, and carry her into the jungle. More than he'd ever wanted anything in his life, Jake wanted to see her on a bed of green springy ferns, her white legs spread and a woman's smile of welcome in her luminous blue-green eyes. He ached to lose himself in the damp valley between her thighs.

She couldn't know, he thought savagely. She couldn't know how that wet shirt clung to her skin. She couldn't know what the sight of her beautiful body did to a man. She couldn't have any idea of the searing lust that blazed in his belly.

Or could she?

The vague, unspecified tension that had kept him awake most of the night sharpened into a sudden, gut-wrenching doubt. He stared at Sarah a moment longer, then forced himself to turn away. He moved slowly, as if the smallest step pained him—which it did.

"Here," he said brusquely, handing Eduard the canteen he'd forgotten to leave with him earlier. "The pool water is probably safe, but there's no need to take chances."

He left the clearing without looking at Sarah again. He didn't have to. Her image hovered in front of him as he retraced his steps down the trail and rejoined Xavier. With each step, suspicion curled in Jake's mind like a damp, pervasive mist. Just what exactly did he know about Sister Sarah Josepha?

Suppressing the aching male need that had gripped him the moment he saw her wrapped in that wet blouse, Jake forced himself to step back and assess the situation. Methodically, ruthlessly, he reviewed every moment since he'd parted those damn palmettos and seen her white, terrified face staring back at him. Had he missed something vital, something he should have seen?

He'd shrugged off her stumbling Spanish with the explanation that she was new to the area, not long in country. That made sense. The dialect used here in the mountains was difficult even for Cartoza's coastal city dwellers to understand, let alone outsiders.

He'd understood when she gritted her teeth and treated the minor ills of the men in the camp with a superficial skill. They'd murdered her friends, after all. He didn't expect her to show a tender, caring bedside manner.

He'd ascribed her sometimes gentle, sometimes exasperated care of the children to the natural stress of their situation. She'd cleansed them, fed them, heard their prayers with a determination he could only call dedication.

No, Sister Sarah hadn't given Jake any reason to think she wasn't the frightened nun he thought her to be.

Until last night. Last night, when she'd blazed with fury and challenged him, woman to man.

And today, when her eyes had met his across the silvery green surface of the pool. When she had responded to the raw hunger that must have shown on his face by straightening her shoulders.

At the vivid image of Sarah's small, rounded breasts thrusting up against the wet cotton, the ruthless agent and the fierce, hungry male in Jake merged once more, painfully. Swearing viciously, he concentrated on placing one foot in front of the other.

A hundred meters down the trail, he stopped in his tracks.

Ahead of him, Xavier froze and dropped into a crouch. "What is it, gringo?" he whispered, pivoting on the balls of his feet.

"I thought I heard something," Jake answered quietly. He jerked his chin toward the left. "In there."

Xavier swung the barrel of his weapon toward the area Jake had indicated.

"Don't fire!" Jake ordered. "You'll detonate the charges."

The man's thin shoulders slumped even more as he swallowed and stared, wide-eyed, at the dense undergrowth.

"Do you want me to check it," Jake asked, "or will you do it yourself?"

Xavier glanced from Jake to the jungle, then back to Jake. "You do it, gringo. I will cover you."

Jake eased his machete out of its scabbard. "Give me ten minutes. If I'm not back by then, get the woman and children back to camp, pronto."

The rebel's fingers tightened on his weapon. *"Sí!"*

Ten minutes was all Jake needed. It would take him two minutes to reach the huge strangler fig where he'd stashed his backup transceiver. Even less to update his OMEGA control on the operation. And that would leave him plenty of time to pump Maggie for details about Sister Sarah Josepha.

Jake knew Maggie wouldn't have wasted these past few days. By now, she would've uncovered every existing detail about the nun's life. How much Sarah had weighed at birth. The exact date she'd had her wisdom teeth extracted. And, Jake was sure, she'd have an explanation for why a woman with Sarah's delicate beauty and plucky courage had chosen to become a nun. Jake wanted to hear the explanation. Badly.

Jaws clenched, he reached into the dark cavity formed by the roots put down by the strangler fig from its perch on a high branch of the host tree.

"OMEGA control, this is Jaguar."

"Howdy, Jaguar. This is Cowboy. Good to hear from you, pal."

Jake's brow furrowed. He'd recognized Cowboy's distinctive Wyoming twang even before the agent identified himself. Tall, rangy, and seemingly easygoing, Cowboy disguised a razor-sharp mind with a sleepy smile and tanned, weathered skin. Jake had worked with the former air force fighter jock on a couple of operations and thoroughly respected him. Still, it was disconcerting to change controls in midoperation.

"Where's Chameleon?"

"She's on-scene, close enough to spit. Stand by while I patch you through."

Maggie was here? In Cartoza? The knowledge that she would lead the extraction team to pick up Sarah and the children sent a shaft of relief shooting through Jake.

"Chameleon here. Glad you finally decided to check in, Jaguar. What took you so long?"

"My transmitter experienced a slight... technical malfunction. I had to wait a few days until it was safe to recover the backup unit."

"Anything you want me to relay to the lab?" Cowboy inquired. "They'll go nuts when they hear their equipment failed."

As Jake recapped the problem with the boot, Maggie's laughter echoed Cowboy's.

"They're going to love that," she said, still chuckling. "Now they'll have to come up with a seal that's waterproof and piddleproof. I'm glad to have confirmation that the children are with you, though. The Cartozan authorities only had a sketchy ID on the kids and weren't sure they were with the woman when she was taken. How's she holding up, by the way?"

Jake's muscles tensed. "As well as can be expected," he replied evenly.

"Good. Given her background, I was afraid you'd have your hands full."

Chapter 9

Still shaken by the intensity of what had passed between her and Jack, Sarah sat cross-legged on the flat rock. She barely heard the children's splashing pursuit of an orange-colored frog or Eleanor's murmured response to their gleeful shouts. All she could think of was the way she'd responded to the raw hunger she saw in the mercenary's eyes.

She couldn't want him, she told herself fiercely. She *couldn't!*

Her fingernails dug into the bar of soap she clutched as she tried to convince herself once more that what she felt for him sprang from hostage-dependency syndrome. From the emotional upheavals she'd been through. From sheer proximity!

She couldn't be on fire for a man who refused to take her and the children to safety because he still had some blood money to earn. She couldn't want to feel his mouth against hers, his legs entwined with hers.

She *couldn't!*

Oh, God, she could! She did!

Sarah gave a silent groan and buried her face in her hands, overwhelmed by the all-consuming desire that coiled in her stomach.

What was wrong with her? Hadn't she learned anything from her busy, brittle, empty life? She'd been courted and flattered and stroked by men of charm. Men of power and wealth. But none of the men who'd said they loved her—not even the one she had loved so desperately in return—could make her pulse hammer and her thighs clench together in a spasm of desire with just a look. How could this one man wake instincts in her she'd thought well buried? He was grimy and hard and made his living in a way she despised. He...

"Sometimes it's best for a woman not to fight what happens."

The soft murmur pierced Sarah's swirling, chaotic thoughts. She lifted her head sharply and turned to find Eleanora watching her. To her surprise, she saw that the woman's brown eyes had lost their dull flatness and held a deep, soul-shattering awareness.

"He is much a man, the gringo. At least if he takes you to his bed, you will find pleasure in it."

Sarah gaped at Eleanora, translating and retranslating the older woman's words in her mind. "He... he won't take me to his bed," she answered in halting Spanish. "He thinks I'm a... I mean, he respects that I'm a sister."

Something incredibly close to amusement flickered across Eleanora's face. "We are all sisters," she said softly. "Here, give it to me."

"Huh?" Sarah struggled stupidly with the other woman's thick mountain accent and her own astonishment.

"The soap. Give me the soap. I will wash your hair for you. Then we will wash the children, yes?"

Dazed, Sarah passed her the yellowed bar of soap. At Eleanora's nod, she slipped off the rock and sank to her knees in the shallow basin. Miraculously cool water eddied around her thighs.

Sarah sat back on her heels, then slowly bent forward and dunked her head under the surface. She was too confused to sort out the emotions whirling through her right now. She decided not to think, not to try to understand anything that had happened in the past few minutes. She'd just remove her layers of sweat and dust, one by one. She'd let Eleanora wash her hair. She'd play with the children. That was about all she could handle at this particular moment.

Sarah sensed rather than saw Jack's return a half hour later. One minute she was sitting quietly on the flat rock, her knees tucked under her chin, her hair clean and damp under the veil that covered it once more. The next moment the skin on the back of her neck began to prickle.

Sarah didn't move for a long moment, alarmed but not unduly frightened by the odd sensation. When it didn't go away, she swiveled slowly on the rock, trying to discover its source.

At first she didn't see anything that would account for it. Two squeaky-clean children sat on the bank and made cakes out of wet, soggy fern leaves with Eleanora's quiet assistance. Eduard dozed, his back against a tree trunk and his still-bandaged arm cradled against his chest.

Sarah swiveled a few more degrees.

For the second time in less than an hour, she met Jack's eyes across the width of the pool. Only this time they didn't glitter with a searing masculine desire that called to the woman in her. This time they held a deadly rage that made Sarah's throat go dry. She stared at him, stunned by his anger.

A shadow moved behind him, and then Xavier appeared at his shoulder. Jack's expression became so swiftly, so carefully, blank that for a moment Sarah thought she'd imagined the cold fury in his eyes.

"Eduard," he called softly.

The boy sat up, rubbing a hand over his face. *"Sí?"*

"Xavier will take you and Eleanora and the children back to camp."

Both Sarah and the slope-shouldered rebel stared at him in surprise.

"I will stay with the *religiosa* while she gathers the white fungus that she needs for treating fevers," he said, in a low, deliberate tone that rasped along Sarah's nerve endings. She didn't understand why just the sound of his voice should suddenly make her so nervous.

The guerrilla glanced from her to Jack, then shrugged and walked toward the boy. Sarah knew that the men weren't quite sure about her relationship with the mercenary, but no one had challenged him or tried to molest her since the big, beefy lieutenant. After catching a glimpse of his face, Sarah wasn't surprised.

"Go with Xavier, Eduard."

The boy rose, clearly not happy at leaving them.

"Now."

The absolute authority in the single syllable convinced Eduard. He walked over to Eleanora, who stood watching the scene with the children. Lifting Ricci onto his hip, Eduard turned without another word and started back down the trail. Eleanora hesitated, then took Teresa's hand and followed silently.

The small sounds they made as they left seemed unnaturally loud to Sarah. Teresa's protest that she hadn't finished making her cake echoed hollowly. Ricci's sleepy murmur seemed to reverberate in Sarah's ears. The flap of a toucanette's wings as it soared off the branch Eleanora brushed against sounded like a rattle of distant thunder.

Then there was only stillness.

And Jack.

He watched her with the silent intensity of a predator that had spotted its prey. Just as silently, he began to move toward her. His lean, taut body radiated an aura of barely leashed power.

The nervous tension that had collected along Sarah's nerve endings seemed to explode in tiny, stinging pinpricks. She tried to think of something to say to break the tense silence between them, but no words came.

Never taking his eyes from her face, he circled the edge of the pool. Slowly, deliberately, he stalked her.

With each step, Sarah felt the fluttering of some primitive inner fear. She wet her lips nervously, not understanding either his menacing approach or her reaction to it. The sunlight reflected from the pool cast his face in hard, uncompromising planes and angles. His eyes glittered with a fierce light that seemed to sear her skin wherever it touched. A maleness so raw, so potent, emanated from him that Sarah reacted instinctively.

She whirled and tried to flee.

Before she'd taken three steps, his fingers closed over her wrist and spun her around. She struggled against his hold, panting with fear and some indescribable, undefinable emotion.

"Jack, what—what is it?"

The noise he made far back in his throat sent ripples of sensation down Sarah's spine. Without speaking, he pulled her slowly toward him.

Sarah battled his hold, like a frightened creature staked out at the end of a rope. She resisted his pull with all her strength, but knew even before his other arm wrapped around her waist that it was hopeless.

Still without saying a word, he hauled her up against him. His arm tightened, banding her, molding her. His free hand reached up and tore the veil away. Sarah gasped and flung her head back.

"Jack, for God's sake..."

"Oh, no," he snarled. "This is for my sake."

The hand tangled in the fall of her hair. Wrapping a length of it around his fist, he held her steady while his mouth took hers.

There was no other way to describe it. Sarah had kissed and been kissed by her share of boys and men in her time. She been made love to by a skilled, considerate Frenchman. But she'd never felt so *taken* before. This was a kiss meant to dominate, to subdue, to possess. And it did.

Thoroughly alarmed now and deeply ashamed of the liquid heat that rose inside her, Sarah wedged both hands against his chest. Using all her strength, she managed to lever her upper body a few inches away. She was bent backward over his arm and her hips were thrust intimately up against his, but at least she could see his eyes. What she saw in them made her heart trip.

"What are you doing?" she panted. "Have you lost the last shred of decency you possessed? I'm a nun! A— a bride of Christ!"

A sharp, slicing derision hardened his eyes to tempered steel. "Some bride," he sneered. "No, don't bother to protest. I know all about you, *Sister Sarah.*"

"Wh-what do you know?"

"I know that three months ago you were caught in bed with a French diplomat. A very married French diplomat."

Sarah felt the blood drain from her face.

"I know that the wife who'd come to Washington to surprise him ended up being very surprised herself. She subsequently tried to OD on sleeping pills."

Sarah fought to force some sound out of her closed throat. "Jack, how did—?"

Relentlessly he ignored her feeble whisper. "I also know that the son of a bitch returned to France with his wife. At which point the spoiled, pampered little socialite he'd been screwing felt so sorry for herself she went on a bender and slammed her Mercedes into a busload of Girl Scouts who were touring the capital."

For a bleak, endless moment, Sarah felt as though she were back in Washington. She cringed as she relived those moments of devastating shame when she'd realized that André had never told his wife he wanted a divorce, as he'd led her to believe. When his young wife's shocked, stunned face had burned itself into her conscience forever.

She could see again her father's pain as he'd come to the darkened bedroom she'd retreated to, bringing her the news that Madame Foutier was in Georgetown Medical Center's emergency room and had linked Sarah to her hysterical, sobbing suicide attempt.

She saw the flash of cameras, heard the shouts of the reporters who'd dogged her every step for weeks, until she'd refused to leave the house. Until, finally, alcohol had brought a stupid, foolish bravado that made her say to hell with them.

She gave a little moan as she heard the sickening sound of metal crunching and glass shattering.

His arm tightened around her waist, bringing her up on her toes, until her face was within inches of his. "You want to tell me I'm mistaken, *Sister Sarah?* You want to deny that was your picture plastered across the front page of the *Washington Post?*"

She wanted desperately to deny it. Staring up at his hard, chiseled face, she would have given her soul to deny it. Instead, she could only press her lips together and, to her shame, make a little whimpering sound far back in her throat.

"Oh, no," he growled. "Don't get all white-faced and piteous on me. Not now. Not when we've got something to settle between us."

He loosened the fist that had tangled in her hair and released her. Sarah stumbled back a pace or two, her legs unsteady and her heart aching. She sucked in a long, ragged breath, then let it out again in a rush. Swallowing, she gaped as Jack began to unbutton his shirt. He shrugged out of it and tossed it onto the springy mat of ferns at his feet. His hands moved to the buckle that held the web belt slung low on his hips.

"Wh-what are you doing?"

The belt thudded down on top of the shirt. "What does it look like?" He lifted a foot and planted it against a rock, bending to untie the laces.

Sarah stared at his dark head, stunned. Her lips worked, but she couldn't force any word out.

One boot, then the other, followed the belt. He peeled off thick white socks and straightened.

Sarah couldn't breathe as she watched his hands work the fastening at his waist. A thousand tumultuous emotions surged through her—astonishment, incredulity, heart-hammering disbelief. But not fear. One small corner of her psyche noted that fact, and her rational mind grabbed it with both hands.

"You won't rape me," she said, in a small, breathy voice. "Not after these past days together. I don't know much about you, but I know that much. You won't rape me."

His hands paused on the zipper. One corner of his lip lifted in a smile that made shivers race along Sarah's nerve endings. "No, I won't rape you. I won't have to."

That stiffened her spine a little. She lifted her chin a small notch. "Listen, Mr. Macho Mercenary, you may think..."

"Save it, *Sister Sarah*. I've done all the listening to you I'm going to do."

"Stop calling me that!"

"I felt your heart thumping against my cheek when you held me last night." His voice low and harsh, he stepped toward her. "I saw the look that flashed into your eyes when I held you."

Sarah stepped back.

He took another forward. "I saw the way you displayed yourself to me a little while ago."

Heat surged into her face. She clenched her fists and refused to move another inch.

"I didn't know what it meant then, *Sister Sarah*, that little display of yours. Those tender little touches. Like a fool, a blind, stupid fool, I assumed your actions were those of a woman who didn't know what she was doing to me. A woman who didn't realize that her slightest touch made my nerves sizzle. That one look from those eyes of yours tied my gut into knots."

Sarah's stomach did a little twist of its own at his admission. "Jack..."

The single word hung on the air between them. He stopped a heartbeat away from her, his face stark, his mouth grim, waiting for her to say more. When she didn't, something flared in his eyes that Sarah couldn't even begin to interpret.

"I held myself on so short a leash these past days I was almost doubled over with it," he said slowly, "and all the time you were playing with me. Well, Sarah Chandler, it's time to stop playing."

Sarah held her breath.

"Put your arms around me."

The soft, steely command surprised her. And aroused her as nothing else could have. She'd known deep within her heart that he wouldn't force her, but only this hard-edged mercenary would stand there and expect her to initiate her own seduction.

No, it wouldn't be a seduction. With a deep, visceral sureness, Sarah knew that if she touched him, the small, steady fire he seemed to have sparked within her would leap into flame and consume her. Consume them both.

In that moment, she felt the need to strip away all pretense between them. She wouldn't lie to him anymore.

She wet her lips and gave the only answer she could. "I...I don't know if I want this, Jack."

A muscle twitched in one side of his jaw. "Put your arms around me and find out."

For what seemed like an eternity, Sarah didn't move. She tried to deny the desire that arced between them like summer lightning slicing through a hot, sultry night. She tried to tell herself that she despised this man, this hard, unyielding man who called to the primitive and elemental in her.

But she refused to lie to herself any longer. Or to him. Swallowing, she lifted a trembling hand. Her fingers grazed the warm, rounded muscle of his chest. Her other hand lifted to join the first. Flattening her palms, she slid them upward. The light dusting of chest hair teased her fingertips. The strong column of his neck shaped her hands.

Sarah gave a little sigh of surrender and stepped forward. Her breasts brushed his chest, their nipples peaking with the rasp of the scratchy black robe. The flame flickering deep within her gathered heat and intensity. Wrapping her arms tighter around his neck, she brought his mouth down to hers.

Any vague idea that he would hold back and make her pay for the way she'd supposedly teased him vanished immediately. At the touch of their lips, Jack's arms banded her waist once more. He shifted his stance and brought her into hard, intimate contact with his hips. Through the fullness of her robe, Sarah felt his rigid member leap against her stomach, even as his mouth slanted more fully over hers. His lips took her touch and gave it back, magnified a hundredfold. Firm, warm, slick, they fueled Sarah's own need.

Straining, she arched against him. His hand slid down to cup her breast. He mounded it in his palm, shaping it, kneading it through the rough fabric that covered it. His handling added to the friction that made her taut nipple ache.

Leaving one arm curled around his neck and her lips molded to his, Sarah ran her other hand over his shoulders, his arm, his ribs. His skin burned under her fingers. She stroked and kneaded it with the same intense, exploratory touch he gave her breast. When her hand slid down and encountered the waistband of his pants, Sarah went crazy with the need to get rid of all barriers between them.

She pushed herself out of his arms. They stood for a moment, their breath harsh and ragged on the air, their eyes hot and wild. Then Sarah's hands lifted to the top fastening of her habit.

"No, let me." His hands brushed hers aside. A slow, sardonic grin twisted his lips. "You have no idea how many times I've fantasized about doing this."

Sarah bit her lip to still the quivers that raced through her as he unfastened the hooks, one by one, then pushed the heavy weight off her shoulders. It slipped down her arms, caught for a moment on the stiff peaks of her nipples, then slithered over her hips. She stood before him, clad only in her still-damp bikini briefs.

He swallowed, raking her with his eyes. "You mean that's all you've been wearing under that robe?"

Sarah felt pinpoints of fire everywhere his gaze lingered. "This is what I was was wearing under my sleep shirt the night of the raid. I . . . I didn't have time to do anything except yank off the shirt and pull on the habit."

"I'm sure glad I didn't know that. I lost enough sleep trying not to think about what was under those folds of material as it was."

Sarah gave a strangled laugh and stepped toward him. "I've lost a little sleep myself the past few nights."

She reached out and traced a finger down the line of soft, springy hair. His stomach muscles jumped under her touch.

"You've no idea how much I've fantasized about this," she whispered.

The small sound broke the last of Jack's restraints. With a smothered groan, he pulled her to him. Mouths hard against each other, they sank to their knees. His weight tumbled Sarah over onto her back, then crushed her into the bed of ferns. Within moments, they'd shed the last of his clothes.

Sarah matched him kiss for kiss, stroke for stroke. When his knee pried her legs apart and his hand tangled in the curls at the juncture of her thighs, she arched upward, seeking his touch. Hot, slick wetness eased the way for the fingers he slid into her. Sarah moaned as he stroked and primed her. Her hand closed around his satiny shaft, priming him, as well.

Jake felt her caress and willed himself not to explode in her hand. He'd never felt a need so great, or such a savage desire to possess a woman. No, not any woman. This woman. Sarah.

He raised himself up on one elbow and stared down into her flushed face. If he'd allowed his fantasies full rein, if he hadn't always jerked himself up short whenever the insidious need for Sarah spiraled in his groin, he would have imagined taking her here, like this. With her shining, spun-gold hair spread out against the lush green of the ferns. Her eyes wide, and shimmering with the same incredible blue-green as the pool. Her lips red and swollen. Her skin flushed with need. For all her delicate beauty, Sarah responded with a primal, elemental directness to his touch. The sight of her sent a shaft of fierce male satisfaction shooting through him.

Although... Jake had spent half his life in the jungle. It occurred to him that he'd never seen anything as beautiful or as pagan as the woman who stared up at him.

That was his last rational thought. Suddenly fiercely impatient, Sarah curled both arms around his neck and brought him down to her. Jake needed no further prompting. Spreading her legs farther, he reached down to position himself, then thrust forward.

Sarah arched her neck and gasped at the intrusion. Within seconds, her tight sheath had fit itself to him, and she gave herself up to the slow pace Jake set. His deliberate approach didn't last long. Her muscles gripped him, almost shredding the last of his control. He gritted his teeth and reached down between their sweat-slick bodies. His hand found the small, hard bud at her center.

Moments, or maybe hours, later, Sarah felt her climax coming. She groaned, arching under him. A slow, dark wave swept up her belly, then receded. Another followed, and then another, until they washed over her in a sudden rush of pure, shattering sensation.

Before the spasms of pleasure subsided, Jack's weight crushed down on her. He shoved his fingers through the hair on either side of her head, held her steady while his mouth plundered hers, and thrust into her. Seconds, or maybe years, later, he followed her over the edge.

Chapter 10

Sarah had never experienced such shattering intimacy. Nor, she admitted in startled surprise, such a swift transition from all-consuming passion to intense, immediate alertness.

The dark head that had been buried in the juncture of her neck and shoulder lifted suddenly. Eyes narrowed, Jack stared at the narrow path from the camp. Before Sarah could gather her uneven breath to ask what was the matter, he'd rolled off her, scooped up his pants, and pulled them on.

"Get dressed."

The low command and the smooth, efficient way Jack slid the .45 out of its holster had Sarah scrabbling for her clothes. She pulled them on with fumbling fingers, then snatched up her veil.

"What is it?"

"I'm not sure. Get behind me and keep quiet."

Her heart pounding, Sarah complied. She didn't much care for Jack's peremptory habit of ordering people around, but in this instance she decided not to take issue with it.

A faint rustle sounded in the undergrowth. The smooth, broad back in front of her stiffened. Sarah could see every ridge in his spine, the delineation of every hard, roped muscle under his skin.

"Señor Creighton?"

The muscles twitched. Jack sent Sarah a disgusted look over his shoulder, then called a response, "*Sí,* Eduard."

The boy hurried into view, his young face scrunched into worried lines. He stuttered a few quick sentences in idiomatic Spanish. Sarah caught Eleanora's name, and Teresa's. She pushed past Jack and ran across the clearing.

"What is it, Eduard? What's happening?"

"It is trouble. Eleanora's man, he hit her face because she didn't do the rice and the beans for him."

"*What?*"

"She bleeds, and Teresa cries. Ricci cries, also. I put them in the hut and came for you."

Although he spoke to Sarah, his eyes sought approval from the man standing behind her.

"You did good," Jack told the boy, laying a hand on his thin shoulder before turning to Sarah. "Get your gear."

She didn't need his quiet order this time. She was already running to the bush where she'd spread the wet cotton blouse to dry. She snatched it and was back beside the waiting pair within minutes.

"Eduard thinks Eleanora's nose may be broken," Jack told her as they hurried toward camp. "If so, you'll have to pack it until the swelling goes down."

Sarah threw him a stricken look.

His mouth twisted. "Just how much medical expertise do you have, *Sister?*"

Her hands fisted on the wet blouse. "I worked in a clinic for two weeks with Sister Maria, the nun whose clothes these are. Were."

"Two weeks! Christ!"

"She was a good teacher," Sarah snapped. "I managed well enough yesterday, if you recall, when I treated your so-called soldiers of the revolution."

Jack shook his head in disgust. "Right. One case of heat exhaustion and another of foot immersion. Good thing they didn't bring back one of their *compadres* with a nice bullet wound in the gut for you to test your skills on." He glanced at the boy ahead. "Could you have sutured Eduard's arm?"

Sarah hated to admit her own inadequacy, but she was past the point of pretense. "No, not with a needle, or with ants. Nor would I have tried. I wouldn't have done that to Eduard. I was going to tell you then, but..."

"Yeah, sure."

"Honestly."

"So why didn't you?"

"Because you handled the situation yourself," she retorted, "and because I didn't trust you."

He slanted her a quick look.

Sarah saw the unspoken question in his eyes, and knew the answer immediately. She still didn't trust him. Even now, after she'd lost herself in his arms. After the shattering union of their bodies. She wanted him, but she didn't trust him. The realization stunned her. And shamed her.

Something of what she was feeling must have shown on her face. His eyes narrowed, and the skin across his cheeks seemed to tighten. A bend in the trail brought them within sight of the camp, however, and he bit off whatever he'd intended to say. Instead, his mouth firmed and he said only, "We'll talk about it later. And about what happened at the pool."

Sarah swept past him. "No, we won't. We won't talk about that. We won't discuss it. We won't mention it, ever again."

She was too confused, too overwhelmed, by what had just happened to talk about it. She needed time to sort through her incredible, explosive response to this man. She needed time and space and privacy. None of which she was likely to get, Sarah thought glumly.

She waited impatiently while he sent Eduard back to the hut to stay with the children. Passing the boy her wet blouse, Sarah gave him what she hoped was a reassuring smile, then walked beside Jake to the lean-to Eleanora shared with the man who claimed her.

They saw him first, a short, wiry little bantam with mean eyes, a scraggly brown mustache, and an evil-looking knife strapped to his thigh. He sat on an up-turned crate just outside the lean-to, with the disassembled pieces of the automatic rifle he'd been cleaning scattered on a rubber poncho in front of him.

"Let me do the talking," Jake warned softly.

"All right. Just get him to let me take a look at... Good God!"

Sarah stopped abruptly, her mouth dropping in shock. Eleanora huddled in a corner of the lean-to. Her battered, bloody face was almost unrecognizable.

"I'll handle..."

Paying no heed to Jake's murmured words, Sarah stomped forward.

"You pig!" she snarled at the little man who stood and blocked her entry. "You stupid, sniveling, slimy pig."

Stifling a curse, Jake considered his options.

He could let the guerrilla handle his adversary, or vice versa.

He could haul Sarah away before she attracted a crowd and gave every man in camp a glimpse of her magnificent fury.

Or he could... Oh, hell. He couldn't. Jake knew there was no way he could walk away from Eleanora's wounded face. Or from Sarah.

She threw an imperious look over her shoulder, summoning him to her side. "You tell this little bastard that I'm taking Eleanora back to our hut. He's not to touch her or speak to her or even come near her without my permission."

Jake's translation was far more succinct. "The *religiosa* will see to your woman's hurts."

The man's eyes shifted from him to the bristling figure in black. "The woman has no need of this one's attentions."

"She's of no use to you like that. Nor to anyone else," Jake added casually. "No one will want her, looking like that. You'll make no money off her until she's healed."

As he'd anticipated, an appeal to the little man's greed had more effect than any appeal to his nonexistent humanity could have. A speculative gleam entered his black eyes.

"You think so, gringo?"

Jake knew this was going to cost him. Big-time. He gave a small nod, signaling his acceptance of the deal. "I think so."

The guerrilla didn't bother to turn around. "Go with the *religiosa*, woman," he called over his shoulder.

"Maybe if she works on you long enough she can make you pretty, eh?"

Eleanora rose slowly, like an old woman, using one hand to pull herself up. Jake's stomach knotted at the sight of the red, swelling bruises that were already starting to discolor, but he'd been in enough brawls to see that she had no smashed or broken bones.

Sarah ran forward and wrapped an arm around the older woman's waist. Without a word to either man, she led Eleanora back to the storage hut. Jake watched them make their way across the clearing, then turned back to face the wiry, mustached little man.

The rebel reached behind the crate and pulled out a half-full bottle. "So, gringo, sit down, sit down. Have some tequila."

The bottle's contents sloshed as he gestured toward the automatic rifle lying in pieces on the poncho. "You must give me your expert opinion on this weapon of mine. It's a Russian model, shipped to Cuba before the capitalists undermined the Soviet economy and they stopped producing altogether. It's ancient, eh? Not fast and efficient, like the one you carry."

Jake stifled a sigh and hooked a boot around another crate to drag it forward. He suspected it was going to be a long afternoon.

And an even longer night.

Listening with half an ear as Eleanora's "husband" began bartering for her, Jake knew that the cramped little hut was about to acquire another occupant. Sarah would no doubt bed the injured woman down next to her, leaving Jake to make room for himself somewhere else. A sharp disappointment lanced through him. He didn't like the prospect of sleeping where he couldn't see the outline of Sarah's pale, high-cheekboned face in the dim light or hear the breathy little smacking noise she made when she settled into sleep or fold her soft body into his. After his one taste of her body's honeyed sweetness, Jake found himself craving it, like a man given a thimbleful of water to slack a raging thirst.

Frowning, Jake reached for the tequila bottle. He suddenly realized that he'd crossed some invisible line in the past few hours, a line he'd never allowed himself to step over before. Always before, he'd been able to resist any personal involvement while in the field. Not that it had been easy.

During any operation, OMEGA's agents lived on the edge. Every emotion was magnified, every reaction could lead to either success or quick death—if they were lucky. Jake knew from textbook studies and from long experience that danger was debilitating in some instances, a powerful aphrodisiac in others. People clung to each other in desperate situations, seeking to affirm life in the face of death. Sometimes that transitory need solidified into a stronger emotion.

One of his fellow agents had almost compromised his mission and his life by falling hard for a laboratory researcher suspected of selling the latest information on genetic engineering to a well-armed and particularly vicious neo-Nazi group. As it turned out, the woman had stumbled onto her lab's suspicious research accidentally, but the agent had gone through twenty stages of hell before he discovered that.

As Jake had with Sarah. He'd desired her, and he'd been so disgusted with himself because of that desire that he tied himself into knots. When he found out she wasn't really a nun, he'd allowed his tight control to slip. Slipped, hell. It had shredded completely. Which wasn't exactly smart for a man who wanted not only to walk out of this jungle alive, but to make sure one woman and three children made it out, as well. Two women, he corrected with an inner grimace. Somehow he suspected Sarah wouldn't leave the compound without Eleanora.

Jake took another swig of the tequila as the little weasel across from him shook his head despairingly over the much-dented stock of his aged weapon. Jake grunted noncommittally, making a mental note to inform Maggie that she might have an additional neutral to extract when she led the team in.

Thank God Sinclair was in the field! She wouldn't blink an eye if she learned she had to extract the entire Cartozan World Cup soccer team from this little camp perched halfway up a mountain. Jake would have to find a few moments to slip away and contact Maggie tomorrow. He didn't dare leave the women alone in camp, though. Maybe he'd take them back to the pool. Have another damn picnic!

Despite his disgust at the way he'd lost control, Jake couldn't prevent the sudden tightening in his groin as he thought of Sarah beside the pool. Her shining hair bright against the green ferns. Her small, delicate body open and welcoming. His hand clenched around the neck of the bottle.

It was going to be a long afternoon.

And an even longer night.

For the first time, Jake began to think beyond this mission. Beyond the moment Maggie plucked Sarah and the children from this little compound.

"You will be back before the evening meal, Sister?"

Maggie smiled to herself. If the evening meal was anything like the noon one, she would certainly not be back.

She needed more than a small bowl of rice and beans to sustain her high energy levels.

"No, Sister," she told the earnest young postulant who'd escorted her to the gate. "If I'm to travel into the interior tomorrow or the next day, I have many arrangements to make and people to see."

That much was true, anyway.

"I'm surprised the mother house sent you to make these arrangements yourself. Usually such matters are taken care of before a new sister arrives to take over a mission."

"This is a rather special mission."

"Oh. I see."

A sudden boom made Maggie jump.

The young sister didn't even blink. "There's the call to afternoon meditation. Go with God."

Maggie returned the benediction, shut the wooden gate behind her and set off down the dirt road. She sighed with relief as the echoes of the thundering bell died away. It still amazed her that a community of women didn't choose a more melodious sound to mark their hours. A bell that chimed, perhaps, or tinkled, or pinged. Not one that shook the rafters with its booming clamor every thirty minutes. The realization that she had to endure the sound for two more days was enough to put a momentary dent in Maggie's soaring spirits.

As she plodded along, however, her hands tucked in her sleeve and her black skirts swishing, Maggie soon put all thoughts of the bell behind her. The excitement that had bubbled in her veins ever since Jake had made contact with her an hour ago brought a gleam to her coffee-brown eyes.

The operation was still viable. Jaguar had confirmed that a new shipment of heat-seeking missiles would be delivered to an unspecified location on the twenty-seventh, two days from now. He would accompany the party that went to the drop site, while Maggie herself hit the camp. Jake had briefed her on the precise layout of all buildings and where he'd have the woman and the children positioned.

The gleam in Maggie's eyes deepened as she remembered Jake's terse rundown of the situation in the camp. He'd confirmed that Sarah Chandler was safe, that she'd donned the dead nun's robes as cover the night of the raid to protect herself and the three children. According to Jake, the disguise had kept her from being molested. So far. At that moment, however, he'd sounded as though he wanted to strangle the woman himself.

He probably did. After five days in Sarah Chandler's company, Jake no doubt couldn't wait to see the last of the socialite. Maggie grinned, wondering just what the other woman made of the terse, hard-eyed mercenary. Jake wasn't exactly sociable, even when he wasn't in the field. In this undercover role, he must terrify the poor woman.

Although... Maggie had to admit Sarah Chandler had shown real courage and ingenuity in carrying off her disguise this long. The media had painted her as weak-willed and shallow, but Maggie knew that no one was that one dimensional. Maybe, just maybe, there was more to Sarah Chandler than anyone realized. After all, she was Senator Chandler's daughter.

Maggie's grin deepened as she pictured Adam Ridgeway facing down the big, bluff senator, who never appeared in public without an unlit cigar clamped in one corner of his mouth. That would be a confrontation worth seeing. Unleashed, unrestrained energy versus absolute control. Raw power colliding with unshakable authority. Maggie put her money on Adam, hands down.

Still, she thought, if she had to choose between witnessing a spectacular demonstration of two civilized, sophisticated males locking horns like bull elks or walking down a dusty road in a colorful, sweltering tropical city, she'd choose to be here. Cartoza's capital—called confusingly enough, Cartoza City—teemed with life.

City dwellers shouted as they alternately zoomed their vehicles for a few yards, then braked to a screeching halt a few inches from the pedestrians clogging the streets. People, taxis, buses, trucks, donkeys and one or two pigs streamed in or out of the city. Traffic was snarled hopelessly around the plaza that housed the colorful open-air market, Cartoza's center of commerce.

Concentrating on her role, Maggie settled her face into calm, quiet lines and shrank within herself. Someone with her height would stand out in a crowd unless she made herself inconspicuous. Head bowed, shoulders slightly slumped, hands folded over the .22 tucked into her sleeve, she entered the throng of people swarming through the market. She had a couple of days before the drop. She intended to use them.

By the time she joined the women who invited her to share their evening meal at a rickety table set in a patch of shade cast by a market stall, Maggie had gathered a cache of informational nuggets. Cartoza was a small country, barely a hundred miles from the Pacific to the Atlantic coast. Everyone was related to everyone else in some remote way. And everyone knew what happened in the interior, although few talked about it openly to outsiders.

Of course, the sisters of Our Lady of Sorrows weren't really outsiders. The nuns understood how difficult it was for a woman to stretch a little bit of milk among five children. Their work brought them into contact with the grinding poverty of the working people.

"One does what one must, Sister," a tired, once-pretty young woman said, scrupulously dividing her dish of paella to give Maggie half.

Maggie ate slowly, listening while the women described the hardships since the guerrillas had begun battling government troops, with the peasants caught between.

"The *federales,* they make it so hard on us," another woman said with a sigh. "They set up roadblocks. They stop our trucks. They search everything for chemicals. We were four hours getting home from market last week."

The mention of chemicals set Maggie's pulse tripping. She knew that cocaine-processing plants needed a steady supply of hydrochloric acid, sulfuric acid and ether to leach the coca leaves and extract a paste that could be shaped into bricks for shipping to refineries. She also knew that a good percentage of the population in many Latin American countries had become economically dependent on coca production. There weren't any programs like welfare or unemployment or food stamps in these countries. People starved to death every day. As a result, many peasants worked the coca fields or tried desperately to make a living by smuggling chemicals to the plants hidden deep in the interior. It wasn't a matter of right or wrong. It was a matter of survival.

Jake's initial reports had confirmed the report that a drug lord had set up a processing plant in Cartoza's interior. The same lord supplied the funds to arm the rebels, thus keeping the government too busy to mount a major search for his plant. Although this part of the operation was outside OMEGA's area of responsibility, Maggie couldn't let slip the chance to gather any useful information. Washing down the paella that had suddenly lodged in her throat with tepid orangeade, she turned a gentle, inquiring look on the woman who'd just spoken.

"It took you four hours to get home, *señora?* You must have traveled far."

"No, Sister, it was those pesky *federales,* I tell you. They set up a checkpoint on the only road into the mountains. Traffic was backed up for two or three miles. They searched everyone, everything. Everyone had to get off the bus in front of us and open every bundle. Then the searchers found some gallon containers under a load of manure on the truck ahead of us." She shook her head. "As soon as the police would unload a container, the husband would flap his arms and argue while the wife snatched it up, ran around to the other side and shoved it back on the truck."

The younger woman chuckled. "My sister-in-law's cousin tried sitting on a container last month. The woman weighs well over two hundred pounds. The *federales* didn't find that container."

She caught herself and threw an embarrassed glance at Maggie. "She does not do that often, Sister. But her baby was sick and needed medicines."

Maggie couldn't condemn these women for their obvious acceptance of the illegal trade. They were caught in a system perpetuated by her own country's insatiable appetite for a deadly, destructive drug. But neither could she condone their support. So she simply nodded and tried to steer the conversation toward the destination of these chemical containers.

Two hours later, Maggie waited for the reverberations of the lights-out bell to stop bouncing off the walls of her small room at the convent, then punched the code for OMEGA control into her satellite transceiver. As soon as Cowboy came on-line, Maggie pressed the transmit button with her thumb.

"Tell Thunder that I have something he might be interested in."

"He's downstairs. Want to talk to him?"

"Yes."

"Hang tight. I'll call him."

Maggie propped one foot up on the chair beside the narrow bed, hunched a shoulder and pressed the transceiver to her ear. She'd guessed that Adam—code name Thunder—would still be at OMEGA headquarters. There was only two hours' time difference between Cartoza's capital and D.C. It wasn't yet eight o'clock in the evening there. Adam was probably just getting ready to attend some diplomatic dinner or political fund-raiser—no doubt with that sleek, ultraelegant redhead who usually accompanied him to such functions. The one pictured hanging on Adam's arm in a glossy magazine that had featured a story about Washington's most eligible bachelors. The one in the yellow silk sheath that contained less than a yard of material, probably cost more than Maggie had taken home last month, and left no doubt in anyone's mind that underwear was a quaint, if outmoded, custom of the middle classes.

Maggie glanced down at her white, unadorned underwear and grinned.

"Thunder here." Adam's low, steady voice came over the receiver. "What do you have?"

Maggie summarized her conversation with the women. "It's all coming together," she concluded, trying hard to keep the excitement out of her voice. "Once we extract the neutrals and Jaguar springs the trap on the middleman, we should go for these druggies."

"No. Under no circumstances."

Maggie frowned at the denial. "I think I can pin down their location in the next day or so."

"I can't authorize extending the operation."

Adam paused, and Maggie waited for the explanation she knew would follow. For all his cool authority, Adam wasn't arbitrary. Most of the time.

"Despite Senator Chandler's cooperation, rumors are starting to circulate about the raid and the fact that his daughter was serving in the area. It's only a matter of time until one of the wire services picks up the story and plasters her picture across the front page again. That flimsy disguise Jaguar told us about won't last. Your mission is to get her out of there in one piece."

"I've got the extraction laid on," Maggie reminded him. "A joint U.S. and Cartozan force, in unmarked helicopters, will be ready to move the moment Jaguar signals."

"Good. Concentrate on the extraction, not on the drug lords," Adam reiterated in his precise way. He hesitated. "We'll pass your information on to the appropriate narcotics agencies. Good work, Chameleon."

"Thanks," Maggie responded dryly.

She signed off a few moments later. Tucking the transceiver under her pillow, next to her .22, she stretched out on the narrow bed.

Maggie was a professional. She understood the importance of focusing on the operation she was responsible for and letting others handle theirs. She knew that Adam would ensure the information she uncovered was passed to people who would use it.

Still, she couldn't rid herself of the conviction that a little more digging, a few more casual contacts, and she'd have the location and maybe the name of the man who was supplying Jake's band of guerillas.

She nibbled on her lower lip, wide awake and staring up into the darkness.

It was going to be a long night.

Chapter 11

Sarah rolled over on her side and wiggled, trying to find a little padding in the thin bedroll to cushion her hips. She sighed, wondering if this long night would ever end.

She'd spent what was left of the daylight hours caring for Eleanora. The woman had refused to speak, refused to even look at Sarah as she bathed her face and dabbed it with antiseptic.

Jack had come back to the hut briefly. He'd stayed only long enough to kneel in front of Eleanora and press her cheekbones with a gentle finger. They weren't broken, he'd informed Sarah. He wouldn't be able to tell about the nose until the swelling went down, but then, there wasn't much they could do about it even if it was broken. Then he'd grabbed his automatic rifle and left.

When he returned a little while ago, minus the weapon, Sarah had already fed the children and Eleanora and had them bedded down. He'd frowned at Sarah across the hut, as if wanting to have that talk he'd promised, but a small moan from Eleanora had broken the shimmering tension between them.

Now Sarah lay restless and on edge, her ear tuned to the labored breathing of the woman beside her, but every other sense achingly aware of the man who'd rigged a hammock in the far corner of the shack.

She'd had so little time to think, so little time to let herself recall what had happened this afternoon beside the pool. Now she found that she couldn't think about it without wanting to creep across the quiet hut and touch Jack lightly on the arm to awaken him. Everything in her wanted to lead him out into the dark privacy of the night. The realization that she desired him, that she ached for him with an intensity she'd never known, filled her with confusion and kept sleep at bay.

A sobbing whimper wrenched Sarah from her self-absorption. Teresa twitched in her hammock, caught in the throes of a bad dream. Sarah rolled over and started to rise, then hesitated as a dark shadow moved toward the girl.

"Hush, *niña,* it's okay," Jack whispered. "Don't be afraid."

His low, calming voice sent waves of longing rippling along Sarah's nerves. She would've given anything she possessed, which admittedly wasn't much at that particular moment, to hear him whisper like that to her. To have him hold her gently and soothe away her fears.

She watched, breath suspended, while he stooped to pick up something from the floor. Sarah couldn't see the object, but she knew instinctively it was the root, in its frilly dress. Jack tucked the doll in Teresa's arm, then melted back into the darkness.

Oh, God, Sarah groaned to herself as she eased back down onto the bedroll. Why did the blasted, infuriating man have to be so damned contradictory? Why couldn't he be totally evil, so she could hate him? Or totally good, so she could love him?

Her thought came zinging back to mock her. She couldn't love Jack if he was a plaster saint. She couldn't love him if he didn't possess the hard, biting edge that made him so different, so unlike any other man she'd ever known.

She loved him just the way he was.

Sarah's stomach lurched, and she flung up an arm to cover her eyes. She'd done some stupid, useless things in her life, and this ranked right up there among the worst of them. For all her so-called sophistication, for all her determination not to become emotionally dependent on this man, she'd merged more than her body with him this afternoon. Somehow, sometime during those searing, soaring moments, she'd merged her soul.

What in the world was she going to do about it?

What *could* she do about it?

She groaned again, not quite as silently this time, and flopped over to bury her face in the bedroll.

The sharp tang of cosmolene, the grease used for packing and shipping weapons, permeated the still morning air outside the hut. Jake wiped the last residue of grease from a blue steel barrel, frowning slightly. He'd dug through several crates to find something halfway acceptable as a replacement for his bartered rifle.

"I need to talk to you."

He glanced up at the sound of Sarah's voice. She stood in the doorway of the shack, one foot tapping under the skirts of that damn black robe.

"So talk," he said, resting the barrel across his knees.

Her gaze flicked to the children playing in the shade a few feet away. "Not here. We need to speak privately. About . . . about yesterday."

He sent her a mocking look. "I thought you didn't want to discuss yesterday. Ever."

"Yes, well, I've had some time to think, to come to a few decisions. I didn't get much rest last night."

"No kidding. Do you always toss and turn in bed like that? You keep a man awake all night just listening to you."

As soon as the words were out of his mouth, Jake could've kicked himself. Who was he kidding? Any man who shared a bed with Sarah wouldn't want to get much sleep. His hormones shot into overdrive at the vivid image that leaped into his mind, an image of a small, curved body sprawled across a wide, rumpled bed.

A flush stained her face. "I didn't realize I was such a restless sleeper. No one's ever mentioned it before."

"No one, Miss Chandler?"

His soft, taunting drawl surprised Jake as much as it did Sarah. He cursed himself when she drew back, hurt reflected in her expressive eyes.

Dammit, what was the matter with him this morning? Jake's hand tightened on the gun barrel as he realized exactly what had triggered his mocking response. Old-fashioned, gut-level jealousy. A destructive emotion he hadn't known he was capable of, and sure as hell didn't like acknowledging.

With brutal honesty, Jake forced himself to admit he'd spent the long hours of the night struggling to reconcile the Sarah he knew with the one whose picture had been plastered across the dailies for so many weeks. The woman the press had crucified had been made to look shallow, selfish, immoral. The woman he knew was no saint, but her courage and determination to care for the children had tugged at Jake's heart. It had taken him a while to accept that whatever she'd been or done before had shaped her into the remarkable woman she now was. But that was as far as he'd gotten.

Sarah, however, tackled the issue head-on. She came to stand before him, planted both hands on her hips and sent him a steely look.

"That's another thing I want to talk to you about. How you discovered who I am. And how my identity figures into this little . . . situation we have."

"Situation?"

Jake didn't much care for her choice of words. He wasn't exactly sure what was between them or where it was going, but he'd describe it differently.

Not *affair*. It was too intense to call an affair.

Not *relationship*. That was too pansy.

"Situation," she replied firmly, then ran out of patience. "Are you going to get off that crate and take a walk with me, or do I have to do something totally un-nunlike and knock you on your backside?"

Jake stared at the diminutive figure before him. Whatever had kept Sarah tossing and turning, whatever decision she'd come to in the dark hours of the night, had put a fierce spark of determination in her eyes. He stared at her, impressed in spite of himself.

There probably weren't two women in the world more dissimilar than Sarah Chandler and Maggie Sinclair in appearance, background, or current employment, but at that moment he could have sworn they were sisters. Maggie was the only woman who'd ever taken Jake down during the defensive-maneuvers training he conducted for OMEGA agents. Right now, Sarah could probably toss him on his head—and would definitely enjoy doing it.

The fierce protectiveness that had colored Jake's feelings for Sarah since the night of the raid shifted, altering subtly in shape and substance. Jake hadn't planned to tell her about the extraction until just before he left camp tomorrow. He'd hoped to minimize her worry and fear and lessen the chance that she might inadvertently let something slip. But, seeing the determination in her eyes, he knew it was time.

Jake set the gun barrel aside and wiped his hands on the stiff khaki shirt he'd been using as a rag, the one so stained with Eduard's blood that it was good for nothing else, and rose.

"You're right. We need to talk. Is Eleanora well enough to walk to the pool?"

She nodded. "I think so. She doesn't speak, but she got up and insisted on dressing herself this morning."

"I'll go let Pig-face know I'm taking you out of camp for a little while." Jake thought rapidly. "I'll tell him you need to gather some fiddlewood bark to soak and use on Eleanora's face."

Sarah slanted him a wry look. "More prehistoric medicine?"

He grinned down at her, feeling the tension that had sprung up between them ease. "Indian shamans in the Amazon rain forest still use the bark in a sort of herbal bath to cure sores caused by tropical parasites. I doubt if it would have any real usefulness on bruises, but I'm betting that Pig-face won't know that."

He didn't.

The big man grunted, not happy at being awakened this early to be informed of Jake's plans. The animosity between the two men hadn't lessened since the night the lieutenant had stumbled into the little hut, but he'd kept his distance since then. Still, Jake knew it was only a matter of time until Enrique erupted.

Twenty minutes later, he left the smaller children splashing happily in the pool, Eleanora sitting silently on the rock, and Eduard on guard.

"We'll only go a little way down this trail," Jake told the boy. "You just have to call out, and I'll be back within seconds."

The boy nodded.

"Wait for us here. We may be a while. Sarah and I have much to discuss, but we'll hear you if you need us."

Jake led the way down the narrow, twisting trail. After the first bend, they were out of sight, but not out of earshot. He could hear Ricci shrieking as Teresa splashed him, and Teresa's answering cry when the boy dunked her precious doll. Using his machete, Jake hacked the twisting vines from a toppled tree trunk, then whacked the wood once or twice with the flat of his blade to dislodge any occupants.

Nothing more threatening than a small ctenosaur emerged, its scaly, blue-banded skin and spiny back quivering in outrage. The lizard, which Jake knew could grow to the size of a small dog, bobbed its head up and down as a signal that the tree trunk was private territory. Jake smiled at Sarah's involuntary "Ugh," and nudged the creature on its waddling way with the toe of his boot.

Holding her skirts up with both hands to make sure nothing slithered underneath them, Sarah approached the trunk. She settled herself gingerly, then reached behind her neck to untie the strings of the veil.

Jake stabbed the machete into the dirt beside the tree to keep it close at hand and propped a foot up on the impromptu bench. Leaning easily on arms crossed over his knee, he watched while Sarah loosened the tie that held her hair. Her fingers raked through it, lifting the soft, fine curtain of pale silk off her neck. Sighing, she unhooked the top few buttons of her habit and flapped the material against her heated skin.

"When and if I get back to civilization, I don't think I'll ever wear black again," she murmured.

Jake, who had entertained more than one fantasy about Sarah's small, deliciously curved body in a black lace garter belt and little else, smiled ruefully to himself.

"You'll get back," he told her quietly.

She stopped fanning the material and tilted her head to look up at him. "Will I?"

"I'm doing my best to make it happen."

Jake hesitated, then took the first step in what he knew would be a difficult explanation. There was so much he wasn't cleared to tell her—about OMEGA, about the mission, about himself.

"I contacted someone yesterday who'll arrange to take you out of here," he told her slowly.

Her fingers curled around the fabric, scrunching it in her fist. "You contacted someone yesterday?" She wet her lips. "Was that before or after you recognized me?"

He shrugged. "Let's just say my contact confirmed the doubts I had about Sister Sarah."

"And from the description you gave him, he recognized Sarah Chandler."

The bitterness in her voice made Jake frown.

"It couldn't have been that difficult," she continued when he didn't respond. "I suppose the press has already picked up the story of the raid. My picture is no doubt splashed all over the dailies again."

She shivered. It was a quick, involuntary shake, so much like that of a small, trapped animal that Jake's jaw tightened.

"There aren't any news stories. Not yet."

"Never mind. I guess it doesn't really matter how you recognized me. What matters is what you're going to do about it." She rose and faced him, nose to nose. "Just tell me how much this is costing my father."

"Your father?"

"My father. How much are you and this contact of yours charging him to arrange this little escape of mine?"

Jake straightened. "What the hell are you talking about?"

Her chin jutted out. "It didn't take you long to cash in on the prize that was right under your nose, did it? You wouldn't let the welfare of a nun and three children interfere with your business deals, but you can arrange something overnight for a senator's daughter."

"Oh, for crissakes!"

"So how much did you ask for, gringo? You can tell me. I'd like to know what you think a senator's daughter is worth."

"I'm not ransoming you, dammit."

"Keep your voice down!" she hissed. "I don't want the children running down here until you and I get a few things settled between us."

"It sounds to me like you've already got everything settled in your mind."

Jake told himself that he shouldn't blame her for leaping to conclusions. Hell, he'd done everything in his power to make her think he was a conscienceless expatriate who'd sell his country for a few dollars. But somehow the fact that he'd succeeded so well didn't give him one iota of satisfaction.

She drew in a deep breath, as though steeling herself for some unpleasant task. Jake sensed that he was about to learn what had kept her—and him—awake so long into the night.

"I don't want you to do it, Jack. I don't want you to blackmail my father. I don't want you to sell yourself to the scum you're working with. I have some money of my own. Not a lot, but enough to stake you until you find some...some other line of work."

Jake's eyes narrowed. A sudden, incredible suspicion curled in his belly and wound its way up to his heart. "What makes you think I want some other line of work? What if I told you I make a good living at what I do?"

"Look at you!" she exclaimed, flinging out her arms in exasperation. "You call this living? You haven't shaved in three days, your shirt looks like something that...that lizard wouldn't even wear. Obviously you haven't had a good whiff of yourself from downwind, and...and..."

"And?" he prompted, his pulse pounding a slow, heavy rhythm.

"And you act about as civilized as some jungle creature," she finished in a huff. Then she sighed, and put a hand on his arm. "All the money in the world isn't going to make up for what this place and these people you work with are doing to you, Jack."

Jake stared down at the small, fine-boned hand. He remembered suddenly that that was the first glimpse of Sarah he'd had in the daylight, that morning after the raid—her work-roughened fingers trembling as she lifted a black sleeve to wipe her face.

He remembered, also, how that same hand had touched him yesterday. How it had speared through the hair on his chest. Slid up to his neck. Pulled his head down for her kiss. The pounding rhythm of his blood grew more intense.

He smiled down at her, wanting to hear just how she'd decided to reform him. "You didn't have any complaints about my uncivilized actions yesterday."

She sucked in a quick breath and snatched her hand away. "Okay, so I didn't exactly scream in maidenly outrage when you touched me. So I, uh..."

"So you went up in flames, and took me with you." A grin tugged at Jake's lips. "I've been in the arms business a long time, Sarah, but I've never seen or felt a detonation quite like that one."

Flushing, she turned away. "Let's not get too technical here."

Jake laughed and slid his arm around her waist, drawing her back against his chest. "It was good between us, Sarah. More than good. I couldn't sleep last night, either, thinking about it."

She laid her head back against his shoulder, sighing. "I don't know how or why I let that happen between us. I'm confused by it. I'm confused by you, and by my responses to you. I only know that I can't run away from it, like I've run away from everything in my life."

She twisted in his arms and placed her palms on his chest. "Let me help you, Jack. Don't extort money from my father. Don't do whatever it is these men want you to do with that arms shipment. Have this contact of yours arrange to pull you out of here at the same time he pulls me and the kids and Eleanora out."

Jake smiled. He'd known she would consider it a package deal. Her and the kids and Eleanora.

"I can't do that," he told her gently. "I can't leave with you."

"Why not?"

"I have a job to do here." He firmed his hold when she would have pushed herself away. "No, not the one you think. I'm here on government business."

"Right," she said bitterly. "You and Ollie North."

"Sarah, listen to me. . . ."

"No, you listen to me. My father heads the Senate Intelligence Subcommittee on Latin-American Affairs, remember? I know darn well that no government agency would be selling arms to this scruffy little band of guerrillas, not when official U.S. policy is to support the Cartozan government."

"We're not selling. We're trying to stop the sale. I've been undercover with this group for almost three weeks now."

Sarah's face registered first disbelief, then skepticism.

Jake kept his voice low and deliberate, trying to convince her. "My mission is to take out the middle link in the international chain that trades stolen U.S. arms for drug dollars. I intend to do that tomorrow night, when he makes his drop."

"My God!" she breathed, staring up at him. "You're . . . you're serious?"

This, time when she pushed away from him, he let her go. Jake felt a wrench at the dazed expression in her eyes.

"I'm deadly serious. You know how shaky this country is. If we don't stop the arms flow, fast, Cartoza will probably see the same wave of political assassinations and drug wars that have torn Peru and Colombia apart."

"You . . . you really are under cover? With the CIA?"

"Close enough."

Jake felt a curious sense of relief to have it out at last. He waited for some confirmation, some sigh of relief, or a welcome laugh.

"You *bastard!*"

Jake was so surprised by her explosive fury that he didn't even see the punch coming.

In any other circumstance, a blow from Sarah's small fist wouldn't have even dented stomach muscles that were conditioned to take karate kicks and powerhouse punches. But she hit him with just enough unexpected speed and force to send him stumbling backward.

His heel thumped against the fallen tree trunk, and his momentum carried him the rest of the way over. Jake landed on his duff on the dense, springy layer of vegetation, his breath whooshing out of his lungs.

Chest heaving, fiery blue-green sparks shooting from her eyes, Sarah clambered over the log.

"You rat! You despicable, chauvinistic, arrogant rat!"

Jake levered himself up. "What in the—?"

Her foot planted itself square on his chest and shoved him back down. "How dare you! How dare you let me think you were the scum of the earth!"

"Sarah..."

"Don't *Sarah* me. You made me ache with wanting you, and I loathed myself for it!"

"Well, I wasn't exactly thrilled to find myself lusting after a nun."

"And that's another thing. Where did you get off being so angry over *my* disguise? I can't believe all the bristling male indignation you displayed yesterday. The way you stalked me. The way you made *me* feel guilty about *your* unbridled lust!"

"Unbridled lust?" Despite himself, Jake felt his shoulders shake.

"Don't you dare laugh!" She spit the words out. "If you do, I swear, I'll...I'll..."

She looked around wildly. Jake saw her glance fall on the machete stuck in the dirt beside the tree trunk.

"Oh, no," he warned. His hand snaked out and caught her ankle, just in case. She kicked her foot, trying to break his hold.

"How could you make love to me yesterday and not tell me the truth?"

Jake hung on to her flailing leg while he scooted back and pushed himself into a sitting position. "Look, I'm sorry about yesterday."

"You should be!"

"It was a mistake," Jake admitted.

She halted in midkick. "What do you mean, it was a mistake?"

"I should never have allowed myself to lose control like that. It was stupid and dangerous."

"Stupid and dangerous," she repeated blankly, taking a little hop to maintain her balance. "Making love to me was stupid and dangerous?"

"In the middle of a mission, yes. I won't let it happen again, at least not until we get out of here."

"*You* won't let it happen again?" She closed her eyes. "Let go of my leg."

Jake decided he'd better hang on until he figured just what was putting that choked quality in her voice.

Sarah opened her eyes and pinned him with a scathing look. "You know, Mr. Gringo-Creighton-Jack-whatever-your-name-is, I'm beginning to think I liked you better as a sleaze. At least I had hopes of reforming you then. This new you might just turn out to be hopeless."

At that moment, with his butt planted in a bed of jungle vegetation, his stomach throbbing and his fist wrapped around the ankle of the woman hovering over him like a vengeful angel, Jake knew he loved her.

This Sarah wasn't the heartless socialite the media had crucified. She wasn't the spoiled daughter of a powerful senator who protected her at every turn. Whatever she might have been before, this woman with the jewellike eyes and the straggling hair was magnificent.

In the time Jake had known her, she'd spent every waking moment caring for three kids who had no claim on her. She'd championed a battered, helpless woman. She'd given herself to a mercenary, with an open, searing passion that still stunned him, then set out with Sarah-like determination to reform him.

Jake would just have to convince her that the real him was far from hopeless. Admittedly, he might have one or two rough edges that needed filing down. When he got them all out of Cartoza, he intended to give her plenty of opportunity to work on them. Right now, however, he needed to soothe her ruffled feathers.

"You may prefer me in my undercover persona, Miss Sarah-Josepha-Sarita Chandler, but I much prefer knowing you're not a nun."

Grinning, he gave her ankle a little yank, pulled her off balance and tumbled her down on top of him.

Chapter 12

Sarah's bottom landed with a solid *whump* on Jake's stomach. He was prepared for the blow this time, however, and barely registered her weight as he rolled over, taking her with him. Before she could do much more than utter a few sputtering protests, he pinned her against the verdant earth.

Holding her easily with one leg thrown over hers and an arm across her waist, Jake waited patiently for her halfhearted struggles to still. When they did, he lifted a hand to smooth away the strands of pale blond hair that had twisted across her cheek.

"Don't write me off as hopeless just yet, Sarah. I must have one or two salvageable traits."

She glared up at him. "I haven't seen any."

"Is that so?" He brushed the back of a knuckle along her chin. "What about the fact that I'm a great cook? Are you forgetting those bananas and cold beans you scarfed up?"

Folding her lips together, Sarah declined to respond.

"And I carve a pretty decent mango root, if I do say so myself."

That won a grudging response. "Well, it wasn't bad."

He smiled down at her. "When we get out of here, you'll have all the time in the world to find some sterling character traits among my less admirable tendencies."

She frowned up at him for a moment or two longer, but then the fight went out of her in a long, huffy sigh.

"When we get out of here," she repeated slowly, as if testing the feel of the words, the concept of some time and some place after these days in the humid jungle and the squalid little hut. "Jack, I... What *is* your name, anyway?"

Jake smiled down at her. "Does it really matter?"

Sarah searched his eyes. Their gray depths held lingering laughter, a rueful tenderness, and something deeper, something that made her heart suddenly slam against her ribs. The doubts and uncertainties that had haunted her for so long melted away. Whatever else she'd done wrong in the past, however poor her judgment had been, she knew she wasn't mistaken about what she saw in his eyes and felt in her own.

"No," she said, after a long, breathless moment. "It doesn't really matter."

Jake told himself he couldn't kiss her. He warned himself that if he bent his head and covered those soft lips with his, he might not be able to stop there. The tendons in his neck corded with the effort of holding back.

Sarah took the matter out of his hands. Curling an arm around his shoulders, she pulled him down.

The touch of her mouth on his sent slow, sweet tendrils of desire spiraling through Jake's chest. He let himself savor them for as long as he dared, then raised his head. He drew in a harsh, ragged breath.

"Sarah, let's just consider the options for a moment."

She planted a line of little kisses along the underside of his chin. "You consider them."

"This is too dangerous. I can't let myself lose control again like I did yesterday."

"So stay in control," she murmured against his skin. "If you can."

"The kids are just a shout away. They might— Hey!"

She laved the little bite she'd given him with her tongue. "You told Eduard to call if there's trouble. He'll call."

"You could get pregnant."

She went still under him, then laid her head back on the springy grass. For once Jake couldn't decipher the expression in her luminous eyes.

"I could," she acknowledged at last. "If I'm lucky."

Jake almost lost it then. He hadn't thought in terms of a family for years. Since his divorce, he'd immersed himself in his work, in OMEGA, in teaching newer, less experienced agents the skills they needed to survive in the dark worlds they inhabited. But the idea of Sarah swelling with his child stirred some long-buried, atavistic need. For the first time, he realized that his feelings for her went beyond desire, beyond the tentative, hazy emotion he'd identified as love earlier. He wanted to mate with her in the most elemental, essential way. He wanted to merge his body and his life with hers. But first, he reminded himself savagely, he needed to make sure they had lives to merge.

Disentangling the arm she had wrapped around his neck, Jake sat up. He ignored her reproachful look and drew her up beside him.

"We don't have much time," he said quietly. "We need to talk about tomorrow."

Sarah wasn't ready. She didn't want to shatter the sweet, sensual moment with the fear his words engendered, but she knew she had no choice. She'd run away from her fears too many times in the past. She couldn't, wouldn't, run away from these.

"Yes, we do," she agreed.

"When I leave for the drop site, my contact will..."

"When you leave?" She swallowed. "Sorry, just a small panic attack. Go on."

He raked a hand through his dark hair. "I've been through this a thousand times in my mind. I don't like it any more than you do, but it's the safest extraction I can arrange for you and the kids."

"And Eleanora," Sarah added. "I'll talk to her as soon as you tell me it's safe, but I know she'll want to go with us."

"And Eleanora," Jake said. "Look, Sarah, the choices were simple. The first was to risk an assault on the camp while the men were still there. I could've held them off until the team landed, but it would've meant a heavy firefight."

She thought of the arsenal of deadly weapons that each man carried and suppressed a shudder.

"The second choice was to get you away from camp and try an extraction through the jungle canopy."

Sarah tilted her head back to look up at the dense, leafy roof. So little sunlight penetrated that she couldn't see through it to the sky. She estimated that the overhead carpet must be three hundred feet above the ground.

"What you're seeing is only the first layer, the canopy," Jake told her. "Above that is the emergent layer, where the crowns of the tallest trees stick out. The chopper would have to hover above that, which is dangerous in itself. This hot, sticky humidity increases density altitude and reduces the rotor blade's lift. Which makes it doubly dangerous to try to hoist anyone through that thick, impenetrable screen. I've seen it tried several times. I've seen it done. Once."

She swallowed. "So what's the third choice?"

"The third choice is for me to take all but a few of the men out of camp to reduce the opposition. My contact will lead the extraction team in moments after we depart."

"He better be good," Sarah mumbled.

A smile lightened the shadows in Jack's eyes. "She's the best. I trained her myself."

Sarah told herself that the spurt of jealousy that shot through her was childish and unreasoning. There was too much at stake here to let personal feelings interfere.

"Tell me exactly what will happen," she said evenly.

She was glad he didn't insult her intelligence by minimizing the risks. Rubbing her damp palms down her thighs, Sarah memorized every detail, every brief instruction.

Jack had her repeat the procedure in her own words, then run through it one more time.

When she had it down to his satisfaction, he eased back against the log and drew up one knee. His dark brows knit, as if he were examining the plan yet again, looking for holes.

Sarah let the silence between them spin out like a gossamer web, until it surrounded them in a silken cocoon, shutting out the sounds of the birds in the trees overhead and the faint echo of childish laughter. For this moment, at least, there was just her and this man whose name she didn't need to know.

He looked so hard, she thought, studying the angles of his face. So self-contained and withdrawn. His flinty eyes were distant behind their screen of black lashes. Driven by a need to bring him back to her, Sarah reached out to touch him.

She froze with her hand half-out, startled by the flash of color that flew past. A huge bird swooped down on what looked like a wild avocado plant a few feet away and plucked a fat ripe fruit with its bill.

"What is it?" Sarah whispered, mesmerized by its long, streaming emerald tail feathers and brilliant red breast.

"It's a quetzal," Jack murmured. "Pretty rare around here."

"I've never seen anything like it."

He smiled at her awed expression as the bird tilted its head back, puffed out its shimmering ruby chest and swallowed the fruit whole.

"Indian legend says its breast wasn't always red."

She slanted him a quick, amused look. "More prehistoric lore?"

"No, this tale's more modern. Supposedly the Spaniards who invaded this area in the 1500s attacked a Mayan chief. The quetzal swooped down and landed on the dying man's chest, either to protect him or to mourn him. When it flew away again, its breast was colored with the chieftain's blood."

Sarah glanced back at the exotic creature, feeling her pleasure in its exotic beauty slowly fade. When it took off with a flap of emerald wings, she sat still for a long moment. Then she reached up and began to work the fastenings on her robe.

Jake eyed her lazily, reluctant to see this interlude of quiet between them end. She was right, though. They needed to get back to the kids. Back to camp. Jake straightened, only to realize that she wasn't hooking the few fastenings she'd undone earlier to fan herself. She was unhooking the remaining ones.

"What are you doing?"

She pulled another hook open. "I'm taking this off. Then I'm going to make love to you."

"We talked about this earlier," Jake said gently. "I can't let myself lose control like that again. Much as I want you, I can't cross that line again—not until I get you out of here."

"What makes you think the decision is yours alone to make?" She jiggled her shoulders. The black gown slid down her arms and pooled around her hips.

Lord, she was beautiful, Jake admitted ruefully. He'd never seen anyone so small and perfectly proportioned. All gold and tan and white in places he damn well shouldn't be staring at.

"Sarah, this isn't smart."

"No," she replied, leaning forward to brush the edges of his shirt aside and lay her palms against his heart. "But it's necessary. Maybe not for you, but for me. I need you, Jack. I need you to hold me and kiss me and know that, whatever happens tomorrow, we had this time together."

He felt the soft touch of her fingertips against his bare skin and drew in a ragged breath. "I don't think I can just hold you."

Her lips curved in a slow, wicked grin. "Why don't you put your arms around me and find out?"

Maybe it *was* time for him to find another line of work, Jake thought. He couldn't ever remember making a conscious decision to put his own desire ahead of operational needs before. The thought worried him for the few seconds it took to reach out and pull Sarah into his lap.

She nestled against him, her arms wrapped around his waist, her head tucked under his chin. He breathed in the sun-warmed scent of her hair. Her skin was damp with the humidity of the jungle and incredibly soft against his.

Jake rested his chin on the top of her head, content for the moment just to absorb the tactile sensations Sarah's mere touch generated. Content, that is, until her hands began to move on his back. With feather-light strokes, she explored his skin, his spine. Her hips shifted, and the lazy sensuality of the moment suddenly sharpened. He felt himself hardening against the rounded curve of her bottom.

She straightened, leaning a little bit away from him. Her eyes gleamed up at him, as shimmering and brilliant as any of the birds that swooped through the canopy.

"Well, I guess that settles that," she declared solemnly. "Holding is definitely not an option for us."

Jake groaned and bent his head.

Sarah responded by wrapping her arms around his neck and kissing him with all the warm eagerness that characterized her. Her lips opened under his. She tasted and explored his mouth with a hunger that matched his. Her breasts pressed against his chest, their small, round centers peaking against his flesh.

This time, when they shed their clothes and rolled onto the green, springy carpet of ferns, their loving wasn't hard and fast and furious. This time it was slow and indescribably sweet. At least at first.

Sarah herself set the pace. Smiling, she pushed Jake onto his back. She stretched out at his side and explored him, tasting, touching, teasing with her hands and mouth. Her hair formed a silvery puddle on his stomach as she left a trail of kisses from his navel to his chin, then back down again. Her fingers speared through the light mat of hair on his chest, twisting it and tugging lightly.

Jake lay with one knee bent, the woman he now considered his own cradled at his side. He closed his eyes, savoring the feel of her body pressed to his and wondering at the crazy junction of time and circumstance that had brought them to this place and this moment.

"Are you going to sleep?"

He opened one eye to see Sarah propped on her elbow, staring down at him with a rueful smile.

"No, ma'am. I'm just lying here thinking about that nun who whacked me over the head all those years ago."

"The one with the umbrella?"

"Mmm...."

She pursed her lips. "I'm not sure I want to hear why you're thinking of her at this particular moment."

He grinned and reached up to twist a strand of her hair around one finger. "If she hadn't scared the bejesus out of me, I might not have been so intimidated by your little disguise for so long."

"And?"

He tugged gently on her hair, bringing her face closer to his. "And I might not have been so angry when I discovered that the woman who'd been twisting me in knots wasn't little Sister Sarah Josepha after all."

"And?"

He brushed his lips across hers. "And I might not have forced the issue between us yesterday."

"No," she whispered against his mouth, "but I might have. In fact, if you hadn't forced it, I probably would've done exactly what I'm going to do now."

Jake's stomach muscles jumped as her seeking fingers slid through the thick hair at his groin and closed around his shaft.

"Now you just close your eyes again," Sarah murmured in between tiny, wet kisses, "and let me give you something else to think about besides being whacked with an umbrella."

She definitely did that. Within moments, she had him rigid and aching and straining against her hold. Her mouth teased and nipped at him with the same erotic impact as her hands. As much as he ached to roll her over into the thick green carpet, Jake held back, giving her the time she wanted, needed. Every muscle quivered with the effort. When his low, strangled growl gave evidence that he couldn't restrain himself any longer, she took him into her body, her hips straddling his and her back arching as she met his slow, driving thrusts with a strength that stunned him.

Jake saw his hands, dark against the pale skin of her breasts. He heard her breathless, panting cries as her passion deepened. He felt her moist heat surround him, clench him. When she braced her hands on his shoulders and brought her mouth to his, Jake drank in her dark, sweet taste.

Sarah was right, Jake thought—while he could still think at all. Whatever happened tomorrow, they'd have this. They'd always have this.

Slowly, reluctantly, they rejoined the universe they'd left behind for a moment out of time. Jake brought Sarah up into his arms for a last touch of his lips against hers, then turned away to reach for their clothes.

She clutched at his shoulders, achingly reluctant to allow even a breath of space between their sweat-slicked bodies.

"Jack, I . . . I want you to know that everything you heard or read about me was true."

He stopped her with a brush of his thumb over the soft skin of her lips. "We both have things in our past that are best forgotten."

She took his hand in both of hers, needing to tell him what was in her heart. "I was stupid and self-centered and uncaring who I hurt, before. I . . . I thought I was in love. But now . . . now I'm just beginning to understand what the word means."

His thumb shaped her lower lip. "When we get out of here, Sarah Josepha, we're going to take a long, slow, cool shower in the biggest, most decadent hotel room money can buy. We're going to make wild, sweet love on a bed with clean sheets. And then we're going to do some serious talking about the future."

Not five minutes later, the future reached out to grab them by the throat.

They'd collected the children and Eleanora and were only a few hundred meters from the camp when the sharp crack of a gunshot set the parrots overhead squawking. The dense undergrowth shielded the camp from view, but there was no mistaking the source of the sound.

"Get down!" Jake ordered instantly. Eleanora dropped like a sack of ballast, tugging Teresa down with her. Sarah grabbed Eduard's good arm and pulled him down with her and Ricci. Tucking the toddler under the shelter of her body, she wrapped a protective arm across Eduard's thin shoulders.

Jake strained to hear above the noise of the birds. No other sound reached him from camp. He straightened slowly, rapidly assessing the possibilities. One of the men could've shot a viper. Or amused himself by taking a potshot at one of the monkeys that occasionally darted into camp to snatch at shiny objects in the debris. Or an argument between a couple of the rebels could've taken a personal, ugly twist. It had happened before.

He turned and crouched beside Sarah. "I don't think it's anything to panic over. I'm going in. Stay here until I signal for you."

He pulled the palm-size pistol from his boot. She hesitated, swallowing hard, then reached out a shaky hand and took it.

"It's ready to fire," Jake warned softly. "If I'm not back in five minutes, take the children back to the pool. I'll call in what help I can and try to hold off the others as long as possible."

"Jack, I—" She broke off, unable to articulate her thoughts. Her eyes expressed them for her.

"Me too," Jake answered, smiling. Ruffling Eduard's hair, he rose and moved down the trail with the silent, swift tread of a hunter.

Che met him at the edge of the clearing, his pistol drawn and a cold, flat rage in his eyes. A half-dozen men were strung out behind him, their expressions nervous. Jake caught the stoop-shouldered Xavier's frowning look. Clearly the leader's unexpected return had shaken the camp.

For several tense moments, they faced each other. Jake's finger curled around the trigger.

At last the rebel leader broke the crackling tension. "I was just coming to look for you."

Jake let his eyes drift to the leader's drawn gun. "Did you think I'd gone somewhere? Without getting paid?"

Che straightened slowly, contempt replacing some of the rage in his eyes. "That was what Enrique said, when he tried to justify letting you go into the jungle with only the women."

"You still don't trust me?" Jake asked mockingly.

"I don't trust anyone who's not dedicated to the revolution," the rebel said flatly. "Nor do I tolerate those who disregard my orders."

Jake knew then what had caused the single pistol shot. He wouldn't have to worry about Pig-face any longer.

Che uncocked his weapon and slid it into its holster. "Where is the woman?"

Jake lowered the barrel of his own weapon. "Where I left her."

The other man eyed him for a long moment. "You've taken your responsibility for her welfare most seriously, gringo."

"You put it on my neck, remember?"

"Call her in. We're abandoning this camp. We leave immediately."

Jake's stomach clenched. "Why?"

"The *patrón* has sources in the city. They tell him people, unknown people, have been asking questions. Too many questions. He is not nervous, you understand, but cautious. He's bringing in the shipment we've been waiting for tonight...."

Tonight, not tomorrow! Beads of sweat collected in the hollow between Jake's shoulder blades.

"After tonight, we will have what we need to bring this decadent government to its knees." The intense fanaticism that characterized the leader vibrated in his voice. "After tonight, we will not need this camp. We will take the revolution out of these hills and into the city."

And take the heat off the *patrón*'s little operation, Jake thought in gut-twisting disgust.

"Call in the woman," Che said impatiently.

Jake slung his weapon over his shoulder. "Why not let her go?" he suggested casually. "She and the children will only slow us on the march. She has served her purpose here."

"I would as soon put a bullet in her head. The church she serves is nothing but a tool of the corrupt government that suppresses our people. But the *patrón* has said to bring her."

"Bring her where?"

"You have no need to know our destination, only that your job with us ends tonight."

It was going to end, all right. One way or another.

"Come, collect the woman and your gear. You will take the point. I have need of a man who's good with his eyes and his weapon out in front."

In other words, Jake thought grimly, Che intended to put the gringo where he could watch him every minute. With Xavier dogging his footsteps, Jake went to collect Sarah and the others, his mind racing with possible options.

Chapter 13

"OMEGA control, this is Chameleon."

Maggie tucked the tiny transceiver between her shoulder and her ear and leaned against the rest room wall. While she waited for Cowboy to respond, she glanced around the dingy room.

As unisex bathrooms went, this one contained all the essentials. A grimy, once-white stool with an old-fashioned overhead flush unit. A urinal hanging crookedly on one wall. A rusted faucet set over an equally rusted sink. A sliver of mirror nailed above the tap. Maggie caught sight of herself in the mirror and grimaced. She fit right in with the rest of the clientele in this raunchy café, but she was ready to wipe off the half pound of green eye shadow that weighted her lids, slip out the back door to retrieve her discreetly concealed habit and make her way back to the relative quiet of the convent. Even the raucous chapter house bell was melodious compared to the disco music booming off the walls of the Café El Caribe.

"This is Cowboy, Chameleon. What's happening? We thought you'd— What's that noise?" His voice sharpened. "Are you under assault?"

"Not me, just my ears," Maggie responded quickly. "I'm at the local night spot."

"Let me guess," Cowboy drawled. "You're soliciting contributions from the patrons for the sisters' welfare fund?"

Maggie glanced down at the skintight glowing-pink tube of slinky fabric that hugged her from well below her collarbone to well above her knees. "Let's just say I'm soliciting...information. Heard anything from Jaguar in the last few hours?"

"No, nothing."

She nibbled on her well-glossed lower lip. Everything was set for tomorrow. She really didn't need Jake's confirmation. Still, Maggie would like to talk to him one last time before going in.

"Did you pick up anything interesting at that end?" Cowboy asked.

"Very. I've been sharing a table for the last half hour with a runner."

"One of the big guys?"

"No, just a mule. A small-time carrier trying to earn enough for a stake for herself in Hollywood."

"Aren't they all?"

Maggie frowned, thinking of the young wives and mothers she'd talked to yesterday. They were simply trying to feed their families.

"No, not all the ones down here, anyway. But this one is definitely in it for the thrills, as well as the money. She makes a run to the States every month or so, ferrying about ten kilos each time. She's also a personal friend—a *very* personal friend—of the man the folks around here call the *patrón*."

Cowboy's low whistle was audible even over the boom of disco. "The same *patrón* who's funding the arms for Jaguar's little band?"

"Right the first time. She mentioned that she paid him a visit a couple of nights ago. Bragged about a chopper flying her in. She also let drop that our friend Che was visiting at the same time."

Maggie hesitated, still not sure of the import of her next tidbit of information. "She said that Che mentioned a nun his band had taken, and that the *patrón* was very interested in her."

"Interested how?"

"I'm not sure. I'm going to follow this up, though. I have this funny feeling..."

Cowboy groaned. "You and your feelings."

"Look, I have to go. I've tied up this rest room long enough. Tell the chief—"

She broke off as the door handle rattled. "Gotta go, Cowboy. Talk at you later."

Flipping the tiny, flat transceiver shut, Maggie hitched up her short skirt and clipped it to the garter belt she'd filched at the same time as the stockings and the high spiked heels. She shimmied her hips to smooth the tight fabric down over them and grinned, remembering the ridiculous ease with which she'd acquired her new wardrobe.

She'd made the rounds of the tawdry shops this afternoon with the young novice to hand out pamphlets describing a free clinic the sisters were offering next week. While the earnest young novice explained the various treatments, Maggie had collected her present outfit, bit by bit. She'd tucked the items under her robe and left notes where the shopkeepers could find them directing them to present a bill to the U.S. consulate. Maggie grinned, imagining the expression on some State Department rep's face when he had to issue a voucher for a black lace garter belt and net stockings.

The door handle rattled once more.

"Just a minute," she called, taking a quick peek in the mirror. She poked her fingers a few times in the mass of hair she'd pulled to one side and teased mercilessly, fluffing it even more. She applied another layer of scarlet lipstick and dusted more green on her lids. Satisfied that even Adam would have had to look twice to recognize her under her layers of paint, Maggie opened the door.

Waves of pulsing music hit her with hurricane force. She stopped on the threshold, wincing, and waited for her eyes to adjust to the flashing lights that cut through an otherwise murky darkness. She saw with disgust that the woman she'd been subtly pumping had left the club.

"It's all yours," she shouted to the figure lounging beside the door. She started to step forward, but found her way blocked by an arm planted across the door jamb.

Maggie glanced down at the white-sleeved arm. Arching one brow, she followed its line to a solid, broad-shouldered body. The shoulders strained against a tailored white linen sports coat. Maggie noted the gold medallion gleaming at the open neck of the shirt. A square, faintly shadowed chin. A luxuriant black mustache. Gleaming brown eyes.

It was only after the tall, dark-haired figure stepped out of the shadows that Maggie saw how the collection of individual features all added up to the most handsome man she'd ever seen. No, not handsome. This guy was drop-dead gorgeous. She managed to keep her mouth from sagging—barely. He was Omar Sharif and Julio Iglesias and Emilio Estevez all rolled into one.

He was also, she discovered, smiling at her in a way that raised the hairs on her arms.

"You want something, my friend?" she asked coolly

The dark mustache lifted, showing white, even teeth. "Perhaps."

His deliberate move forward crowded Maggie's space too much for her liking. She took a quick couple of steps backward, deciding that she needed some distance between her and this hunk.

He stepped into the dingy rest room and closed the door, cutting the noise down from mind-bending to merely ear-splitting. Leaning his shoulders back against the door, he folded his arms over his chest. Maggie saw the flash of a gold Rolex on his wrist.

She didn't make the mistake of thinking this was some wealthy aristocrat out cruising Cartoza's only night spot. Until he showed his hand, however, she would play her role. She gave him a slow half smile. "So, my friend, what is it you want?"

His dark eyes lingered on her mouth for a moment, then traced a slow, casual path down her body. Maggie willed herself not to stiffen, not to react in any way. In his own good time, he brought his gaze back to her face.

"Maybe I wish a few moments of your company."

She flicked a quick glance around the dingy bathroom. The small disparaging smile on her face said she didn't think much of his choice of a trysting place. Maggie used the few seconds to catalog possible escape routes. There weren't any. The rest room had no window. No other door. No crack in the graffiti-covered plaster walls.

"Or maybe I just want to know why you ask so many questions," he said lazily. He jerked his chin toward the outer room. "Our little friend out there says you have an interest in the interior."

Maggie shrugged. "I was just making small talk."

"A particular interest."

She took her lower lip between her teeth, hesitating. "All right, I admit I am interested. I'm new here, you understand. Just down from Mexico. I have need of funds."

When he didn't answer, she pouted and turned to survey herself in the piece of mirror. Running one finger along the line of her darkened brow, Maggie watched him in the cracked glass.

"I understand there is money to be made," she said to his reflection. "Much money. You will tell your *patrón* I am interested, yes?"

He smiled and levered his shoulders off the door.

"Perhaps you can tell him yourself. You will come with me, I think."

At that moment, Maggie would've given everything she possessed to be primary agent on this mission. If it was her operation, she could've followed this promising lead and walked out of the Café El Caribe with this man she suspected was one of the *patrón*'s lieutenants. But she was Jaguar's backup. She was here, as Adam had so succinctly pointed out, to work Sarah Chandler's extraction.

She sighed with real regret. "No, I think not."

He had quick reflexes, Maggie had to give him that. He blocked her first blow with an upflung arm. That gave her just the opening she needed for a swift, sharp jab to the solar plexus. He bent over in an involuntary reaction, his breath rushing out in a startled grunt. Maggie finished him with a chop to the back of the neck. He crumpled to the cement floor without a sound.

She stared down at his sprawled figure, regretting the waste of such magnificent malehood. Too bad the men she met in this job were either first class weirdoes or all-around scumbags. She dropped to one knee and quickly, expertly searched him.

The lethal little Benelli she found in a holster tucked under his arm didn't surprise her, but the small leather case she extracted from a hidden pocket did. When she flipped it open, Maggie's eyes narrowed.

He came awake with a little jerk of one leg. Maggie leaned her shoulders comfortably against the wall and watched with interest as his muscular thigh bunched, then drew up, until his knee was bent and an expensive alligator boot was planted firmly on the floor. He propped himself up on one elbow and shook his head. He must have caught sight of her orange-and-pink-striped shoes out of one corner of his eye. His head tilted, studying the shoe for a moment. Then he rose to his feet with an athletic grace and dusted off the seat of his linen slacks.

Maggie had had plenty of opportunity to study him while he lay sprawled on the less-than-clean cement floor. She discovered, however, that a handsome, unconscious man, and one whose eyes held a reluctant gleam of admiration for a worthy adversary, were two different creatures altogether. She held the Benelli easily in her left hand, hoping she wouldn't have to use it, and flipped open the leather case with the other.

"So, Colonel, do you care to tell me why the chief of security for Cartoza was going to take me to the one called the *patrón*?"

His mustache lifted. "I wasn't. I was going to...shall we say, convince you to take *me* to *him*."

"What makes you think I know his location?"

"My men listened via a remote device the whole time the little songbird poured her heart out to you. Unfortunately, the noise levels drowned out all but a few words. Those were enough, however, for me to pay a little visit to my favorite night spot to check out the latest arrival."

"You come here often? The chief of security?"

"Often enough." He saw the skepticism in her eyes and shrugged. "This is a small country. Everyone knows who I am. I don't hide from the men who seek to destroy our government. It is better to let them see me, and know that they are watched."

He was either incredibly brave or had reasons not to worry about the political assassinations that regularly rocked this part of the world. Maggie's face remained bland, but the Benelli never wavered.

"You're Chameleon, I take it." His eyes flickered down her miniskirted length once more. "I understood you were good, but I didn't realize how good. Or how attractive."

He wasn't exactly dog food himself, Maggie thought with an inner smile.

"You're wise not to trust me," he continued smoothly. "Check with your headquarters. They will verify what I say, who I am."

"I know who you are," she admitted at last. "Luis Barbedo Esteban. Educated here and at Oxford. Colonel, Cartozan army. Former instructor in counterterrorist tactics at the Inter-American Defense College in Washington. Appointed by the president as chief of security two years ago."

"You don't seem particularly impressed," he commented, his white teeth gleaming.

"Oh, I am. I'm also impressed by your off-duty uniform. You appear to have expensive tastes, Colonel. Or was that watch you're wearing a gift from a grateful citizen?"

"Actually, it was a gift from the president. Yours, not mine."

Maggie notched a brow.

"For a slight service I rendered him some years ago," Esteban said with a shrug. "He was a private citizen at the time."

"That was you? You're the one who swam two miles out to the boat where he was being held hostage? You took the terrorists out, single-handed?"

The incident had occurred long before Maggie was recruited by OMEGA, but a few of the older heads still cited it as a textbook example of surprise and brains triumphing over armed brawn.

The colonel grinned. "Your president managed to assist quite ably with one or two."

Well, hell! Adam had stated in no uncertain terms during the mission prebrief that Colonel Esteban was to be trusted, but he'd left out a couple of rather pertinent details about the man. Maggie's mouth twisted at the thought of what her boss would say when he learned that she'd dropped the colonel and held him at gun point in a sleazy little nightclub.

She lowered the Benelli, thumbing the safety before she handed it to him. "I hope the men who'll be with me on the extraction team tomorrow night will have the same skill as you and my president."

"Perhaps I will find it necessary to accompany the team myself," Esteban murmured, holstering his weapon.

"Perhaps you should."

He buttoned his coat and lifted his broad shoulders once or twice to settle the linen smoothly over the holster. With the simple action, he seemed to assumed a different persona. Harder, more precise, more authoritarian.

"Tell me what you learned from the woman you were speaking with."

Maggie arched a brow.

He caught her look and moderated both his voice and his stance. "I know my country's interior. I was raised in the mountains. Perhaps I can recognize some hint of where she went to visit this friend of hers, identify some feature."

Knowing that someone could pound on the rest room door at any moment, Maggie ran through every detail quickly, precisely.

"Are you sure she said this *patrón*'s hacienda was only fifteen minutes by helicopter?"

"I'm sure. Does that help?"

"It would help more if I knew the exact airspeed and wind direction at the time of the flight," he answered with a grin, "but it narrows the search area considerably."

"Perhaps we can narrow it even more. There are three major roads leading out of Cartoza City into the interior. My source—Juana's sister-in-law's cousin, you understand—says the road heading north is the shortest way to get chemicals such as hydrochloric acid and ether to their destination."

Surprise etched his aristocratic features. "You have been busy, haven't you?"

"It's my job."

"You do it well, Chameleon."

"Thanks," Maggie said, tipping two fingers to her brow. "Glad to be of service, Colonel. Now, if there's nothing else, we'd better free up this room before someone wonders just exactly what's going on in here."

He gave a leer that was only half feigned. "They won't wonder."

Maggie tossed a smile over her shoulder and opened the door. She winced as fresh waves of music assaulted her ears. She hadn't taken two steps before the colonel grabbed her arm and hauled her back. Maggie found herself wedged between the hard concrete wall and a body that was every bit as unyielding.

"Do not fight me," he ordered swiftly, then covered her mouth with his.

In the curious way the human brain has, Maggie's processed a half-dozen sensory perceptions all at once. She felt his belt buckle press against her stomach. She tasted the golden hint of rum on his breath. She saw his dark head slant to take her mouth more fully. And she heard the faint thud of footsteps passing.

"Who was that?" Maggie whispered against his mouth when she could breathe again. Barely.

"I don't know," he murmured, brushing his lips across hers.

"But...why...this?"

"Because...I've been wanting...'this'...since the first moment I saw you."

He muffled her indignant little huff with another kiss, feather-light this time, but just as devastating as the first.

From the tensile strength of the body pressed against hers, Maggie knew that she wouldn't take him down as easily as she had before. Assuming she wanted to. She was still debating the issue when he raised his head and smiled down at her.

"Until tomorrow."

"Until tomorrow."

Breathless, she watched him make his leisurely way through the crowd in the club. Several of the patrons sent curious looks at Maggie, still lounging against the door jamb. She sighed. She wouldn't get much out of them now, not after they'd seen her in the arms of Cartoza's chief of security.

She sauntered toward the end of the crowded bar, waiting for the right moment to melt into the shadows and slip out the door. She flicked a quick glance up at the clock embedded in neon palm trees above the bar. Not even eight o'clock. She thought of the convent bell and shuddered. This could turn out to be another long night.

In fact, it turned out to be far shorter than Maggie anticipated. She was only halfway back to the convent house when a discreet ping signaled an incoming transmission. She ducked into a nearby alley and whipped the transceiver out of her side pocket.

"Hold on, Chameleon. Jaguar's on the line."

Maggie's fingers curled around the tiny instrument.

"I've only got a few seconds." Jake's disembodied whisper vibrated with tension. "We've been on the march most of the day. Che hasn't let me out of his sight until now. He won't say where we're going, only that the drop has been moved up to tonight. Sarah and the children are with us, and a woman named Eleanora, who will be extracted, as well.''

Great, Maggie thought. Just great. Two women. Three kids. Unknown location. Unspecified time. Uncertain size of opposition. She reassessed the size of her team and of the strike team that Jake would call in at the drop site. If he made it to the drop site.

''I've got the GPS unit on,'' Jake continued, low and fast, referring to the Global Positioning Satellite compass built into his digital watch. The GPS could pinpoint a location anywhere in the world to within a few square meters, as the tank commanders who used it in the vast, featureless deserts of Iraq during Desert Storm had discovered. With GPS, Maggie would be able to track Jake's exact location, and try to anticipate where he was heading.

''Be ready to come in on my call. I'll give you more detail when I can. Out.''

Five minutes later, Maggie gave a heartfelt prayer of thanks and shed her scratchy habit for the last time. Pulling a pair of dark slacks and a black cotton turtleneck from the small cardboard suitcase she'd carried into the country, she dressed hurriedly and slipped out the convent gates for the last time. She climbed into the Jeep she'd had Cowboy summon via his channels and sped through the night to the army's heavily guarded airfield outside town.

Despite the black-and-green camouflage paint on his face and the stark, utilitarian fatigues that had replaced his white linen suit, Maggie recognized the tall man who strode forward to meet her immediately.

''You look much different,'' he said, eyeing her scrubbed face and tumbled hair.

"So do you, big guy. Have you got the gear I requested?"

"It's all here."

"Then let's go."

Chapter 14

"Are you all right?"

Jake pointed the powerful beam of the flashlight at the ground, but enough peripheral light filtered upward to illuminate Sarah's pale, strained face.

"I'm all right," she answered stiffly, leaning her shoulders against the withers of the patient packhorse that carried the two smaller children. Eduard stood beside her, silent and watchful. Eleanora's solid figure loomed in the darkness just behind them.

Jake bit back a curse, wishing he could offer the little group some words of encouragement, but Che and the woman he shared the revolution and his bed with weren't three yards away. One or the other of them had been at Sarah's side throughout the long, exhausting day. The woman had even gone with Sarah and Eleanora into the bushes the few times the rebel leader allowed a stop so that they could rest and attend to personal needs.

Jake himself had been under close watch, as well. He'd managed to take a few unguarded moments to send his hurried transmission to Maggie an hour ago, but not much else.

The children, however, were not watched quite as closely. Eduard had varied his pace, sometimes walking silently beside Jake, sometimes falling back to lay a reassuring hand on the bewildered Ricci's stubby leg. Occasionally he'd marched beside Sarah. Using the boy as an intermediary, Jake had made what plans he could with her. This would be their last stop, he guessed. It was time to implement those plans.

Under the watchful eyes of the leader, Jake studied Sarah's face. "You don't look all right. You look like something the jungle scavengers would pass by."

Her chin lifted. "Thanks. That's just what I needed to hear right now."

He gave an exasperated grunt. "Look, I've put my neck on the line for you about as long as I intend to. I don't have the time or the energy to deal with a fainting female. You've got to keep up."

"I'll keep up."

Jake flashed the powerful beam into her face, causing Sarah to flinch back against the horse and throw up an arm to shield her eyes. He swung the beam down again, shaking his head in disgust.

"Drink some water, dammit. From the look of your face, you're half a step away from dehydration."

"I don't have any. I gave it all to the children."

"Christ!"

He unhooked the canteen that hung from his web belt and shoved it at her. Jake heard Teresa's little sob of fright at the roughness in his voice and hardened his heart.

"Here," he snarled. "Take it."

Sarah's fingers trembled as she took the canteen and fumbled with the cap.

"You just unscrew it," Jake said caustically. "Two turns to the left. Think you can manage that?"

She flashed him a look of scorn that was visible even in the dim light. "I can manage it."

Deliberately she wiped the mouth of the canteen with a corner of her sleeve. The folds of the dark habit fell over her fingers and covered the small, flat box that Jake had passed her with the canteen.

As he watched Sarah tilt her head and drink greedily, Jake felt a sharp, lancing pride in her courage. He'd shared some desperate moments with a wide spectrum of people in his lifetime. Some of them had crumpled under the stress of fear and imminent death, but many had found resources within themselves they didn't know they possessed to challenge it with. Sarah definitely fell into the latter category. He wanted, he *needed* to tell her so.

Jake pulled off his floppy hat and raked a hand through his sweat-dampened hair. "Look, I'm sorry I snapped at you. I'm a little uptight knowing I'll finally be able to get my business done and get out of this steam bath."

She wiped the canteen's mouth once more and passed it to the children, saying nothing.

"You've done okay, Sister," Jake offered, putting his hat on again. "In fact, I know of only one other woman who would've stood up as well as you have. Maybe you'll get a chance to know her someday."

Oh, she would, Sarah thought with a tight, inner smile. She would definitely get to know this partner/contact/ special friend of Jack's. In fact, that was one of her top priorities after they got out of this nightmare. She wanted to check this woman out and make sure she understood that Jack had some new priorities in his life now. Sarah had already begun planning her campaign to smooth out those rough edges he'd mentioned. And she was a master at laying out campaign plans. She'd spent half her life helping her father in his bids for reelection. Jack didn't know it yet, but he was going to have to make a few major career decisions in the very near future.

If there was a future.

Sarah managed a shaky smile. "Maybe I will. Get to know her, I mean."

"We'll see what we can work out." He sent her a look of silent command. "Just do as I tell you, and we'll both get through the next few hours."

"Enough of this." Che stepped out of the darkness. "We must move."

Jake wrenched his attention away from Sarah. Turning slowly, he faced the rebel leader. "Isn't it about time you tell me just where the hell we're moving to?"

"You will collect your fee by the time the night is over. That's all you need to know."

"Wrong. The last time I went to a drop with your trigger-happy little band, the site was almost overrun with *federales*. What guarantees do I have that I'm not walking into the same kind of situation tonight?"

"This site is well protected."

"Yeah? Who says?"

"The *patrón*." Che gave a thin smile when he saw Jake's narrowed eyes. "We go to his headquarters, you see. Your countryman, the one who brings the missiles, is as anxious as you to collect his money. There is an airstrip at the hacienda he will use to off-load, and then perhaps take on a different cargo."

Jake's mind whirled with the implications. Instead of an isolated airstrip hacked out of the jungle, they were heading for one that would be well defended. He had to get word to Maggie. There was no way he was going to let Sarah walk into what he knew would be a self-contained fortress.

"Come," the rebel leader said impatiently. "It's not far now."

Jake lifted his weapon, his eyes on Sarah.

Her gaze flickered to Che, and then to Jake's face. "I'm glad we're almost there," she said calmly. "I'm ready for this to be over."

Jake smiled at her. "So am I, Sister Sarah, so am I."

His hungry gaze raked her face once more, and then he laid a casual hand on Eduard's thin shoulder. "Come on, kid. Let's get this show on the road."

Maggie had experienced some real thrills in her life, even before joining OMEGA. One of her earliest memories was of sneaking away from her mother to watch her father's crew bring in a well. She'd been standing only a few feet away from the rig when the earth began to rumble and black liquid leaped into the air. She'd clapped her hands in delight. Her father had shouted something she learned the meaning of only years later and dashed across the burning desert sands to snatch her up. Afterward he'd shown her how she could've been weighted down and drowned by the viscous liquid, but at the time she'd thought it was a great adventure.

As adventures went, however, skimming along at ninety knots a mere twenty-five feet above the impenetrable jungle canopy had that little escapade beat hands down. The pilot had explained that they'd fly a contour pattern until they reached the target area, then drop down to nap of the earth. From that point on, they'd slink in at a death-defying five to ten knots, with their skids brushing the top of the trees, leaving just enough clearance above the branches for the rotor blades. Their only safety systems would be their night-vision goggles and the pilot's skill. Maggie tried not to think about nap of the earth. This contour stuff was bad enough.

Lifting off her goggles for a moment, she wiped the perspiration from around her eyes. She stole a glance at the figure beside her. If Colonel Esteban was nervous about dodging around treetops in the black of night at ninety knots, he sure didn't show it. He flashed her a smile that won an answering grin and a thumbs-up from Maggie.

She settled the goggles over her eyes again and peered out the helicopter's side hatch into the hazy green sea below. The magnification of the lenses was so powerful that the copilot had bragged he could read a name tag on a soldier's chest. At night. From the air. Maggie didn't want to read any name tags. She just wanted some sight, some signal from Jaguar.

He was down there, only a few minutes' flight time away. The copilot was tracking his coordinates and relaying position updates to Maggie. In between his reports, an air surveillance officer in the Big Bird aircraft orbiting high above the Caribbean was providing regular updates on the approaching suspect smuggler. He was a half hour out and closing fast. The strike team that would take him down was on his tail, also sending Maggie periodic updates via a secure ultra-high-frequency data link.

Cowboy was tracking everything at the control center, as well. Maggie knew she could call him for confirmation if she missed anything, but she doubted she would.

Things happened too fast, decisions would have to be made in split seconds. She'd have to coordinate the two prongs of this operation with the information she processed in her own, internal computers.

It would sure help matters, though, if Jake would let her know just how he planned to deploy his little ground cadre when he reached his destination.

She got her wish some ten minutes later.

Maggie jerked upright in her web seat as a thin, frightened voice came over the secure voice link. The first words were so garbled she didn't catch them.

"Retransmit your ID," she rapped out. "Over."

"Is there anyone there?"

"Repeat your last transmission. Over."

"Can anyone hear me? Please," the frightened voice sobbed. "Please, someone hear me."

Maggie groaned into the mike. It was one of Jake's kids. He was pushing the transmit button, but either didn't know or had forgotten to release it so that he could receive.

"If you are there, please listen. I have not much time. My friend, Señor Creighton, he talks with the one called Che while I am in the jungle."

Señor Creighton? Maggie shook her head. It had to be Jake. Only he could set the transceiver to this frequency. Her mouth went dry as she thought of the courage it must have taken for this child to slip into the dark, impenetrable jungle on his own.

"He says to tell you we go to the hacienda of the *patrón*," the boy whispered. "It is not far, he thinks."

Maggie's heart jumped into her throat. Jake and company were on their way to the drug lord's hideaway!

Their operation didn't have just two prongs. It now had three, all of which were about to slam together with the force of three freight trains colliding. The extraction of the senator's daughter. The takedown of the middleman, the link to the United States that the president wanted to sever. And the elimination of the big man, the one who supplied the money. If Maggie had been any less of a professional, she would've shouted her excitement. Instead, she listened intently while the boy stumbled on.

"Señor Creighton says to tell you we will separate when we arrive there. Sarita...the woman Sarah...she has the st...str..."

The strobe! She had the strobe, Maggie thought exultantly. Smaller and flatter than a cigarette package, the strobe packed enough power to fire a pulsing halogen light that could be seen for miles.

"She use this light to signal our location. Señor Creighton will create a noise..."

A diversion, Maggie interpreted.

"He has red pins to tell you where he is."

What he had were .38 caliber pin-gun flares, no bigger than a cigarette. One twist of the spring mechanism and they shot out a flare that would light up the target area like a string of high-powered Christmas lights.

"I must go. Please, please, you must help us."

A faint, flat hum came over the earphones.

Wetting her lips, Maggie turned to the man beside her. "Did you hear?"

"Every word." Excitement threaded the colonel's smooth voice. He spread an aerial map across his lap and drew a rough vector with a grease pencil borrowed from the copilot. "This is where your Jaguar is now, according to the GPS signals. And this is the location of a plantation house owned by one of Cartoza's most influential businessmen, an exporter of tropical fruit."

He pointed to a wide, flat valley surrounded on all sides by steep hills. Maggie saw at once the thin, straggling line that led from the plantation to the capital city. A road. A road that would transport produce out. And bring chemicals in.

"Maybe this businessman grows more than fruit."

Esteban's white teeth gleamed as his mustache lifted in a slow, dangerous smile. "I think perhaps he does. I sent a man in undercover to infiltrate his operation a few weeks ago, but he met with an unfortunate accident. It will give me great pleasure to take this *bastardo* down. I thank you for this one."

Maggie grinned. "Anytime, Colonel."

"So, my Chameleon, we will direct the strike team to the plantation and have them waiting when our friends arrive, will we not?"

Maggie's grin faded. This was the crucial moment. The irrevocable decision point that came in almost every operation. Normally the field agent made the call about when and where to direct the strike team, regardless of whether that consisted of a single sharpshooter, a civilian SWAT team, or, as in this case, a combined military and civilian force from two nations.

Jake had passed every scrap of information he had to Maggie, which was all he could do at this point. The decision was now hers.

She nodded to Esteban. "Send them to the plantation."

Sarah knew they were only minutes away from their destination. She sensed it by the ripple of preparation in the men strung out ahead of and behind her. By the low murmurs and coarse jokes they exchanged. By the sharp admonishment Eleanora's "husband" gave her to move her carcass.

She wondered vaguely why she wasn't more afraid. She couldn't work up enough moisture in her throat to swallow. By contrast, her palms were so damp she wiped them continually on the sides of her habit. But the physical manifestations of fear didn't penetrate to her inner self.

Her entire being was focused on the dim silhouettes moving ahead of her, intermittently illuminated by the flashlights they carried. Every few steps she'd catch a glimpse of Jack. He wasn't hard to distinguish from the other shadowy shapes. If she hadn't been able to pick out the broad shoulders that strained against his disreputable khaki shirt, she would have recognized him from the way he moved. With a silent, self-contained coordination. A smooth, easy grace that belied his size.

The memory of their afternoon by the glistening, silvered pool flashed into Sarah's mind. Jack had circled the water with the same deadly grace, stalking her like some kind of predator that had spotted its prey. She hadn't been afraid then, either, Sarah remembered.

She should have been, but she hadn't.

She should be now, but she wasn't. She'd passed beyond fear to that curious state where every sense is heightened, every emotion suspended, every faculty focused on one thing and one thing only.

She ran over the simple instructions Jack had passed to her, repeating them over and over in her mind like a litany.

By the time they halted at the edge of a vast clearing, she was as ready as she'd ever be.

Her heart began to thump against her ribs as her eyes swept the scene. For a moment, Sarah thought they'd stumbled by mistake onto a movie set. Spotlights mounted on high towers bathed the clearing in light and illuminated the cluster of buildings that occupied it. Set square in the middle was a tile-roofed two-story house, surrounded by an arched veranda on the upper floor. Gauzy curtains fluttered at the open windows upstairs, while light spilled out of the patio doors on the ground floor. Sarah caught the brief, intermittent flare of insects grilled by the bug lights that guarded the windows and, incredibly, the sound of chamber music floating from one of the downstairs rooms.

Only someone with supreme self-confidence would leave his home open to the night, Sarah thought, her gaze sweeping the neat, orderly complex once more. Only someone of indomitable strength could force the jungle back and bend it to his will.

The music rose to a polite crescendo. A cello led the chorus, followed by a trill of violins. Sarah felt an eerie sense of displacement. She was standing on the edge of a tropical rain forest, surrounded by men who carried their automatic rifles with the ease and nonchalance with which the men of her world carried their briefcases, listening to a sonata that she'd last heard performed by an ensemble at the Kennedy Center.

The strange sensation heightened, until Sarah clutched at Ricci's leg to anchor herself in reality. She tore her eyes from the surreal scene before her and searched the dim figures at the edge of the clearing. Jack stood out among them, tall, solid, a dark shape barely visible in the wash of the lights from the hacienda. He faced the far end of the clearing, his body taut and stiff. Sarah followed his line of sight and saw what he'd come for. What he'd risked his life for.

There, at the end of a grassy runway, sat a medium-size plane, propellers still whirling. Portable spotlights ringed it, washing it in a bright, incandescent light. Sarah couldn't tell the make, and wouldn't have recognized it in any case. But even from this distance she recognized the U.S. markings on the crates being unloaded by a scruffy-looking crew.

Slowly, her arms feeling as though they were weighted with lead, Sarah reached up and lifted Ricci from the packhorse. She wrapped her arms around his small body, pressing his face against her shoulder. He trembled against her but made no sound.

Eleanora moved up to lift Teresa down. The girl burrowed into the woman's legs, clutching her skirt with one hand and the root doll with her other. Eduard stood stiff and silent beside them.

Sarah searched the other woman's bruised, swollen face in the dim light, wondering if she had any hint of what was to come, wishing desperately she could explain it. Eleanora met her look and gave a slow, silent nod.

The stillness of the moment was broken when one of the men from the rear guard edged past their small, still group, anxious for a better view of the clearing. A second followed, then a third. The plane and its rich haul drew them like a magnet, as Jack had hoped it would. Over the pounding of her heart, Sarah heard their excited murmurs.

Their eyes were locked on the prize they'd waited for.

Hers were on Jack.

Che and the woman in fatigues stepped into the clearing.

Jack took one step with them. Two.

The other men followed.

Jack half turned, searching the dimness for her face.

Sarah tightened her arms around Ricci and pressed his head more firmly into her shoulder. She watched Jack lift his hand, slowly, deliberately... then freeze as a new sound cut through the night.

He whirled to meet this unexpected threat, as did the men around him. The snicker and click of bolts being drawn back competed with the rhythmic pounding of a horse's hooves.

"It is the *patrón!*" someone called.

A white stallion danced to a halt.

"You are late, Che," a cultured voice called out. The speaker didn't use the mountain dialect, but instead a pure, flowing Spanish that Sarah had no trouble following. "Did you bring the woman?"

"Yes, as you instructed. She is back there, with the packhorses."

The rider shifted in his saddle. Sarah heard the creak of leather. The thud of a hoof dropping against the hard-packed earth.

"Welcome to my humble *estancia,* Miss Chandler," the rider said in clear, unaccented English. "I've been anticipating your arrival with great eagerness."

Chapter 15

Sarah stood frozen for an endless moment, her arms wrapped around Ricci. If Jack gave the signal, she didn't see it.

Her stunned gaze was riveted on the horseman. A thousand conflicting, chaotic thoughts chased through her mind. Out of them all, only one emerged to impress itself on her numbed consciousness. She and Jack and the children hadn't been brought here because of a rescheduled drop. Nor because the rebels had decided to abandon camp. They'd been brought here because this criminal had somehow learned her identity.

The fear that Sarah had held at bay earlier swamped through her. Her stomach knotted as she watched the horseman swing off his mount with a lithe, easy confidence. He was a short man, she noted, and rather heavy, yet fluid in his movements. He drew the reins over the stallion's head and patted its muzzle with absent affection.

"I met your father once, some years ago," he said conversationally, moving toward Sarah. "A most forceful and invigorating man. Very strong in his opinions. When you're rested and recovered from your ordeal, you must tell me how best to deal with him."

Jack stepped forward to block the man's path. "Nobody's going to be telling—"

"I'll handle this."

Ever afterward, Sarah would wonder at the cool authority in her voice. It stopped Jack in his tracks. He spun on his heel, staring through the dark shadows. Before he could say anything, the *patrón* signaled his approval.

"Very wise, Miss Chandler."

"What the hell is going on here?"

Jake's low growl raised the hairs on the back of Sarah's neck. "Isn't it obvious?" she said, only the faintest tremor in her voice. "You have your business to conduct, and so, apparently, does this gentleman."

"Very perceptive, my dear. You are indeed your father's daughter."

Sarah didn't acknowledge the compliment, if it was one. "Take Ricci, Eduard."

A thin, small shadow materialized at her side. Her hands shaking, Sarah passed the child to Eduard. At the same time, she pressed the small, flat box Jake had given her under the older boy's elbow.

Her low murmur was for Eduard's ears alone. "Just turn the top. To the left. Understand?"

"*Sí.*"

"Sarita?" Ricci's childish treble quavered. "Do we die, Sarita?"

Sarah closed her eyes, swallowing. "No, of course not. You stay here with Eduard and Teresa and Eleanora until I see what is to be done."

"I want to go with Señor Creighton." Teresa tugged against Eleanora's hand, a hiccup of fear in her voice.

"No!" Tension sharpened Sarah's reply. "You will stay here! Señor Creighton has...has business to conduct. You will be in the way."

"Creighton?" Amusement tinted the *patrón*'s voice. "Is that what he told you his name was?"

"That's what she calls him," Che volunteered with a sneer, coming forward to join the other two men. All three turned to watch Sarah approach.

She stepped out of the jungle shadows and walked toward them. Light from the spotlights across the clearing caught the skirts of her robe and moved higher with each step, until it fell across her face. Seeing the *patrón*'s narrowed, speculative eyes on her, Sarah reached up to tug off the veil.

The short, heavyset man drew in an appreciative breath. "The pictures in the newspapers didn't do you justice, my dear."

She forced a small shrug. "They weren't taken at my best moment."

"Nor does that habit particularly become you," he murmured.

At the man's soft, almost caressing tone, a sick feeling curled in Sarah's stomach. She sensed, rather than saw, Jack stiffening beside her.

Sarah ignored Jack, concentrating on the man she faced. She recognized his type. Urbane, cultured, confident of himself and his power. She'd dealt with men like him all her life. Summoning the slow half smile she'd so often used to good effect with lecherous ambassadors and interested politicians, she plucked at the black skirts.

"The habit served its purpose. I must confess it is rather uncomfortable, however."

She reached up to unhook the top fastening. Then the second. She fanned her heated skin with the fold of material. The *patrón*'s eyes narrowed on the patch of flesh she bared to the glare of the spotlights.

"I apologize that you had to endure such discomfort for so long," he murmured. "My sources were a bit slow in passing me the information I sought about the medical sister my friend Che held in his camp."

Sarah lifted one shoulder. "The camp is behind us now. Perhaps you have something at the hacienda that I might change into."

"Perhaps I do." He gave a little bow. "Please, allow me to escort you."

Sarah didn't move. "First we must settle the issue of the children. They were taken with me in the raid. They're tired and frightened. I would ask your—" She choked a bit. "I would ask your word that you will send them back to their village with the woman, Eleanora."

He flicked a glance at Eleanora and the three youngsters and gave a dismissive shrug. "I have no interest in the children or the woman."

Sarah nodded and started forward.

Jack caught her wrist, swinging her around. "What the hell do you think you're doing?"

"I'm going with him."

"Just like that? You're going with him?"

She searched his eyes, pleading with him to understand. "It's best for the children, and for—"

"And for Miss Sarah Chandler." Jack sneered. "Do you think I'm going to let you just walk away? After all I did for you?"

"I'm grateful, truly grateful. But—"

He gave a vicious oath. Twisting her arm behind her waist, he brought her slamming up against his chest.

"Want to know what you can do with your gratitude, lady?"

Jack's explosive violence startled Sarah. For a moment, she feared he didn't understand her motives. Didn't realize that she couldn't jeopardize the children for her own safety. She couldn't add to the risks he himself already faced.

At that moment, she felt him slip the small, palm-size gun into the hand twisted behind her back. For the space of a heartbeat, Sarah sagged against him, relieved that he understood, afraid to leave the safety of his arms. She wanted so much to wrap her free arm around his neck, to burrow into his strength and let him shield her.

The old Sarah might have done just that.

This Sarah had learned that she had strengths within herself she hadn't been aware of before. If she'd learned nothing else in these past days, it was that she could no longer hide.

Summoning her will, Sarah wrenched free and faced him, her fists buried in the folds of her skirts.

"All right, gringo. If my gratitude isn't sufficient, then perhaps you'll accept some more tangible form of thanks. I'm sure the *patrón* will give you a bonus for taking care of us, as an advance on what he'll receive from my father. Will you not?"

The man nodded politely, his eyes on Sarah's face. "Certainly, my dear. You will have to tell me, of course, just what specific...services...he performed for you, and what you think they're worth. Come, let us go to the hacienda and discuss this more comfortably."

Sarah threw a last look over her shoulder at the children, swept her gaze past Jack's tight, rigid features, then turned and started across the clearing without another word. Covered by the heavy folds of her skirt, her finger curled around the trigger of the small gun.

Holding his horse's reins, the *patrón* fell into step beside her.

The steady plopping of the animal's hooves thundered in Sarah's ears. She strained to hear some other sound, some movement behind her.

Jake watched her walk away, a slight figure in black, identifiable only by the silvery-gold hair that tumbled around her shoulders. He turned slowly, one thumb hooked in his belt. He would have reassessed his options, but Sarah had just preempted them all.

Che wore a tight, satisfied expression on his face, as though the the sight of the woman walking away from Jake pleased him enormously. Which it probably did, the bastard.

"So, gringo," he said with a sneer, "let us now turn to the business at hand."

"Yes," Jake responded. "Let us turn to the business at hand."

His finger tapped a single coded signal on the metal gusset next to his buckle.

When it came, the attack took Sarah by surprise, even though she was expecting it. Halfway across the clearing she heard a low, steady *whump-whump-whump*. Suddenly the treetops rattled, as though a violent wind had just blown in. The man beside her froze, then spun in the direction of the sound. Sarah swung around, as well, gasping at the sight that greeted her.

Like a giant moth rising from the jungle canopy, a huge, black-painted helicopter lifted out of the trees and hovered over the clearing. Powerful spotlights switched on, and what Sarah later learned was a million footcandles of brilliant white light lit the entire area.

Sarah brought the little pistol up. "I wouldn't do that if I were you!"

The heavyset man paused with one foot in the stirrup and a hand on the saddle horn. Squinting against the glare, Sarah saw rage seize his features.

"You will not shoot." He sneered. "Your hand is shaking so badly you would not hit me if you did. You hold that as though you've never fired a weapon before."

Sarah wrapped her second hand around the first. "I haven't," she admitted. "I've never touched a gun before in my life, and I'm extremely nervous about this."

In the wash of bright light, Sarah couldn't tell if the man paled, but he did take an involuntary step backward, his eyes wide and fixed on her trembling hand. She heard the first shouts from the compound, and a sudden rattle of gunfire.

"Get down," she ordered. "On your face."

A sudden explosion rocked the earth back, far down the grassy runway. The horse, already skittish, danced sideways a few steps, threw up its head to avoid the piercing light, then galloped away. The *patrón* swore savagely and started toward her.

"Get down!" Sarah shouted. "Get down, or I'll..."

She wasn't sure what she'd do. She didn't have to make the decision, however. The *patrón* was only a few yards away when a figure launched itself from behind her and took him down in a flying tackle. Sarah sobbed in relief as Jack's fist slammed into the man's face. Before she could say a word, he reached behind her, grabbed a handful of her skirts and yanked her down. Sarah fell beside him just as a brilliant red flare soared into the sky, marking their place.

Red, she thought dazedly, her face pressed to the earth. As red as the quetzal's breast, stained by the blood of the dying Mayan chief.

It seemed to Sarah as though the red flare must have been a signal. The noise all around her suddenly intensified a thousandfold. A sudden whizzing sound split the night overhead. Rockets were launched from the helicopter, leaving bright trails as they arced overhead. Small explosions detonated all around the cluster of buildings. The hiss of escaping gas was added to the shouts and gunfire exploding all around.

Her ear pressed to the earth, Sarah felt the reverberations of footsteps thudding toward them. Her fingers tightened around the little pistol.

"Jaguar! Have you got her?"

Sarah assimilated the sound of the woman's voice and the name she used for Jack in the same second. She twisted her head and collected a confused picture of a tall, long-legged woman in black, with paint smeared across her face and a lethal-looking weapon in her hands. Incredibly, she was grinning at Sarah.

"I've got her," Jack replied, scrambling to his feet. "What about the kids?"

"They're already in the chopper. The strobe guided us right to them."

The tight, choking tension that had gripped Jake by the throat eased enough for him to swallow. He reached down and hauled Sarah to her feet. Her knees shook so badly that she sagged in his hold and would have crumpled to the ground.

Jake swore, then bent and scooped her over his shoulder. He wrapped one arm around her legs, keeping his other hand free for the weapon he snatched up from the ground.

"Take care of this guy. I'll put Sarah in the chopper, then join you. We've got work to do."

He raced to the helicopter, bent low, protecting Sarah's body with his own. When he reached the side hatch, he tossed her inside. She scrambled to her knees, hampered by her skirts and the three year old who launched himself at her and wrapped both arms around her neck.

"Jack!"

"Stay here! Don't try any more of your damned cowboy tactics. If you move, if you so much as stick your hand out the door, I swear I'll—"

A rattle of gunfire nearby cut him off. He whirled and ran to Maggie's side.

It was over in minutes.

The gas canisters the assault helicopter had fired into the compound soon stilled all but a weak resistance. A burst of fire from the 50 mm cannons bristling from its nose shredded most of the tail on the smuggler's aircraft and halted its desperate attempt to take off. The combined force of elite Cartozan and U.S. rangers moved through the compound, subduing the dazed, coughing defenders and collecting an arsenal of weapons that would have supplied a small army.

"So, Chameleon, I will leave you now."

Maggie turned at the sound of Colonel Esteban's voice. "Let me guess," she said, grinning. "You've had a chat with one of the prisoners and managed to discover the exact coordinates of the processing plant nearby."

His black mustache lifted. "I have. The rest of my force will arrive within moments. You may see the explosion from here when the chemicals go up."

"I'd give anything to go with you!"

He grinned. "So come."

Maggie shoved a hand through her hair. She was tempted. Lord, she was tempted. The thought of facing Adam held her back. She was going to have enough difficulty explaining to him how her simple extraction mission had expanded so dramatically.

"I'd better not," she said ruefully. "I'll stay here and help clean up."

He stepped forward and curled a finger under her chin. Maggie swallowed—hard!—at the impact of his stunning masculinity at such close quarters.

His thumb brushed her lips. "Perhaps we will work together again sometime, my Chameleon."

"Perhaps we will," she answered, more than a little breathless.

His thumb traced her lips once more, and then he was gone. Maggie watched him climb aboard a Cartozan helicopter. Stifling a small sigh, she went to back to work.

The prisoners—including Jake's middleman, a coldly furious *patrón*, and a superficially wounded Che—were herded aboard waiting choppers.

Gleeful at the rich haul, Maggie greeted Jake with a sweep of one hand. "Do you believe this?"

Fully expecting Jake's usual quiet words of praise after a successful mission, Maggie gaped when he stalked past her toward the open hatch of the helo.

"Jaguar! Wait, what—?"

He reached inside, grabbed a fistful of black skirt and hauled the pseudosister out the open side hatch. She tumbled down into his arms, apparently not at all averse to his rough treatment. The three children scrambled out after her, followed by a heavyset woman.

Maggie watched in astonishment as Sarah Chandler wrapped her hands around Jake's neck and smiled up at him. Her eyes were luminous in the glare of the search-lights, and shining with an emotion that sent a spear of envy through Maggie's heart. She dismissed it immediately. If anyone deserved to win a look like that from a woman, it was Jake. Self-contained, quiet, controlled Jake. A man who had put his duty and his dedication to OMEGA ahead of his own life for so many years.

It occurred to Maggie that she wouldn't have thought a woman with Sarah Chandler's background would tumble into love with someone like Jake. But there wasn't any doubt from the expression on her face that that was exactly what she'd done. Of course, what Maggie had seen tonight made her realize that the senator's daughter was one heck of a lot tougher than her fragile, delicate appearance suggested.

Jake didn't seem to be appeased by the glowing look in Sarah's remarkable eyes. His dark brows were drawn into a slash, and he glared down at her.

"If you ever—*ever*—do anything as harebrained and idiotic as that again, I swear I'll... I'll..."

Maggie, the three children and assorted strike team members all waited with interest to hear what exactly he would do.

So did Sarah. When he appeared unable to articulate his precise intentions, she laughed up at him.

"What you need to do, Mr. Gringo-Creighton-Jack-Jaguar, is consider your options. You can stand here and sputter at me. You can put me down. Or you can kiss me."

Jake gave a strangled groan and bent his dark head.

Maggie folded her arms across her chest and rocked back on her heels, thoroughly fascinated by this new, previously hidden facet of Jaguar's personality. She'd worked with him for two years, seen him operate in every conceivable situation. Except this one. Evidently he was as thorough and as skilled in his lovemaking as he was in everything else, she thought in amusement, wondering when either of them was going to come up for air.

The little girl beside Maggie watched in smug complacency, a strange-looking doll tucked under her chin.

"Sarita is not the *religiosa,* you understand," she explained earnestly. "She just wears the robes. She and Señor Creighton are going to be married. By a padre. A *real* padre."

"I have to make the pee-pee," the smallest child announced.

The helicopter ride back to Cartoza City was considerably less hair-raising than the one that had brought Maggie out. She held the squirming little three year old in her lap. Once assured that they weren't going to die, he squealed in delight every time the aircraft banked, and bounced on her thighs. Maggie noted with some interest that although the little girl clung to Jake like a limpet, he managed to hang on to Sarah's hand, as well.

One of Colonel Esteban's aides met them at the military airstrip outside the city. He came screeching up in a Jeep loaded with an assortment of supplies and a dapper little man in a neat, dark suit and discreet red tie. Maggie jumped out, waiting while Jake unloaded the children. She smiled as the precise, prissy little man wiped a handkerchief across his damp, balding forehead, folded it in neat squares, then tucked it into his breast pocket, leaving an exact half inch showing.

When Jake lifted Sarah out of the chopper, he stepped forward.

"I can't tell you how relieved I am to see you safe, Miss Chandler."

Sarah swung around, her mouth dropping in surprise. "What on earth are you doing here?"

The man minced forward. There was no other word to describe it, Maggie decided. He definitely minced.

"I came at your father's behest, of course." He folded his lips in a thin, prim smile. "I was prepared to go into the jungle to search for you, but these gentlemen assured me their colonel would bring you back safely. In fact, they forcibly restrained me." His nose wrinkled. "In a rather disgusting cell."

Sarah stepped forward to lay a hand on the man's shoulder. "Thank you for coming for me, Creighton."

Jake gave a strangled choke.

Sarah ignored him and smiled down at the balding little man. "I know from past experience that you would've whisked me out from under those guerrilla's noses with the same efficiency you use when you extract my father from the political messes he's forever creating."

He preened under her generous and quite sincere praise.

Maggie had to admire Sarah Chandler's style. She was good. Damn good. She exuded an aura of charm and elegance, despite the ragged black robe that hung shapelessly around her and her limp, straggling hair. Maggie hid a grin. Jake was *not* going to know what hit him when Miss Chandler got back to Washington and was once more in her own element.

Then again, she thought as Jake stepped forward and slid a proprietary arm around Sarah's waist, maybe he already had a pretty good idea.

"A jet is waiting for you," the aide informed them, then waved toward the Jeep. "My colonel told me you may wish some fresh clothing and food for the journey. He also sent some gifts for you. And something for the one called Chameleon."

He reached into the back seat and pulled out a cardboard box. Maggie took it with a smile of thanks, then jumped when the box moved in her hands.

The aide turned to address Sarah. "We have a padre standing by at headquarters to take the children. He will see they are cared for until they find homes. The colonel said to tell you he himself will ensure that the woman finds a place to live and good employment."

Sarah nodded numbly. She turned, her throat closing at the sight of Teresa standing beside Jack, the root doll dangling from one hand. Eduard, still, silent, brave Eduard, stood at his other side. Eleanora held Ricci in her arms, her face impassive.

"I . . ." She wet her lips and tried again. "I . . ."

"We have to go, Miss Chandler," Creighton—the *real* Creighton—said kindly, clearly understanding her distress. "I've arranged for an air-force jet to take us back to Washington. Your father is most anxious to have you home."

"Do not worry, they will be well cared for," the aide assured her.

Sarah ignored both men. Her eyes met Jack's across a few feet of concrete runway. "I can't do it. I can't leave them."

"Miss Chandler!"

She stepped around Creighton. Two steps brought her to within a heartbeat of the tall, lean mercenary.

"I love you, Jack. I love you more than I ever dreamed it was possible to love in any lifetime. But I can't leave them here."

He reached for her. "Sarah, I don't want—"

She grasped his arms, her eyes pleading, needing this settled before she walked into his hold. Once there, she knew, she'd never want to leave.

"I know we haven't had time to talk about the future, our future. You're so self-sufficient, so independent, I don't even know if you want me in your life."

"Just try getting out of it," he growled.

Her fingers dug into his arm. "Can't you make room for all of us? We've been through so much together. We're a family. We . . . we need each other."

He slid his hands around her waist, drawing her up against him. "Sarah, listen to me. I love you, too. I don't want to leave the children or Eleanora behind, either. I have no *intention* of leaving them behind. And there's plenty of room in my life for all of you."

He tightened his hold. "In fact, I didn't realize how empty it was until I met you and your assorted charges, Sarita Sarah Josepha."

Sarah stared up into his shadowed eyes, wondering how she'd ever thought them cold and hard. At this moment, they gleamed with a warmth and a love that Sarah knew was reflected in her own eyes.

A small hand tugged at her much-tried black robe. "There is a padre here," Teresa reminded them both solemnly. "I heard the man with the Jeep say so. If he is a *real* padre, he can make us a *real* family."

"Yes," Sarah said slowly, "he can." She turned back to Jack, a question in her eyes.

"Miss Chandler, really." Creighton materialized behind Teresa, his mouth pursed disapprovingly. "This is all highly irregular."

"Go get him," Jake ordered quietly, his eyes never leaving Sarah's face.

"I beg your pardon?"

"Go get the padre."

"Now see here, Senator Chandler would hardly approve. I suggest you—"

"Move it, Creighton. Now!"

Sarah bit her lip as the little man huffed off and clambered into the Jeep. It roared away into the darkness, leaving them wrapped in silence for a moment.

"You know," Sarah said softly, "this means you'll finally have to blow your cover. You're going to have a tough enough time convincing the padre to perform a marriage for someone wearing a nun's habit. Somehow I don't think he'll consent to do it if you give your name as Mr. Gringo Jaguar."

His lips twitched. "No, I guess not."

She leaned back in his arms. "Well?"

"Jake?"

"Jake what?"

"Jake MacKenzie."

She shook her head. "Not good enough. I want the whole thing. Exactly as it appears on your birth certificate. The one you had before it was no doubt altered by this agency you work for."

He grinned down at her. "You sure you're ready for this?"

"I'm ready for anything."

"Stonewall Jackson Duncan MacKenzie."

"Oh, my," she said faintly.

Jake nodded, his eyes gleaming with laughter. "My father was a great admirer of men of action."

She answered with a smile of her own. "So am I, my darling. So am I."

Chapter 16

An afternoon breeze rustled the branches of the oak trees that lined the quiet side street just off Massachusetts Avenue. A small family of tourists wandered down the brick sidewalk, obviously lost. The sandy-haired mother consulted her tour guide, then peered at the discreet bronze plaque beside the door of one of the elegant town houses. She shook her head. The father grimaced, hitching his heavy camera bag higher on his shoulder. Taking one of the towheaded youngsters by the hand, he turned around and headed back toward the main avenue. The mother and the two other protesting children followed.

Maggie watched from the town house's second-story window as the family trudged past. The children looked cranky and bored, the father exasperated and the mother tired. Right now she would have exchanged places with any one of them.

"The special envoy will see you now,"

She swiveled around and returned Elizabeth's smile. Jake rose from one of the high wing-backed chairs placed on either side of an exquisite and extremely rare Queen Anne table. Maggie, no expert in antiques, knew it was Queen Anne because the knowledgeable, gray-haired Elizabeth had told her so. She could discern for herself the beauty in the rectangular thumb-molded marble top and delicately carved walnut legs.

"I've cleared his calendar for the next two hours," Elizabeth said, giving Jake and Maggie a kind, grandmotherly look. "The security folks downstairs have been alerted to seal this floor until I signal."

"Two hours, huh?" Maggie shoved a hand through the neat, shining mass of her chestnut hair.

Elizabeth nodded sympathetically. "He requested it."

Maggie threw Jake a quick, wry glance. "Why do I suddenly wish I had stayed in Cartoza for an extended vacation?"

He laughed and opened the door that led to Adam's inner office. "Come on, it can't be too bad. We survived the postmission debrief last night."

"You know he never lets loose in front of the other team members. In fact," Maggie added gloomily, "he never lets loose at all."

She preceded Jake down the short corridor between the inner and outer doors, paying no attention to the lights that pulsed discreetly as she passed. Had they not recognized her, any one of those sensors could have activated a lethal variety of devices that the security people euphemistically, if accurately, termed "stoppers." Although the second floor was open to the public who came to see the special envoy, the security systems made sure that the public was well screened.

As always, the sight of Adam upped Maggie's awareness quotient by several degrees. She frowned, wondering why. While Jake accepted Adam's offer of coffee and poured himself a cup, Maggie studied her boss.

He certainly looked distinguished enough in his expertly tailored navy suit and white shirt, but he wasn't as handsome as Colonel Luis Esteban. Or rather he was handsome in a different way. Where Esteban's classic male-model perfection could stop a woman in her tracks at fifty yards, Adam Ridgeway's attraction stemmed not so much from his lean, dark looks as from his aura of cool, unshakable authority. He was a man in charge. Of himself and of the agents he directed.

Maggie settled comfortably in her chair, knowing that she had a darned good chance of shaking him out of his customary control in the next two hours.

Adam sat on the edge of his mahogany desk, one knee bent as he scanned the papers in a plain manila folder. Shutting the folder, he laid it aside.

"All right, Jake. Let's start with you. I've reread the summaries of the debrief you gave us last night, but there are some key points I'd like cleared up."

Maggie steepled her fingers while Jake and Adam worked through his phase of the operation, from the initial botched drop to the takedown of the white-faced, stuttering businessman who had just happened to be delivering a shipment of stolen U.S. arms to a Cartozan drug lord. She caught Adam's brief smile as Jake recounted the "equipment failure" that had led to his periods of noncommunication. Adam nodded once or twice, listening intently while Jake answered each question in precise technical terms.

Maggie's admiration for her fellow agent, already profound, deepened as he unemotionally detailed his own decisions during the operation—including the very emotional one to step over that invisible line separating an operative from those he dealt with in the field. Her admiration for Sarah Chandler also increased with every passing moment.

Maggie wasn't fooled by the flat, expressionless tone Jake used when he described Sarah's actions during the days they'd been together. Maggie had worked with him long enough to hear what he tried so hard to suppress. Besides, she'd been part of the appreciative audience that witnessed that spectacular kiss beside the helicopter. A tiny thread of envy wiggled through her veins once more. Someday, she thought, she just might find what Jake seemed to have found with Sarah Chandler.

"Maggie?"

Maggie blinked, surprised to realize that Jake had finished and both men were looking at her expectantly.

Adam listened without interrupting while she ran through her part of the operation. When she finished, he stared at her thoughtfully for a moment.

"I think you may have left out one or two details."

"If I did, they're irrelevant," Maggie stated calmly.

"Perhaps to you, but I'd like just a bit more information."

"What is it you need to know?" Maggie was every bit as cool and professional as Adam when it came to her job.

He reached behind him and lifted the manila folder. Flipping it open, he examined the top document. "Could you explain this interagency memo the State Department forwarded? It requests that we reimburse them for payment, made through diplomatic channels, for a black lace garter belt and, ah, two-inch pink-and-orange spiked heels. Among other things. The bill comes to three hundred dollars."

"Three hundred dollars!" Maggie screeched. "Surely those dunderheaded bureaucrats didn't pay that. Don't they know they're supposed to haggle? The shopkeepers probably weren't expecting a tenth of that."

"Yes, well, it appears the United States government doesn't haggle when presented with a bill through diplomatic channels."

"Well it had better learn how, if I'm going to be operating in the field. I appropriated those clothes as part of the disguise that got me into the Café El Caribe. Where," she added pointedly, "I contacted Colonel Esteban."

"Ah, yes. Luis."

"Do you know him?"

"We've met," Adam said noncommittally. He pulled out another document. "This is an official intergovernmental communiqué. On the advice of his chief of security, the president of Cartoza has requested that a certain agent, code name Chameleon, be detailed to a special inter-American task force he's forming. Our president has asked for my recommendation as to whether you can be spared. For an indefinite period of time."

Maggie felt her breath catch somewhere in midchest. She knew that Adam would support the request if she wanted it. Did she want it? She met Adam's eyes, telegraphing a silent message.

He slipped the document into the folder. "I can't spare you."

Maggie sagged in relief, only to discover she'd relaxed too soon.

Adam pulled yet another document out of the damned folder, this one a faxed memo of some kind.

"Customs is rather upset with us. It seems one of their new, rather inexperienced agents tried to process an international flight that landed at Andrews Air Force Base last night. When he attempted to confiscate a certain..." Adam referred to the fax. "When he tried to

confiscate a certain *agamidae iguanid,* an agent assigned
to this organization told him in rather forceful terms to
back off.''

"It…it was a gift," Maggie explained, biting down on
her lower lip.

Adam's brows rose as he referred to the faxed page.
"A rather repulsive-looking one."

"It's all in the eye of the beholder," Maggie responded, grinning. "Actually, I'm told these lizards
make great house pets. They grow to about the size of a
small dog, and can snatch a fly off the wall with their
tongues from halfway across a room."

"Just don't ask me to baby-sit the thing for you when
you're in the field," Jake said, laughing.

Adam wasn't quite as amused.

Maggie pushed her shoulder-length fall of brown hair
behind one ear. "The lizard changes colors, Adam. It can
blend into any environment. Like me."

"I see. That explains it, then." He slipped the fax inside the folders. "What it doesn't explain, however, is
why an agent whom I directed to focus on one specific
aspect of her mission managed to expand that mission to
include an extraction, a takedown, and a major drug
bust."

Maggie shrugged. "I couldn't let that tripleheader
pass, Adam."

"She brought in three for the price of one," Jake put
in quietly. "That's what makes Maggie one of your best,
Chief."

Adam nodded. "I'm not disputing—"

The phone on Adam's desk chimed discreetly. He
arched a dark brow, clearly not pleased at the interrup-
tion after having left specific instructions. He lifted the
receiver.

Saved by the bell, Maggie thought in relief.

"Yes, Mrs. Wells?"

Adam listened for a moment, then nodded. "Send them in."

Maggie and Jake glanced at each other in surprise.

OMEGA's director stood and fastened the monogrammed button of his navy suit. His blue eyes glinted. "We'll finish later, Chameleon. Right now, it seems Jaguar has more pressing business to attend to."

Maggie and Jake both turned as the inner door opened and Sarah Chandler swept in, followed by what seemed to be half the population of Washington D.C. The children filed in after her, followed by Eleanora in a flowered, lace-trimmed dress. Maggie's favorite, the chubby little Ricci, squealed a rough approximation of "Cammie" and toddled over to her side. She scooped him up, duly admiring his purple-and-green Barney shirt. Although she cuddled the boy until he laughingly protested, Maggie's attention was on the big, bluff senator and his fussy, oh-so-efficient chief of staff.

Sarah's father had been at the airport to meet them yesterday, weak with relief at getting his daughter back and ready to whisk her away. Maggie had felt as though she had a front-row seat at ringside when Sarah calmly explained that she had a prior engagement. She'd just discovered that her husband had exactly three hours before he had to report to his headquarters to debrief his mission. If that was all the honeymoon she was going to get, Sarah didn't intend to waste a minute of it.

And, to judge from the radiant expression on her face today, she hadn't.

If ever there was a woman who looked less like the bedraggled nun Jake had thrown over his shoulder and tossed into the helicopter, it was this one. Poised, confident, stunning in a royal blue suit that hugged her slender figure and deepened her eyes to an astonishing blue-green, she walked over to Jake's side. Her shining silvery-gold hair was swept up in a French twist that revealed the sapphires winking in her earring.

"Sorry to intrude like this, Ridgeway," the senator boomed. "But we have an appointment with the head of Immigration in a half hour. The damn fool insists Sarah and Jake have to sign two reams of documents in front of witnesses and half a dozen notaries. I've got to take a look at this refugee processing procedure," he muttered. "Make a note of that, Creighton."

"Yes, sir."

Maggie hid a grin. She had no doubt that the Immigration Department's procedures were going to be on the Senate agenda next week.

"Actually," Sarah interjected, "we need to make a stop before we go to Immigration."

"What now?" the Senator boomed. "We've hit every department store and toy store between here and Bethesda."

"Yes, but . . ."

"I have a new doll," Teresa put in with a gap-toothed grin. "But I don't like it as much as the one Señor Creight—" She stopped, a look of confusion crossing her face.

"Señor Jake," Sarah reminded her.

Her lips pursed. "I will call him Papa," she announced, then sent an anxious look at the tall, quiet man.

Jake hunkered down before her, his gray eyes alight with pleasure. "That's fine with me, *niña.*"

The senator's huff broke the silence that gripped the office. He chomped on his cigar, shifting it from one corner of his mouth to the other. "Well, let's get this caucus underway."

Reluctantly Maggie let Ricci slip out of her arms. He waddled across the room, stopped to show Adam his

Barney shirt, then reached up to be lifted into Eleanora's arms.

"Here, let me, *señora*." Creighton stepped forward and lifted the child into his arms. To Maggie's surprise, the chief of staff didn't even blink when Ricci tugged his paisley handkerchief out of his pocket and flapped it experimentally.

"It is not *señora*."

Everyone in the room turned to stare at Eleanora.

Her dark eyes held a shy smile as they met Creighton's. "I am not married."

"Really?" He smoothed his free hand over his shiny forehead. "Well, you must let me show you some of Washington's sights. There's an exhibit of pre-Columbian art at the Smithsonian you may be interested in."

He hefted Ricci higher on his hip, took Eleanora's arm and escorted her out of the office.

Sarah wasn't the only one whose mouth dropped in astonishment.

Senator Chandler gaped.

"I'll be damned," Jake murmured.

Even Adam snorted.

Maggie laughed outright. She just might have to recalculate the final success ratio on this operation. It appeared there might have been more takes than she'd originally thought.

She bid repeated affectionate goodbyes to the children, then sighed as the door closed behind the lively group. Sudden, undisturbed silence descended, wrapping her and Adam in a quiet cocoon.

"Listen to this," she said, indicating the quiet room with a wave of one hand. "I don't think Jake's going to hear anything like this ever again. Think he'll be able to handle it?"

"He'll manage."

Maggie turned at the sound of Adam's cool voice. "Still torqued about my little adventures in Cartoza? That's 'upset' in oil-field lingo," she added helpfully.

His blue eyes rested on her face. "I rarely get upset, and have yet to get torqued."

Someday, Maggie thought. Someday.

"You pulled this one off, Maggie, but I don't want any more tripleheaders. I can't afford to lose any of my agents. Particularly a stubborn, independent one with a built-in sixth sense as accurate as radar—who always manages to get the job done in her own inimitable style."

Maggie offered her version of a salute. It brought a pained expression to Adam's face. "Aye, aye, Chief. I promise, I'll be the perfect model of a docile, well-behaved secret agent."

She strolled to the door, tossing him a cheeky grin over one shoulder. "Until the next time I go in the field."

*   *   *   *   *

COMING NEXT MONTH

#643 ANOTHER MAN'S WIFE—Dallas Schulze
Heartbreakers/A Family Circle
Gage Walker knew the value of friendship—enough to have taken responsibility for his best buddy's widow and young son. But his sense of duty had *never* included marriage—or fatherhood. Then he learned that Kelsey had a baby on the way—*his!*

#644 IAIN ROSS'S WOMAN—Emilie Richards
The Men of Midnight
Iain Ross had no idea that the woman he'd saved from drowning was the embodiment of his own destruction. Feisty Billie Harper seemed harmless—and charming—enough, but an age-old curse had rendered her his sworn enemy. But Iain was powerless to resist her—and their destiny....

#645 THE WEDDING VENTURE—Nikki Benjamin
Laura Burke would never give up her son. Timmy was hers, and no mob kingpin would take him away—even if he was the child's grandfather. Desperate, she turned to Devlin Gray, a man shrouded in mystery. Then she learned that Devlin's idea of protection involved trading danger for wedding vows.

#646 THE ONLY WAY OUT—Susan Mallery
Andie Cochran was on the run, struggling to bring herself and her young son to safety. Yet Jeff Markum was the only man she could trust—and the one man who had every reason to hate her.

#647 NOT WITHOUT RISK—Suzanne Brockmann
Emily Marshall had never dreamed of seeing police detective Jim Keegan ever again. He'd dumped her years earlier without warning—or explanation—and now he was masquerading as her "brother" to catch a drug smuggler. But the feelings that stirred between them were anything but familial.

#648 FOR MERCY'S SAKE—Nancy Gideon
Sheriff Spencer Halloway knew a person in hiding when he saw one, and Mercy Pomeroy was one woman who didn't want to be found. He couldn't figure out what a classy lady and her cute daughter could possibly fear, but he would move the heavens to find out....

Silhouette celebrates motherhood in May with...

Debbie Macomber
Jill Marie Landis
Gina Ferris Wilkins

in

Three Mothers & a Cradle

Join three award-winning authors in this beautiful collection you'll treasure forever. The same antique, hand-crafted cradle connects these three heartwarming romances, which celebrate the joys and excitement of motherhood. Makes the perfect gift for yourself or a loved one!

A special celebration of love,

Only from

Silhouette®

—where passion lives.

SILHOUETTE® *Desire*

Don't let the winter months get you down because the heat is about to get turned way up...with the sexiest hunks of 1995!

January: *A NUISANCE*
by Lass Small

February: *COWBOYS DON'T CRY*
by Anne McAllister

March: *THAT BURKE MAN*
the 75th Man of the Month
by Diana Palmer

April: *MR. EASY*
by Cait London

May: *MYSTERIOUS MOUNTAIN MAN*
by Annette Broadrick

June: *SINGLE DAD*
by Jennifer Greene

**MAN OF THE MONTH...
ONLY FROM
SIILHOUETTE DESIRE**

MOM95JJ-R

ANNOUNCING THE

FLYAWAY VACATION SWEEPSTAKES!

This month's destination:

Beautiful SAN FRANCISCO!

This month, as a special surprise, we're offering an exciting FREE VACATION!

Think how much fun it would be to visit San Francisco "on us"! You could ride cable cars, visit Chinatown, see the Golden Gate Bridge and dine in some of the finest restaurants in America!

The facing page contains two Entry Coupons (as does every book you received this shipment). Complete and return *all* the entry coupons; **the more times you enter, the better your chances of winning!**

Then keep your fingers crossed, because you'll find out by June 15, 1995 if you're the winner! If you are, here's what you'll get:

- Round-trip airfare for two to beautiful San Francisco!
- 4 days/3 nights at a first-class hotel!
- $500.00 pocket money for meals and sightseeing!

Remember: The more times you enter, the better your chances of winning!*

*NO PURCHASE OR OBLIGATION TO CONTINUE BEING A SUBSCRIBER NECESSARY TO ENTER. SEE REVERSE SIDE OR ANY ENTRY COUPON FOR ALTERNATIVE MEANS OF ENTRY.

FLYAWAY VACATION
SWEEPSTAKES
OFFICIAL ENTRY COUPON

This entry must be received by: MAY 30, 1995
This month's winner will be notified by: JUNE 15, 1995
Trip must be taken between: JULY 30, 1995-JULY 30, 1996

YES, I want to win the San Francisco vacation for two. I understand the prize includes round-trip airfare, first-class hotel and $500.00 spending money. Please let me know if I'm the winner!

Name_____

Address _____ Apt. _____

City   State/Prov.   Zip/Postal Code

Account #_____

Return entry with invoice in reply envelope.

© 1995 HARLEQUIN ENTERPRISES LTD.   CSF KAL

FLYAWAY VACATION
SWEEPSTAKES
OFFICIAL ENTRY COUPON

This entry must be received by: MAY 30, 1995
This month's winner will be notified by: JUNE 15, 1995
Trip must be taken between: JULY 30, 1995-JULY 30, 1996

YES, I want to win the San Francisco vacation for two. I understand the prize includes round-trip airfare, first-class hotel and $500.00 spending money. Please let me know if I'm the winner!

Name_____

Address _____ Apt. _____

City   State/Prov.   Zip/Postal Code

Account #_____

Return entry with invoice in reply envelope.

© 1995 HARLEQUIN ENTERPRISES LTD.   CSF KAL

OFFICIAL RULES

FLYAWAY VACATION SWEEPSTAKES 3449

NO PURCHASE OR OBLIGATION NECESSARY

Three Harlequin Reader Service 1995 shipments will contain respectively, coupons for entry into three different prize drawings, one for a trip for two to San Francisco, another for a trip for two to Las Vegas and the third for a trip for two to Orlando, Florida. To enter any drawing using an Entry Coupon, simply complete and mail according to directions.

There is no obligation to continue using the Reader Service to enter and be eligible for any prize drawing. You may also enter any drawing by hand printing the words "Flyaway Vacation," your name and address on a 3"x5" card and the destination of the prize you wish that entry to be considered for (i.e., San Francisco trip, Las Vegas trip or Orlando trip). Send your 3"x5" entries via first-class mail (limit: one entry per envelope) to: Flyaway Vacation Sweepstakes 3449, c/o Prize Destination you wish that entry to be considered for, P.O. Box 1315, Buffalo, NY 14269-1315, USA or P.O. Box 610, Fort Erie, Ontario L2A 5X3, Canada.

To be eligible for the San Francisco trip, entries must be received by 5/30/95; for the Las Vegas trip, 7/30/95; and for the Orlando trip, 9/30/95.

Winners will be determined in random drawings conducted under the supervision of D.L. Blair, Inc., an independent judging organization whose decisions are final, from among all eligible entries received for that drawing. San Francisco trip prize includes round-trip airfare for two, 4-day/3-night weekend accommodations at a first-class hotel, and $500 in cash (trip must be taken between 7/30/95—7/30/96, approximate prize value—$3,500); Las Vegas trip includes round-trip airfare for two, 4-day/3-night weekend accommodations at a first-class hotel, and $500 in cash (trip must be taken between 9/30/95—9/30/96, approximate prize value—$3,500); Orlando trip includes round-trip airfare for two, 4-day/3-night weekend accommodations at a first-class hotel, and $500 in cash (trip must be taken between 11/30/95—11/30/96, approximate prize value—$3,500). All travelers must sign and return a Release of Liability prior to travel. Hotel accommodations and flights are subject to accommodation and schedule availability. Sweepstakes open to residents of the U.S. (except Puerto Rico) and Canada, 18 years of age or older. Employees and immediate family members of Harlequin Enterprises, Ltd., D.L. Blair, Inc., their affiliates, subsidiaries and all other agencies, entities and persons connected with the use, marketing or conduct of this sweepstakes are not eligible. Odds of winning a prize are dependent upon the number of eligible entries received for that drawing. Prize drawing and winner notification for each drawing will occur no later than 15 days after deadline for entry eligibility for that drawing. Limit: one prize to an individual, family or organization. All applicable laws and regulations apply. Sweepstakes offer void wherever prohibited by law. Any litigation within the province of Quebec respecting the conduct and awarding of the prizes in this sweepstakes must be submitted to the Regies des loteries et Courses du Quebec. In order to win a prize, residents of Canada will be required to correctly answer a time-limited arithmetical skill-testing question. Value of prizes are in U.S. currency.

Winners will be obligated to sign and return an Affidavit of Eligibility within 30 days of notification. In the event of noncompliance within this time period, prize may not be awarded. If any prize or prize notification is returned as undeliverable, that prize will not be awarded. By acceptance of a prize, winner consents to use of his/her name, photograph or other likeness for purposes of advertising, trade and promotion on behalf of Harlequin Enterprises, Ltd., without further compensation, unless prohibited by law.

For the names of prizewinners (available after 12/31/95), send a self-addressed, stamped envelope to: Flyaway Vacation Sweepstakes 3449 Winners, P.O. Box 4200, Blair, NE 68009.

RVC KAL